A Short Affair

A SHORT AFFAIR

An Anthology

Edited by Simon Oldfield

SCRIBNER

LONDON NEW YORK TORONTO SYDNEY NEW DELHI

pindrop

First published in Great Britain by Scribner,
an imprint of Simon & Schuster UK Ltd, 2018
A CBS COMPANY

1 3 5 7 9 10 8 6 4 2

Simon & Schuster UK Ltd
1st Floor
222 Gray's Inn Road
London WC1X 8HB

Simon & Schuster Australia, Sydney
Simon & Schuster India, New Delhi

www.simonandschuster.co.uk
www.simonandschuster.com.au
www.simonandschuster.co.in

A CIP catalogue record for this book
is available from the British Library

Hardback ISBN: 978-1-4711-4732-6
eBook ISBN: 978-1-4711-4734-0

Typeset in Palatino by M Rules
Printed and bound by CPI Group (UK) Ltd, Croydon CR0 4YY

MIX
Paper from
responsible sources
FSC
www.fsc.org   FSC® C020471

Simon & Schuster UK Ltd are committed to sourcing paper
that is made from wood grown in sustainable forests and support the Forest
Stewardship Council, the leading international forest certification organisation.
Our books displaying the FSC logo are printed on FSC certified paper.

For T.M.J.

CONTENTS

Introduction
by Simon Oldfield   xi
Editor and Co-founder
of Pin Drop Studio

Foreword
by Tim Marlow   xvii
Artistic Director of
the Royal Academy of Arts

'On Heat'
by Elizabeth Day   1
ARTWORK BY KAY HARWOOD

'Ms Featherstone and the Beast'
by Bethan Roberts   21
ARTWORK BY GABRIELLA BOYD

'Didi's'
by Nikesh Shukla   41
ARTWORK BY JONATHAN TRAYTE

'A Quiet Tidy Man'
by Claire Fuller   67
ARTWORK BY LUEY GRAVES

'The Lighting of the Lamp'
by Ben Okri 87
ARTWORK BY MARCO PALMIERI

'These Silver Fish'
by Anne O'Brien 107
ARTWORK BY JOHN ROBERTSON

'Panic Attack'
by A. L. Kennedy 121
ARTWORK BY COCO CRAMPTON

'The Way I Breathed'
by Anna Stewart 141
ARTWORK BY FANI PARALI

'Feathers Thick with Oil'
by Craig Burnett 157
ARTWORK BY MURRAY O'GRADY

'Heart's Last Pass'
by Douglas W. Milliken 169
ARTWORK BY PIO ABAD

'Civilisation'
by Will Self 183
ARTWORK BY EDDIE PEAKE

'Rough Beasts'
by Jarred McGinnis 199
ARTWORK BY DECLAN JENKINS

'Under the Waves'
by Barney Walsh   213
ARTWORK BY MARY RAMSDEN

'Paper Chains'
by Rebecca F. John   231
ARTWORK BY CARLA BUSUTTIL

'Brad's Rooster Food'
by Joanna Campbell   245
ARTWORK BY JESSY JETPACKS

'Freshwater'
by Emily Bullock   261
ARTWORK BY NICK GOSS

'Morelia Spilota'
by Cherise Saywell   275
ARTWORK BY TIM ELLIS

'How They Turned Out'
by Lionel Shriver   293
ARTWORK BY ADAM SHIELD

Author Biographies   331
Artist Biographies   338
About Pin Drop Studio   343
Acknowledgements   344
Copyrights and Credits   347

INTRODUCTION

Simon Oldfield

Standing centre stage in a packed theatre as the sun dipped behind the Hollywood Hills, I gazed out at the audience as they jostled for space and spilled into the aisles, eager for our LA debut. Minutes later a film star broke the silence with the opening lines of a short story, and in that moment I realised something extraordinary was happening. That something is Pin Drop, and its essence is captured here, in *A Short Affair*.

Eighteen original short stories by celebrated authors alongside writers discovered through the Pin Drop Short Story Award, each coupled with a unique artwork by an artist from the Royal Academy Schools and with a jacket especially created by Eddie Peake. The aim is to create a layered book where pictures and words symbiotically entwine.

It is thrilling to be at the helm of Pin Drop, weaving short fiction into everything from film to fashion, music and art, and this anthology is a landmark in our journey. It has been a privilege to compile, edit and curate something as wonderfully tangible as this book, in a world where the fast and temporal reign supreme.

The stories, varied and diverse, offer a remarkable tour of the short-story form with searing prose and powerful narratives that leap off the page. Take these stories with you from place to place, from old home to new home, from sun-drenched holidays to bumpy train journeys. Read them to yourself. Read them to your family, to your lover, to your friends, to your neighbours. Embrace the pleasure of the short story.

A Short Affair opens with 'On Heat' by Elizabeth Day, the story of a marriage teetering dangerously on the brink in the heart of the north London literary set. It is fitting that Elizabeth's story is first in the anthology because Pin Drop began with us sitting in my London gallery with an ambition to put art and short fiction side by side. I invited Elizabeth to be writer in residence at the gallery and shortly afterwards we began to hold live events where short stories, selected or written in response to the exhibitions, were read aloud to keen listeners.

Initially, the audiences were intimate, gathered on an assortment of chairs, benches and window ledges. But the ranks quickly swelled, helped along by a flurry of press coverage, word-of-mouth enthusiasm and a shared interest in rekindling an experience left behind as a preserve of childhood.

Buoyed with excitement, we invited bestselling American author Lionel Shriver to join the gang. The following month, having accepted our invitation, Lionel was standing in the gallery reading her own short story to a full house.

It is especially pleasing that our relationship with Lionel has continued to flourish and, like many other authors, she has remained part of the Pin Drop family. For this anthology, she has written 'How They Turned Out', a story that chronicles the travails of an ageing American pop star.

A. L. Kennedy was next to join our merry band, accepting an invitation to feature in Pin Drop's radio debut and, more recently, writing 'Panic Attack' for this anthology; a portrait of two strangers painfully entangled and thwarted by the circumstances of their private situations. Nikesh Shukla, who also appeared at Pin Drop in the early days and silenced a packed room with his powerful delivery, gives us 'Didi's', an evocative story of a millennial woman living in New York, the daughter of Indian immigrants, wrestling with the friction between two starkly contrasting cultures as she seeks to define her identity in twenty-first-century America.

Pin Drop soon moved to bigger stages, thanks to a far-reaching tapestry of trusted friends and relationships. BAFTA, the Royal Academy of Arts, Burberry, Soho House and many others welcomed us through their doors and embraced the spirit of Pin Drop.

For this anthology our relationship with the Royal Academy of Arts is particularly significant. I have the privilege of curating Pin Drop's live literary programme at the Royal Academy of Arts. The programme has seen us welcome world-leading authors and actors to the stage, including a number of contributors to *A Short Affair*, including Man Booker Prize-winner Ben Okri, who paints a poetic tale of seduction in 'The Lighting of the Lamp', and bestselling author Will Self, who gives us 'Civilisation', a strange and brilliant story of a man, and a society, unravelling at the seams.

The partnership between Pin Drop and the Royal Academy of Arts now extends to the annual Pin Drop Short Story Award, a platform for new writing, open to published and unpublished writers from anywhere across the globe.

It is discovering new voices, with their verve and confidence, that makes the Pin Drop Short Story Award so rewarding. Each year, after hundreds of entries have been read, it is utterly thrilling when a story of exceptional quality emerges as the winner. In the inaugural year, Bethan Roberts took the award for 'Ms Featherstone and the Beast', a richly layered story set against the backdrop of Thatcher's 1980s Britain and the Falklands War. Claire Fuller followed with a modern-gothic tale of cruelty and deceit in 'A Quiet Tidy Man', and then came Cherise Saywell's 'Morelia Spilota', a suspenseful narrative imbued with lust and intrigue, set against the expansive landscape of the Australian outback. These three stories, recorded by Stephen Fry, Juliet Stevenson and Dame Penelope Wilton for our podcast and film series, are featured in *A Short Affair*, alongside a selection of the award's shortlisted writers.

Anna Stewart gives us 'The Way I Breathed', delivered in authentic Scottish dialect. 'These Silver Fish' by Anne O'Brien is a quietly intense story set on the water's edge in Denmark. Craig Burnett, in 'Feathers Thick with Oil', has written a story that is at once peculiar and strangely familiar. 'Paper Chains' by Rebecca F. John, 'Under the Waves' by Barney Walsh and 'Freshwater' by Emily Bullock each tell the story of disturbing family situations. Joanna Campbell's tale of 'Brad's Rooster Food', Jarred McGinnis's dystopian 'Rough Beasts' and Douglas W. Milliken's American odyssey in 'Heart's Last Pass' deliver powerful, compelling narratives.

I am humbled and honoured that Scribner, publisher of the great short-story writers from Ernest Hemingway to F. Scott Fitzgerald, embraced the potential of Pin Drop and *A Short Affair*.

As Pin Drop spreads its wings across America, Europe and beyond, this anthology is part of an extraordinary adventure. I like to imagine that *A Short Affair* and the stories within it will be devoured in countless places: on a flight to Hong Kong, a train into London, a ferry across Sydney Harbour or at the edge of a great American lake.

A Short Affair is a slice of Pin Drop, an anthology of original short fiction, bound and illustrated, for you to treasure and share. May it take you on many journeys.

Simon Oldfield is the Co-founder of Pin Drop Studio and Editor of *A Short Affair*.

FOREWORD

Tim Marlow

The Royal Academy of Arts' collaboration with Pin Drop has been an expansive creative project which began in 2014. Pin Drop, it is fair to say, is a visionary organisation that wants to take literature into places that it hasn't reached before, and it has been an ongoing pleasure to help them find new contexts for the short story and the spoken word, or rather the beautifully written word spoken aloud with intelligence and feeling.

It is very important for an academy that was founded by artists and architects to remain open to other art forms. The interplay between the visual arts and literature has been an interesting one over the Royal Academy of Arts' 250-year history. Charles Dickens famously gave the annual speech here in 1853, and Howard Jacobson more recently, and it is a relationship that we keenly continue with Pin Drop.

We have been immensely fortunate that a number of the illustrious writers in this anthology have come to the Royal Academy of Arts and read their work in public. The results have been both symbiotic and poetically resonant in relationship to what has been on display in the main galleries.

These include Lionel Shriver during Anselm Kiefer's monumental solo show, Ben Okri against the backdrop of *Painting the Modern Garden: Monet to Matisse*, and Will Self during the landmark Ai Weiwei exhibition.

Extending the relationship between the RA and Pin Drop, Simon Oldfield invited us to partner on the annual Pin Drop Short Story Award. Naturally we agreed, and I have had the privilege of being one of the judges for what has become an important short-story competition. It is appropriate that the award has an open-submission policy, in the context and spirit of the Royal Academy's annual Summer Exhibition. It has achieved many things, notably the exploration and celebration of emerging talent.

A Short Affair is, in short, an illustrated anthology that celebrates the marriage (or at least a passionate coupling) of art and literature. It captures between its pages the rich and fruitful collaboration between Pin Drop and the Royal Academy of Arts. It is especially pleasing that many of the stories in the anthology are drawn from the Pin Drop Short Story Award, and that each of the short stories is illustrated by an artist from the RA Schools. We are incredibly proud of the achievements of the students that come through our art school, which – physically as well as metaphorically – lies at the centre of the establishment, and it is inspiring to see some of these young artists bringing their own developing vision and artistic voice so strikingly into play.

Tim Marlow is the Artistic Director of the Royal Academy of Arts.

ON HEAT

Elizabeth Day

Artwork by Kay Harwood

On Heat

Elizabeth Day

James

There is a dog tied to the railings outside his local cafe. James is more of a cat person, normally, but this dog looks like he needs help.

Or it.

Is an animal a he or an it? He's never been sure.

The dog is well kept and glossy, with a red leather collar, and he/she/it is panting in the heat, tongue lolling. The sun is beating down, forming a curiously precise semicircle on the pavement around the animal's shape, so that the effect is rather like a spotlight or a Gestapo interrogation.

Poor beast, he thinks, observing it from the first-floor window of his study. Must be hell to have a fur coat in this weather.

The cafe has put out a scattering of tables on the pavement in an effort to be continental. The chrome surfaces refract prisms of sunlight. In the centre of each are salt and pepper shakers, a fake plant and a white bowl containing sachets of tomato ketchup. A woman sits at one of them, bare legs crossed, her denim cut-offs riding high up her thigh. She shows no interest in the dog, preferring instead to tap at the screen of her phone. She is wearing sunglasses and her skin is the palest brown, like the underside of a mushroom. Her nails are painted dark red, the varnish chewed and flaking at the ends.

She must be nineteen or twenty, he guesses. The perfect age. Ripe, yet unaware of her own beauty.

He's been having an affair with an editorial assistant at his publishing house. She's called Cressida and is absurdly young. Shoulder-length dirty-blonde hair, cut in a blunt fringe across her forehead. Messy skirts and Breton tops. A mouth that never fully closes, even when she's silent.

He doesn't love her. But nor can he stop thinking of her body: the creaseless wonder of her skin; the flatness of her childless stomach.

He returns to the computer screen, where he has typed a few desultory paragraphs of his latest novel.

'She felt the blister against her shoe,' he reads aloud to himself, 'the nuchal-fold tenderness of its pressure.'

Jesus, what an awful sentence.

He contemplates it as he sips the bottled drink his wife had given him. It has a fizzy, fermented taste and is called kombucha. The consensus seems to be that it's terribly good for your digestion. Patsy introduced him to it after his doctor made him stop drinking caffeine. One had to be careful of this kind of thing when one was hurtling towards seventy and did less exercise than one should.

He glances down at his tummy. Automatic reflex. There's more of it there than he'd like.

He pulls up his t-shirt to reveal wrinkly flesh, saggy in unexpected places. And then, because there's no one around, he lifts the waistband of his jogging bottoms and checks his penis. It lies there, limp and curled, conveying defeat. A smattering of grey in his pubic hair.

God he misses the Viagra-free erection. What a luxury it had been, and how little he had appreciated it. The delightful frequency of adolescent tumescence. He wishes he could tell young boys what a gift it is to get hard without even wanting to.

He stares at the kombucha bottle. 'Unpasteurised, unadulterated, wild-ginger sparkle' reads the label. He thinks of a redhead he once bedded who scratched his back in the grip of passion, leaving shallow rivulets of pink.

He misses coffee.

Patsy, his wife, is always trying to make him healthier than he wants to be. The other day, at breakfast, she had presented him with two amber-coloured pills, swollen like maggots.

'What are these?' he'd asked.

'Omega-3 complex.'

'Oh darling. Don't you think I've got enough complexes already?'

She laughed. Patsy obligingly thought all his jokes were funny. It was one of the reasons he had married her. Sometimes he is inclined to think it might have been the only reason.

'Take them,' she said, patting his hand. 'For me.'

He looked at her, at the inconsequential features of her all-too-familiar face. Her eyelids had drooped with age, pulling down at the corners as if they had expended a lifetime's effort and now could no longer be bothered to stay taut. It gave Patsy a perpetually sleepy expression.

She had been pretty once. Not beautiful, but definitely pretty. They had met at a time when James had grown tired of beautiful women.

There had been so many of them when his second novel had been published. In his thirties, he got invited to fashionable parties and did lines of coke with supermodels in the lavatories while, outside, people talked about him as an 'enfant terrible' and a 'loose canon' and a 'wild card' and all those other clichés used to denote someone who is out of control and dangerous in a sexy kind of way.

There was so much sex in the Eighties. One-night stands. Threesomes. Foursomes. Sex on yachts. In hotels. In a cloak-room at a party, pushed up against a rail of coats while the woman's clueless husband greeted guests outside. Once: an encounter with a woman dressed in skin-tight leather who whipped him and talked about his mummy in an underground dungeon in Prague.

Sex was there for the taking. It was so easy.

But the problem with beautiful women, he discovered, was that they never cared as much for him as they did for themselves. He once dated a minor actress who insisted on having sex facing away from him in bed. After a few weeks, James realised it was because she wanted to look at herself in the mirror hanging on the wall.

Patsy was different. Patsy was adoring and sweetly in

8

awe. Patsy, with her tidy bobbed hair and neatly buttoned cardigans, wanted to devote herself to him at the cost of erasing herself. Patsy gave up her job when they got married. It wasn't as if she'd been a high-flyer – she was PA to a successful banker in the city – and times were different then anyway. None of this guff about women being able to 'have it all'. Patsy was perfectly content ministering to her creative husband's needs and raising their two children – a daughter and a son, just as it should be. And James had held up his end of the bargain by reliably producing a novel every two years or so. Some of them were pretty good. One of them had won the Booker. They were comfortably well off and had a house in north London, on a street with a pastoral suffix (Grove) set back from the main traffic but still within easy distance of the urban bustle.

Patsy had everything she wanted, as far as he could see.

As for him? Well, James was very, very fond of her.

And so he had swallowed the Omega-3, even though he had a childhood phobia of pills and was always worried they would get stuck in his throat and he would choke to death. But he had done it. For his loving, pliant little wife. For her.

He doesn't mind the kombucha. If he drinks enough of it, it gives him a pleasant, heady buzz reminiscent of the first stages of daytime tipsiness. There's a light white sediment in the bottom of the bottle, he notices. He screws up his face and swallows it down.

He glares at the screen again. It is the first time he has written a female protagonist, but his agent has been on at him to try something new so he thought he'd give it a go.

Yesterday, realising he had no idea what it felt like to wear a stiletto, he had shuffled to the bedroom and rummaged through Patsy's collection of trainers and sandals until he finally came across a pair of patent-leather court shoes that had a modest block heel. He remembered her wearing them to accompany him to an awards ceremony last year. (He hadn't won. A bisexual twenty-something had scooped the prize for what the judges described as 'a searing memoir of gender fluidity'. His agent had told him that transgender was 'all the rage', but James wasn't quite up to the task of writing that sort of protagonist.)

In the bedroom, James had done his best to squeeze the front half of his foot into the shoes and then, after a few seconds, grunted with satisfaction and returned to his desk to write confidently of blisters and nuchal folds.

He isn't even sure what a nuchal fold is.

He'd written it because it sounded nice and he had a vague sense that it was something to do with Down's Syndrome. He spends another five minutes Googling the term and gazing half-heartedly at pictures of embryos emerging in a cluster of pixelated white dots from the anonymous blackness of the ultrasound.

He looks at the sentence again. His heroine is a single mother with a shadowy past. He hasn't named her yet. He is thinking of Megan. Or Kirsten. Everyone is called Megan or Kirsten nowadays, aren't they? He wants to be modern. Maybe Cressida, he thinks, and he spends a pleasant cluster of minutes thinking of the wetness of her mouth; the excitement of her young tongue.

'It's so weird,' Cressida had said, the first time they'd kissed. 'I studied you for my degree.'

10

He glances out at the dog. It has dropped its head onto its crossed paws. The sun is still beating down. It must be boiling, he thinks. Whose dog is it? Bloody stupid people leaving it out there, suffering in the heat without so much as a bowl of water.

He returns to the screen. Concentrate, Richmond, he tells himself in the voice of his former housemaster. Focus. He looks at the sentence again. It is like looking at the photograph of an ex-girlfriend and he is filled with loathing. He deletes it.

It's no good. He can't do anything with that dog sitting out there, sending him plaintive telepathic messages. He's never been able to resist the dumb stare of a helpless animal.

He clicks 'save' and listens to the resulting whoosh as the document minimises itself on the computer screen. He goes downstairs, opens the front door and, still in his slippers, walks across the road with scant regard for the passing traffic.

The dog cocks its head with interest.

The woman is still staring at her phone, sunglasses pushed up her head.

'Is this your dog?'

She looks at him vaguely.

'Is this your dog?' he repeats.

She shakes her head, tapping something onto the screen with clickety-clack nails.

'Nope,' she says, not looking up.

He feels a surge of antagonism towards her. It comes from the knowledge of his own invisibility. At sixty-eight, he is past the point of her interest. He tells himself he doesn't care and she's clearly thick as pigshit but he sucks in his stomach anyway.

'Do you know whose it is?'

His voice, when he hears it, is shriller than he expects. He sounds like a tremulous elderly busybody and he can't stand it.

'No idea, mate.'

She turns her face towards him, one cool cheek at a time.

Did she actually just call him 'mate'? Extraordinary, the entitlement of the young. All sense of her attractiveness evaporates.

'Well, whoever it is should be ashamed of themselves,' he says, sounding more and more like his housemaster.

He unties the dog's lead. It whimpers apologetically, then stands with scampering paws, aware that something is about to happen.

'Hey, you can't do that!' the woman is saying. She's pushed her sunglasses onto her head. Her eyes are narrowed and black.

'I can,' he mutters, 'and I will.'

He takes the dog further along the railings to a patch of pavement shaded by the leaves of a tall tree and reties the lead. The dog pants appreciatively then sits, wagging its tail.

'There,' James says, satisfied.

He straightens, placing his hands against his sacrum and arching his back, unwittingly emitting a groan as he does so. He is lightheaded and for a moment thinks he will need to sit down to gather himself. But the humiliation would be too much. The woman is still staring at him, hostility emanating from her every pore, so he shuffles back across the street in his slippers.

He can see the front door of the house. It was repainted a duck-egg blue earlier this year at Patsy's request. He wasn't sure about the colour. It seemed to be trying too hard.

He steps up onto the kerb and as he does so, the light bleaches and he can no longer focus on the duck-egg-blue door. It swirls in front of him, just out of reach. Something snaps in his neck and there is an electric river of pain down his right side. He gasps. His chest tightens. He wonders if the dog lead has somehow become entangled around his torso and if the woman outside the cafe is pulling it tighter and tighter until he can no longer breathe. She hates him. She wants him dead. Women. He has never understood them. A car blares past. He stumbles, grazing a knee against the tarmac.

If he could only make it to the door, to press the bell and alert Patsy. She would know immediately what action to take. That's all he needs to do. Get to the door. Ring the bell. Lie down on the cool mosaic tiles of the hallway. Get to the door. Come on, Richmond. Ring the bloody bell, boy. Get to the door, Richmond. Ring the bell. Lie down on the hallway floor. Wait for Patsy who would know what to do. She always knew what to do.

Behind him, a dog barks.

PATSY

A friend has come round for coffee, complete with sympathetic expression and Tupperware box of beef stew. They sit at the kitchen table drinking freshly brewed coffee and Patsy can feel the precise moment it happens; the actual second when she slips from shock into a smooth purveyor

13

of anecdote, sanitised of all unpleasantness so that the other person won't feel uncomfortable.

Always thinking of the other person. That was Patsy's way.

First, there was the usual routine as she started to talk. Kettle. Coffee. Cafetière. Plunge. Pour. Milk. Sip. Automatic motions and social niceties.

And then – pop! There it was: the appalling calmness of her rational mind easing into gear. Patsy can recount the sequence of events with perfect clarity, in chronological narrative order.

It was like a coin dropping onto the shelf of one of those childhood amusement-arcade games she used to play on seaside holidays – the one where mechanical sweepers would slide back and forth and you had to hope that the coin would land in the right spot to dislodge the others.

She can still remember the satisfying rush and clatter when she got it right. Patsy would keep on playing and playing and playing because she thought she was getting better. It was a brilliant game because it gave you the impression of skill while being entirely reliant on luck.

Just like life, really, when you thought about it. You think you're getting a handle on things and then your husband has an affair. And another. And another one after that. The coins drop with a communal clatter. And then you realise you're angry. Not sad – not any more – but absolutely fucking furious.

'So, what happened?' asks her friend at the kitchen table.

A thud on the door was what happened.

She tells the story like this.

At first, Patsy hadn't heard it. She was in the drawing

room at the back of the house, the one which led onto the conservatory they'd put in back in the Nineties, before side-extensions and sliding floor-to-ceiling windows became fashionable. The sun was dappling through the glass and Patsy was sitting on the chintz sofa, flicking through the pages of a novel she was meant to be reading for her book group. It was one of those thrillers which described women as girls in the title and came complete with an out-of-focus picture of a shattered mirror and Patsy couldn't concentrate. She kept thinking of Chloe and whether she would come for lunch next Sunday or not. Patsy had sent an email to her daughter two days ago and had yet to hear back. It was always difficult to know whether to try again or whether such a move would be construed as pushy. Patsy picked at the cuticle of her left thumb.

She'd give it one more day.

It was as Patsy was putting the book aside that she heard the thud. She stiffened, senses alert. She waited to see if it would happen again. No sound came.

She checked her watch. Just after three. Time for her to make him some tea in any case. She switched off the angle-poise lamp and placed the novel on a pile of other unread material – the latest McEwan; a Lonely Planet guide to Southern Spain for a holiday they had never booked, and the flattened crossword page of the *Guardian*. She levered herself out of the sofa, which seemed lower than it had this time a week ago, and popped into the kitchen to put the kettle on. Then she walked upstairs.

'Jamie?'

She was the only person in the world who called him

Jamie. She had a suspicion it made him feel diminished, but she kept on doing it because it was a mark of her possession – one of the few she had.

There was no answer. She pushed the door open to his study. No one was at the desk. An empty bottle of kombucha stood by the computer. So he'd drunk it.

She smiled.

(This smile does not form part of the story she tells her friend. This smile is hers alone.)

She moved towards the desk, reaching automatically for the bottle to put in the recycling, and then she glanced out of the window and saw a dog, tied to the railings outside the cafe on the opposite side of the street, and it was barking loudly and there was a woman in sunglasses waving her arms in a state of high agitation.

Patsy crept closer to the window. She peered out and then, following the dog's gaze, she looked downwards to the path and the flower beds at the front of the house where she saw two legs, twitching against the paving stones. The window-sill was blocking her view of the rest of the human form, but she needed no confirmation. It was James. They were his greying jogging bottoms. His godawful slippers. The cashmere socks she had given him for Christmas, splayed out with odd angularity.

She ran downstairs and opened the front door and her husband's head rolled onto the hallway tiles, speckles of foam at the corner of his mouth, his colour at once both bright red and the whitest pale.

She acted as she was meant to.

'Jamie! Jamie, wake up! Jamie!'

She was on her knees now, cradling his head and willing him to open his eyes. His body was twisted in different directions.

'I've called an ambulance,' a voice said above her. 'Are you okay? Are you okay?'

She didn't register that it was the woman in sunglasses from across the street. Patsy nodded.

She put her hand on his chest. It was hot. His right eye flickered and then he shifted his head to look at her and she could see he was trying to say something, lips moving soundlessly. She bent towards him, straining to make out the words.

'Love,' he slurred.

'I love you too, darling. I love you too.'

His right eyelid twitched. He shook his head, the movement minute.

'C ... C ...'

He was trying to say something, trying to get out a word.

'Chloe?' she said. 'Of course. Of course you love her too. I know, my darling, I know. Just rest now. Help is on the way. You're going to be fine, you're going to be absolutely fine.'

The woman from across the street was still standing there. Her shoes, Patsy noticed, were round-toed, patent leather, and she was wearing white ankle-socks, the rims frilly like the outer edge of a seashell.

'Cress ...' James whispered. And then, again, faintly: 'Cre ...' followed by a steep slope of S's.

Patsy craned forwards.

'What was that, darling? I didn't quite catch ...'

'I think it was "Cress",' the woman with the shoes said.

Patsy glanced up at her. What was she still doing here anyway? Couldn't she keep her nose out of other people's business? Patsy had never been able to abide rubberneckers: those awful people on motorways who slowed down to gawp at accidents and caused long tailbacks.

'That seems unlikely,' Patsy said more forcefully than she'd intended. The shoes stood motionless. 'Thank you for your help.' The woman didn't leave. She seemed to be determined to stay until the ambulance got here.

James's head was heavier now in her lap and he closed his eyes. She took his hand in hers and felt the reassuring coolness of his wedding ring.

He hadn't worn one for the first years of their marriage, claiming he didn't like jewellery on men. But then he'd had an affair and when he'd asked what he could do to make it up to her, Patsy replied that she wanted him to wear a wedding band. He agreed. She bought him one the next day. Platinum. Engraved with their initials.

He said he'd never strayed again, but of course, Patsy knew differently. She pretended not to have minded for years. But the latest one had been the final straw. Young enough to be their daughter. It was enough, she had decided. It needed to be stopped.

The sharp wail of sirens approaching. Patsy sat up straighter, took a breath. She felt her usual capability return. She pressed two fingers against James's neck, searching for a pulse, and then, before the paramedics got to her, she eased herself out from under his weight and gently cupped the back of his head, placing it gently onto the doormat. She kissed his cheek. His face was cold.

The woman with the sunglasses and the shoes and frilly socks offered to come with her in the ambulance but by then, Patsy knew it was too late. He was dead. The love of her life. How she hated him.

Afterwards, sitting in the safety of her kitchen, drinking Waitrose Colombian Blend (Strength: a middling '3'), her friend will reach across and pat the back of Patsy's hand.

'How awful for you. Awful.'

What she doesn't tell her friend is what happened next. She doesn't say that, inventing some excuse about having to get her keys, Patsy had run back into the house. She had checked the kitchen for incriminating evidence and found that she had cleaned up very well. The pestle and mortar had been washed of the crushed-up sleeping pills and were resting on the side, where they usually stood. The empty bottle of kombucha was in the recycling. Yes, she nodded to herself, reassured. It had been a tidy job.

'Did he . . .' the friend asks, hesitantly, '. . . I mean . . . did he . . . *say* anything before he died?'

Patsy looks steadily over the rim of her coffee mug.

'He asked for Chloe,' she says with a small gulp of sadness.

She keeps on telling the story and keeps on not mentioning the name and after a while, it becomes easy to forget that anyone called Cressida ever existed.

Ms Featherstone and the Beast

Bethan Roberts

Artwork by Gabriella Boyd

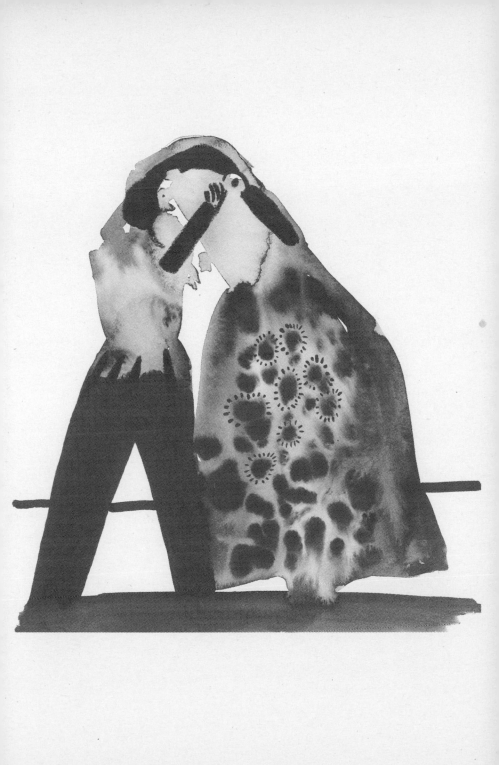

Ms Featherstone
and the Beast

Bethan Roberts

'If women ruled the world,' said his English teacher, 'there would be no more wars.'

Her name was Ms Amber Featherstone.

'But, Miss,' said Wayne Collett (they all called her Miss; even Stevie couldn't bring himself to utter that strange thrumming 's' in *Ms*), 'Maggie Thatcher's a woman, Miss. And you hate *her*, Miss.'

As the class erupted into laughter and argument, Ms Featherstone crossed her pale naked legs. No other adult in the school had naked legs, apart from the PE teachers, and their calves were shaped like bags of golf balls. Today she wore turquoise shoes and a grey skirt that hugged her thighs.

'Thatcher's not a real woman,' said Ms Featherstone.

Sarah Figgs put up her hand and said, 'She's done a lot for the women's cause, Miss.'

'She hates feminists,' said Ms Featherstone.

Stevie had seen Ms Featherstone's first name on a letter, whilst photocopying in the secretary's office – a special privilege reserved only for him, as editor of the school newspaper. *Amber*. Like her, it had seemed too glamorous to be real. He'd looked it up in the dictionary, hoping for poetry. On finding the words *hard translucent fossilised resin* he'd closed the dictionary, unsure if he was disappointed or enthralled.

'*Margaret Thatcher is a powerful woman who hates feminists. Discuss,*' said Ms Featherstone. She smiled, delightedly. At him, it seemed.

A few weeks earlier, Stevie's older brother Mike had left for the Falklands. Stevie didn't miss him much. Mike was noisy, always crunching on a bag of Monster Munch or swigging on a Coke, belching for real or making belching noises with his hand in his armpit. But there was a strange quietness to the house without him. It was a quietness that Stevie's parents did their best to eradicate. Every evening since Mike's departure, Stevie's father would sit in his puffily upholstered armchair and read aloud from newspaper articles about the war. '*I saw my missile hit the back of the enemy aircraft. It exploded as advertised. His plane was in flames . . .*' Above his thick hair, a ceramic screech owl flew across the chimney breast, claws stretched towards the geometric pattern on the carpet. After a few sentences, Stevie's mother would silently remove herself to the kitchen, shut the door and turn on her cassette player. Then she danced. She had a fondness for full-skirted dresses, the like of which Stevie had seen nowhere else in town, and when Stevie watched her dance they seemed to fill the room with their colour and movement. Sometimes he joined her, and had to remember to grimace as she twirled him beneath her outstretched arm.

Last night his father came into the kitchen whilst Stevie was dancing with his mother. A Motown song was playing, and her face was becoming greasy with perspiration. Stevie could smell chip fat and perfume on her collar. His father stood and watched them for a minute before saying, 'Smokey. That's the stuff.' Then he reached for Stevie's mother's arm. 'Give her to me,' he told his son. 'I'll show you how it's done.' And he pulled her into a tight embrace against the plaid of his shirt, which made her close her eyes, and prompted Stevie to leave the room.

At school Stevie was always alert to her presence. You never knew when Ms Featherstone might enter a room unannounced.

And so, when she pushed the double doors open and stood, chin held high, scanning the rows during his Learning for Life lecture, Stevie wasn't that surprised. Mr Roth and the rest of the room watched in silence as, without apology, she caught Stevie's eye, waved a folder in his direction, and began ploughing towards him.

She slapped the folder – the proofs for that month's school newspaper – on the desk and hissed, not quietly enough, 'The masterpiece!'

Stevie's ears burned with shame and pleasure.

Mr Roth said, 'Don't let me interrupt you, *Ms* Featherstone.' The class sniggered. Ms Featherstone exited with a jaunty wave in Stevie's direction.

Later, she caught Stevie in the dinner hall and said she wouldn't be able to make their scheduled final editorial meeting. He should check with his parents first, but her suggestion, therefore, was for a meeting on Saturday morning, at her house. She would pick him up at ten o'clock.

He didn't ask his parents. He told them, the night before, what was happening.

His mother said, 'Isn't she the feminist one?'

Stevie said he thought she was.

'That's all right, then,' she said.

'Why is that all right?' asked his father, from behind his newspaper.

'Well, you know. They're not generally ... predatory.'

His father snorted. 'Not generally pretty, you mean.'

'Oh, I don't know. Some of them are quite attractive.'

'Name one.'

There was a pause. After a while, his mother ventured, 'Miriam Stoppard?'

When he'd stopped laughing, his father re-erected his newspaper and muttered, 'She'll have him up at Greenham before you know it. Waving banners. Burning bras.'

'I don't think men are allowed up there, George.'

'My point exactly, June,' said the newspaper.

Ms Featherstone drew up outside the house. To Stevie's relief, she stayed where she was and peeped the Mini's horn. Hurrying towards the car, he was aware of his mother monitoring his progress down their narrow pathway.

'Is that your mum?' Ms Featherstone asked.

Every fibre of his being wanted to deny that the woman in the loud, huge skirt, standing in the path with her arms crossed, was his mother. But as he secured his seatbelt he could smell Ms Featherstone's hair – deeply soil-like, strangely sweet – and he nodded.

'She looks . . . nurturing,' said Ms Featherstone, driving away.

Alone with Ms Featherstone. He was alone with *Amber*, in a small, enclosed space, the suburbs disappearing behind them. He'd imagined, many times, this kind of journey. He took a breath and tried to remain alert to every detail, so he could replay the scene later on, in the dark.

She wrenched the gearstick, wound down the window to let out her cigarette smoke.

He watched the grey plume disappear and wished he had his own cigarette. They were on a busy shopping street now, lined by Mr Minit, Gateway and several shops with Arabic lettering on the windows. Boxes of red peppers and aubergines spilled onto the pavement.

'Your brother's gone to the Falklands, hasn't he?'

'Cornwall,' blurted Stevie. 'He's actually gone to Cornwall.' She looked puzzled.

'He's in training. The navy. Helston. He wants to go to war, though.'

'I don't understand that,' she said. 'Do you?'

He thought of what his father had said, when Mike made the announcement: *Going to war, for old iron-knickers? Are you insane?* But he'd smiled as he said it, and held his son's shoulder. Then he'd drawn him in for a bear hug. Stevie had shared a bear hug with his father only once, when, after years of trying, he'd finally learned how to ride a bike.

29

'No,' said Stevie. 'I don't understand it at all.'

Mike had later confessed that joining the navy seemed a better option than the dole queue or cutting out medical implements at the local factory.

Her knee – clothed today in a tight pair of pink cotton trousers – brushed the gearstick. 'Well. Let's hope Maggie doesn't bring in conscription,' she said, with a half-smile.

Then she took her hand off the steering wheel and placed it on his arm. He couldn't be sure if she meant to leave her fingers there for longer than a beat. But he was sure that she sighed. Ms Featherstone sighed, and Stevie sighed, too.

Her house was a small terraced place in the east of the town. It reminded him of *Pigeon Street*. All red bricks, multi-coloured fanlights and small cars lining the kerb.

Inside, the smell of damp and fried onions greeted him.

'Hello?' she shouted, swinging her bag and jacket onto the banister and peering up the stairs.

Perhaps she had a housemate. There was certainly no ring on her wedding finger. He'd checked, many times.

Stevie stared as a large man in a fluffy dressing gown descended the stairs.

'Not dressed yet?' Ms Featherstone asked the man.

The man yawned in response.

She tutted. 'Stevie, this is Barney. Barney, Stevie.'

Barney? As in Rubble?

The man raised his chin in greeting. It was as rectangular and definite as a brick. Then he stepped in front of Stevie and ruffled Ms Featherstone's hair. 'Making coffee?' he asked.

She smoothed her blonde bob back into place but made no

other protest. Instead she went through to the kitchen and filled the kettle. Barney slowly climbed back upstairs, the muscles in his calves jostling for space as he walked, leaving Stevie gawping after him in the hallway.

After handing him a mug of coffee, she said, with a roll of her eyes, 'Better take one to the beast.' And she disappeared.

Stevie took the opportunity to look around the living room. A high shelf ran from one end of the room to the other, lined with orange-spined paperbacks. Through the low window hyacinths splayed their greenness onto the path. On the fireplace were a couple of burnt-down candles and a framed black-and-white photograph of a couple on their wedding day.

'Mum and Dad,' said Ms Featherstone, returning and standing close behind him. 'Happiest day of their lives. Or, at least, I hope it was, since they spent the rest of them fighting.'

He took a swig of burning coffee. 'That's usual, though. Isn't it?'

'Is there a usual?'

'There is in my house,' said Stevie. He was aware this sounded more dramatic than it actually was. The truth was his mother and father got along fairly well, despite regular rows. What Stevie had really started to hate were their habitual intimacies. The way his father would often stroke his mother's forearm whilst he spoke, as if, Stevie thought, to silence her. The way his mother would brush his father's hair before he left the house, and tut admiringly at the density of it.

But Ms Featherstone didn't seem to have heard. She

31

was looking towards the doorway, where Barney was now standing, wearing a pair of jogging bottoms and a sweatshirt emblazoned with the words CORPUS CHRISTI.

'I'm off, then.' He raised a hand in salute.

'Where are you going?' she asked.

'Tennis,' he said, bringing his racket out from behind his back, as if displaying the proof.

'With Adam?'

He nodded.

'I thought Adam couldn't play this morning.'

'He changed his mind,' said Barney, gazing at the ceiling.

'He called, did he?' asked Ms Featherstone.

Barney turned on his heel. 'Yep. See you later, newshounds.'

Stevie thought Ms Featherstone might follow Barney. He'd never seen her look as beautiful as she did now. Biting her bottom lip, her cheeks flushed, she seemed to him to tremble, like a wronged heroine in a Thomas Hardy novel. She made an almost imperceptible movement towards the door, then stopped herself. After a moment, she said, 'Tennis,' with the sort of contempt she usually reserved for the word *Tories*.

'Shall we look at the proofs?' he asked, hoping she would see the softness in his eyes.

Their front page headline was CALL FOR REAL TRACING PAPER GOES TO COUNCIL. There was a photograph of Sarah Figgs handing a petition to Councillor Jennings. Ms Featherstone had encouraged them to protest about the school's dwindling tracing-paper supplies (they were often sent from Maths to fetch toilet paper as a substitute), calling it the 'thin end of the funding wedge'. Other stories included a vox pop on the relevance of PE during this time of political unrest and an investigation into the hypocrisy of the school's anti-smoking policy. Stevie knew from previous editions of the paper that it was supposed to be a light-hearted and positive publication. But Ms Featherstone had encouraged him to produce something more challenging for his first issue as editor.

Now, though, she looked at the pages they'd spread on the floor, and seemed unable to recognise any of them.

'Looks great, doesn't it?' Stevie ventured, unsure of what, exactly, he should be doing in an editorial meeting.

She sat back on her heels. 'You've done a good job, Stevie. You should be proud.'

He smiled. She might utter the word *masterpiece* again. His ears began to warm at the thought.

Instead she looked at her watch. 'Why don't you have a last read through? I've got to make a couple of calls. Then we can sign off.'

'Is there anything I should be looking for, in particular?' he asked.

But she was already heading for the door, a hand in her hair.

Whilst she was gone, he strained to hear her conversation, but all he could make out were the words *bloody typical of him*.

The first Stevie knew of the trouble was when Mr Roth approached him in the overheated craft block, a copy of the newspaper held aloft. 'And I quote,' he said, rattling the paper, 'This school's anti-smoking policy is yet another example of the hypocrisy with which the place is riddled. The teachers stink of nicotine. Why shouldn't we sneak the occasional fag behind the bike sheds?'

For a moment, Stevie smirked.

Then Mr Roth said, 'Mr Perlman wants to see you. Now.'

Stevie had never before been summoned to the Deputy Head's office, and he found himself rather excited by the prospect of a showdown with Norman Perlman. Perlman was famous for spitting. As he talked he left foamy globs on his jumper. The problem seemed to be that his lips were too large for his beard.

In his office, which was the size of a cupboard and stacked high with copies of *Deutsch Heute*, they sat at opposite sides of the table, Stevie's heart thudding as Perlman stroked his knitted tie. Between them, the newspaper lay open.

Finally Perlman said, in a sad tone, 'This is your first issue as editor, isn't it, Stevie?'

Stevie nodded.

'That's a shame. Because if there was going to be a next time – which there won't, of course – you'd know better.'

Perlman wiped his spittle-spotted jumper. 'Good journalism means sticking to the facts. No one wants your opinions.' He sighed. 'It's her I blame. Featherstone. I'm presuming it was all her idea?'

'Not really, Sir.'

'But the *tone* of it, Stevie. That's her, isn't it? It's her all over.'

'We wanted it to be challenging, Sir. And entertaining.' He remembered her words: *more quality supplement than local rag.*

34

A bell rang.

'Look,' said Perlman, 'if you like, just tell me that she put you up to it. Then we'll forget it, okay? You'll be off the paper, but there'll be no other punishment.' He leant forwards and spat purposefully. 'We all know what she's like. Show her a line and she'll step over it.'

'But she didn't write any of it, Sir.'

Perlman laughed softly. 'These women. They get a bit of power and they go hysterical.'

'Miss Featherstone had nothing to do with it.' Stevie flushed. He remembered her Thomas Hardy heroine look on Saturday, and felt they had something in common, now. They'd both been wronged. And he was going to make a stand.

'Have it your own way,' said Perlman, 'and you can have two weeks' detention, too. Now get lost.'

In bed that night, Stevie thought about how he'd tell Ms Featherstone what he'd done. *I did it for you*, he'd say. And she would put her fingers on his arm, give that sigh of hers, and say, *You shouldn't have*. Would they kiss? He wasn't sure. This was, he knew, the next logical step in his fantasy, and it was a scenario he tried often to imagine, especially under the covers after eleven o'clock at night. But it seemed slightly jarring – disappointing, even. It wasn't the kiss that he wanted the most – although he did want it – it was something less defined and harder to imagine. On the edge of sleep, a word came to him: *admiration*. He thought that maybe he wanted Ms Featherstone's admiration.

*

The following day, she wasn't at school. She wasn't there the next day, either. Instead, Norman Perlman appeared in Stevie's English lesson and told them that, owing to personal circumstances, Ms Featherstone would not be back that term.

After school, Stevie took the bus to where she lived and loitered outside her house, gathering the courage to walk to her door. He was careful not to lean against her car, even though he wanted to touch the door handle, the petrol cap, the bonnet – any place her fingers had been. A cool wind blew up the street, making the hyacinths that grew up her front path shiver.

As he rang the bell he had some phrase in his head, something like *Now or Never* or *Do or Die*. Some phrase with *or* in the middle that his father or Mike might use. That afternoon, during double physics, he'd written out what he was going to say – *I know what they've done to you, what they do to all powerful women, and we have to fight back* – but now the only thing in his head was this idea of a phrase with *or* in the middle.

She opened the door a crack, leaving the safety chain on, and peered at him. 'Oh,' she said. 'It's you.'

'Can I talk to you?'

'I can't really talk right now, Stevie, I'm sorry.'

'But there's something I need to tell you.'

'Yes?'

He could see only an eye and a slither of her pale neck.

Instead of reciting what he'd written, he blurted: 'I didn't say anything. About the newspaper.'

'What?' She sounded very tired.

'In case you think it was me who got you sacked.' He took a breath, remembered some of his script. 'It's the system, isn't it, the system that can't deal with powerful women. But I stood up for you, Miss.'

She shut the door. He heard the click and slide of the chain coming off, and when she opened it again he gasped. Her right eye was half hidden by purple, swollen flesh, through which ran a deep cut, held together by black slashes of stitch. He shuddered and sucked the air audibly through his teeth. Then he looked away, uncomfortably aware that he was grimacing at the sight of her.

She sighed, and it was a very different sound to the one she'd made when she'd placed a hand on his arm. 'You'd better come in.'

She led him through to the sitting room and sat facing away from the window. With the light behind her, her black eye was no longer so pronounced. Stevie breathed out, relieved to be spared a little of its glaring drama.

'Well,' she said. 'Now you know.'

He wanted to ask her: *What the hell happened? Was it Barney?* But he found himself unable to speak. He hoped she would fill the silence, but she just sat there, staring at him, as if, he thought, in accusation. In his panic, he thought he might cry, and had to put a hand to his mouth to steady himself.

'Oh for Christ's sake . . .' she said. Beneath the bruise, the rest of her face was grey, and her voice sounded grey, too. 'Don't get upset. I can't handle you getting upset. This has nothing to do with you.'

It was as if she, Ms Amber Featherstone, had disappeared and been replaced by this hideous bruise.

'Sorry,' he said, gulping back the tears. To avoid looking at her face, he glanced around the room, and saw Barney's tennis racket balanced against the windowsill. Was he actually here, still in the house? If he wasn't, then he could be back at any moment. Stevie's heart flapped in his chest.

She must have seen him looking at the racket, because she said, 'I keep meaning to burn that bloody thing.'

'So it was ... I mean, is he ... I mean, where ...?'

'Oh,' she said, 'don't worry. He's gone.' She reached for a cigarette and lit up with a shaking hand.

'Right. Good. I mean ...'

She exhaled a long stream of smoke. 'Stevie, why did you come?'

He wondered if the beating had given her amnesia. What about his masterpiece? Was that all forgotten now, too?

'Well,' he began, wiping his sweaty palms on his jeans, 'Like I said, I wanted to check, you know, about them sacking you, and I wanted to help—'

'They haven't sacked me, Stevie. I've taken leave. Due to—' she flicked ash on the carpet, 'a domestic situation. I think that's what this is.' She jabbed her cigarette towards her mangled eye. 'It's nothing to do with you.'

Stevie winced. He knew he should want to comfort and hold her. And, for a moment, he thought of touching her arm the way she had his, and sighing in that sympathetic manner. But he stayed where he was, paralysed on her sofa, his eyes constantly flicking towards the taut strings of Barney's tennis racket.

'Look, could you just go?' she said. 'I'm not really ... I can't have this conversation with a pupil just now.'

He took that in for a second, that word. *Pupil.* Then he rose and bolted for the door, hating himself for the great relief that welled in his chest as he realised that what she'd said was true. This was nothing to do with him.

Out in the street, he was filled with violent thoughts. He pictured himself surprising Barney from behind, plunging a large knife straight through the fluff of his dressing gown and puncturing his lung. He imagined kicking Barney into the mud with an army-issue boot, raising a rifle and waiting whilst the beast begged for mercy before shooting him between the eyes.

That evening, Mike called home from Helston. The training was going well, he said, but it would be a while before he'd be ready to go into combat. Probably the war would be over before he got to the Falklands. He sounded disappointed.

From behind his newspaper, Stevie's father read out the latest news. *The Belgrano, which survived the Pearl Harbor attack when it belonged to the US navy, had been asking for trouble all day . . .*

Stevie and his mother left the room. When they were alone in the kitchen together, she told Stevie that Mike's call reminded her of one he'd made, years ago, whilst on his first school holiday on the Isle of Wight. It was so long-awaited, that call, and yet, when it happened, neither of them knew what to say, so they'd talked about the food, and the weather, and afterwards she'd cried, because she'd forgotten to tell her son that she missed him. Stevie listened, and nodded, and then he handed her a tissue.

'Don't you go away, too, will you?' she said. 'Don't go and fight any stupid wars. I know it's what men do, but . . . you're different, aren't you?'

She traced the outline of his face with a fingertip and looked at him for a long time, and he nodded.

Then she flicked the switch on the cassette player, and a song came into the room. He recognised the voice as Smokey Robinson's. She had to pull him to his feet, but once Stevie was in his mother's arms and could smell the familiar scent of chip fat and perfume on her collar, he rested his head on her warm shoulder and held her as tightly as he could.

His father came in. 'The girls love a man with a woman's voice,' he said. 'Don't they, June?'

But Stevie's mother said nothing, and Stevie didn't let go. Instead he clung to her, letting her dance him around the room, her skirt whirling and whirling like a crazed bird.

DIDI'S

Nikesh Shukla

Artwork by Jonathan Trayte

Didi's

Nikesh Shukla

For Chimene Suleyman

ONE

The way he looks at me, I know he's going to send a drink over and then follow it up three minutes after that with his ass on the seat next to me. Luckily, Teddy knows me and so, when he sits the beer down on the counter next to me, he asks if I want an exit strategy. I look up from my book and shake my head at him.

'I was hoping reading a book would be my exit strategy,' I say.

He laughs and shimmies his shoulders to the Frank Ocean song playing. It's hit the bit with the strained falsetto at the end. Before I look back down at the page, I see Teddy bite his bottom lip and spin around to face the rest of the bar. I cackle. Rohan once said my laugh was the noise a passer-by would least expect me to make. It was, he said, how shy people really sound when no one is paying any attention.

I need new friends.

Teddy, trying to hold my attention, does that cock-hitting lip-biting head shimmy that made *Bad*-era Michael Jackson impossible to look away from.

I found Teddy's Instagram page recently. He's in an all-boy dance troupe called Gravity Bites. They all look ten years too late to be a boyband. Like they've formed a tribute band to N-SYNC now, approaching forty, rather than N-SYNC in their prime. He's their Joey Fat One.

Four minutes after the beer goes untouched, I feel the guy slide onto the seat next to me.

'What are you reading?' he asks, like the book is a major imposition.

I flap up the cover so he can see it, while keeping my eyes on the page, cursing this guy for making me re-read the same sentence four times.

'Any good?' he asks.

I hold my finger up to indicate I'm still reading, let me finish. I carry on staring at the page, long enough to turn it, and stare more. I wait until it becomes awkward.

I hear him let out a slow, deliberate sigh of air.

'Okay, I hear ya,' he says, sliding off his stool and standing. He walks back to his buddy.

'Excuse me,' I say, looking up finally. He turns around expectantly. 'You forgot your beer,' I say louder.

He cuts eyes at me. 'It's on me,' he says.

I want to laugh. I look up at Teddy and he rolls his eyes around, clockwise. I let out a giggle.

The apartment is dark. It doesn't feel like home yet. Everything is placed in an unfamiliar location.

I can hear the dog's tail wagging as I enter. It's come to the door. I haven't taken it out all day.

I refuse to call him Spider-Man. It's a stupid name. Rohan's an idiot.

I switch the light on and there he is, Spider-Man the dog, staring at me. He nods over to where his leash hangs off my bookshelf. I look at the doormat where I stand to pick up the dog-walker's note.

It's written by some guy called Mike. He always leaves something cute.

> *Spider-Man, Spider-Man, does whatever a*
> > *doggie can.*
> *Except a number two. He may be constipated.*
> > *Or superheroes never need the toilet.*
> *Mike*

Sighing, drunk from the free beer I accepted, I grab the lead off the shelf and open the bag with the empanada in it. So much for eating it in front of Twitter in my bed, I think.

Outside, Spider-Man has his nose to the ground. Searching for rivals. Jackson Heights is blissfully still at this time, part of the reason I moved here. I don't know the area too well yet. The empanada is warm in my stomach. I'm thirsty. Spying an open bodega, I walk towards it to buy a bottle of water. Inside, the lights are bright and there is a bustle. I keep looking back at the front door, nervous to leave Spider-Man by himself. I buy a bottle of water, silently, from a guy who barely looks up from the Hindi melodrama he's watching on his phone.

I've downed half the bottle before I've untied Spider-Man.

We walk a couple more blocks. I want to go home but the way Spider-Man tugs at the lead, excited to be out at 4 a.m., makes me feel bad about cutting short his street time. We near a corner and there is a familiar noise.

Someone's listening to the *Dhoom 3* soundtrack. It makes me smile. I remember the song well, Katrina Kaif simulates a chaste lap dance for 50-year-old Aamir Khan, who is wearing a bowler hat and suit vest like a creep. I may have misremembered this. There are voices talking over the soundtrack. The familiar familial sound of shrill, fast Gujarati peppers the night air and for a second I'm transported home.

I haven't been back in months. Not since Papa told me he voted Trump and I yelled that he was a sell-out before hiding in my room and getting not-stoned from a 7-year-old joint I remembered I hid in an old copy of a Jhumpa book. I can barely speak to the man on the phone. I'm sure to send Mom photos of me on every single damn protest, my placards and slogans clear, because I know she's definitely showing them to him. But no way I'm spending time with that apologist for the racist hashtag notmypresident.

Hearing the *Dhoom 3* soundtrack reminds me of a few Christmases ago, being home, with Preeti, listening to it on repeat as we drove around, doing the Greatest Hits of our stupid upstate small town. It reminds me of my mom, standing over the kitchen counter, cutting up okra wheels so small they dissolved in your mouth, while a desi cable channel pumped out the hits.

That song.

> *Ni main kamli, kamli,*
> *Mere yaar di*

With no one to speak to in Gujarati in the city, I've been feeling homesick.

I almost bound around the corner, feeling instantly at home as I hum the chorus, my arrival announced by Spider-Man's relentless enthusiasm.

Seven people, three women and four men, all dressed in jubo lenghas and sarees, wearing NY Yankees puffa jackets, stand around the open trunk of a car, smoking, listening to music and laughing. There are deep silver trays of food, potatoes and onions and okra and gajar pickle and white rice and yello kadhi and my favourite, mounds of khichdi, all stacked next to the trunk.

They all stop talking as I arrive, and look at me.

In unison, they all nod, and I walk on, waving an embarrassed *hi* to the sky, as they resume their conversation.

It's only when I've passed them that I turn around and nod back. None of them is paying any attention.

That communal nod of theirs, it stays with me all the way home. For a second, I don't feel homesick.

TWO

I'm thinking about those people the next morning when Rohan stops by the coffee shop to grab my keys and collect Spider-Man.

He nods at me as he enters and I smile and offer a small wave. The shop is empty. I'm leaning on the counter, reading articles on my phone.

If you have time to lean, you have time to clean, the old barista mantra goes. Not me.

'You have a good time with the pup?' he asks.

'Nah,' I say. 'He definitely shed hair on everything I own. He smells like butt. All my throw pillows look like mohair monstrosities now.'

'At least you're no longer referring to Spider-Man as *it* any more. That tells me you bonded at least.'

'Perhaps,' I say. 'How was your trip?'

'Oh, you know,' Rohan says. 'Shaadis are always four days too long, twenty masis too social and one racist kaka. I brought you a box of samosas though. Shall I leave them in your apartment?'

'Leave me one,' I say. 'I need my fix. God, I can't wait to go to a wedding this year. I need my masi fix.'

'All right, bet,' Rohan says, handing me a baggy with a deliciously brown samosa in it.

An online commentator wrote under my last essay, about the unbearable whiteness of publishing, that I should shut the fuck up because no one cares what a chubby samosa thinks. I thought, my guy, the last thing you want is a thin goddamn samosa.

Rohan leaves as another brown guy enters, wearing a snapback that says Haram on it. They nod at each other.

As the Haram guy approaches the counter, I smile and he nods at me.

'You know Rohan?' I ask.

'Who?' he says.

'What can I get you?' I ask. Maybe I mistook that nod.

THREE

'Where you from?' the Uber driver asks me.

I don't mind answering. Her name is Priyanka. She laughs after everything she says, and in silences flatly says *doo-be-doo*. No tune associated with it. Just *doo-be-doo*. Normally I would find it so irritating but tonight, it sounds utterly charming.

'I'm Gujarati but I grew up in New Jersey,' I tell her.

'Baroda?'

'Rajkot.'

'I have a faiba in Rajkot. You know the Mistrys?'

'No,' I say. 'Should I?'

She laughs. 'It's what you say when you're in strange cities, you try to find the links. It helps you feel connected.'

'Does it?' I say. 'It makes everyone feel so far away.'

'At first,' she says. 'But then, before you know it, you're nodding at every person with brown skin you walk past, and you start to feel like you're near the people who look like you. It helps you put down roots.'

'I miss my mom,' I say.

'Me too,' she says. 'Where is yours?'

'Bergen County. You?'

She taps at her neck. Her taveez.

'I'm sorry. When did she pass?'

'Five years ago. I was not even there. My sister sent this to me in the mail. My mother. Through the mail.'

'All the way from Gujarat?' I say.

'No,' she says, looking in her rear-view. 'Houston.'

She laughs. I smile back. We fall into silence.

Doo-be-doo, she tells me flatly.

We're nearing home. It's late. The amber swell of the streetlights as we approach my street are a comforting welcome-home for my drunk ass. Drunk enough to Uber. At some point tonight, I was sober enough to say yes to one more drink. I got even more excited when that one more drink was at my favourite bar in my old neighbourhood.

As we pass the building a few blocks from my house, Priyanka points at it.

'So glad I took this job,' she says, banging the steering wheel. 'I can go and get some aapna food.'

'Where?' I ask. 'It's 4.20 a.m. Where you gonna get dhal bhatt shaak rotli?'

Priyanka slows the car and looks back at me, leaning with my cheek against the cool window.

'You live here and you don't know about Didi's?' I shake my head. 'Didi's Gujarati food?' I shake my head again. I close my eyes and smile. I want to lie down. I want to drink something fizzy. I want to not be in this car. 'Come on,' she says. 'Let's get some dhal bhatt shaak rotli at 4.23 a.m.'

Priyanka pulls the car over and parks it before I can agree.

I've not heard of Didi's. My mom's rotlis were the best. We all say that of our mom's way of making them. Each mom has their special way. Every chapatti is different. Every family serves their chapattis differently. I know that now. I know that Sheila mami likes them small and thick, that Nisha kaki likes them with lots of ghee. I know that Ba made flying saucers, with the middle all puffy. Mom makes them flat. Like our family is used to. Every family learns to make them their favourite way. The difference is subtle. It can be down to the diameter, thickness, amount of heat. My mom's chapattis were thin and very round, covering the circumference of her circular rolling board. She would cook them on a naked flame, using her asbestos fingers to turn them as needed. They were sometimes burnt and always as they should be. I haven't been home in months. I want rotli.

'Sure thing, Priyanka,' I say.

I open the car door, and wrench myself from the backseat. I've been in this car so long I feel less drunk and more heavy.

'Didi's,' I say to her, as she leads me to the door.

'Aapna,' she says, smiling.

Ours.

FOUR

Meena sends me out from the hotel to get these infamous kebabs. I'm walking down some random street behind the Taj. Every red-flag word of warning Mom gave me about this country is banging through my brain.

But at the same time I can't help but feel like I'm at home.

The two men, hunching over four oil drums, each one blazing, illuminating their faces golden in the night sky, work dough for the naans, keep the kebabs turning, have the right change for you before you've even paid. I order two lamb and two chicken.

Mom said don't eat street food, your poor American stomach won't like it.

I ask where I can buy some beers. It's almost a novelty,

being able to drink at nineteen. One of the kebab-wallahs points down a street.

It's dark and eerie and exactly the type of street Mom told me to never walk down alone. The buoyancy in my feet comes from stepping out of my American shoes into something more ethereal. I get this place. I don't need Mom to patronise me.

Fucking come on. White people come to India to find themselves all the fucking time. A desi girl can't walk down a dark Bombay street and masquerade for a local at all?

I've been instructed to knock on a window. I look around for the window in the side of the warehouse that occupies the majority of the dead-end street I've been sent down. I feel like I'm on the set of *Don't Look Now*.

To be honest, there's only one thing on the side of the building that could be a window. I tap on it, confidently. I need beer goddamnit, my kebabs are going soft, so quick, please.

The window opens, decisively. A man sits at a desk in the window. He nods at me.

'Two Kingfisher,' I ask, peering inside, watching men crate up bottles of beer and eat kebabs from the same place I just stopped at.

'White label or black label?'

'White,' I say, not entirely convinced I'm enough of a connoisseur of any alcohol to know the difference.

Back at the hotel, Meena is nearly ready for our trip to Inferno. I tell her about the warehouse of beer.

'Look at you, badass, with your local knowledge,' she says, laughing.

I've always wanted to call this place home, I think. It feels right.

FIVE

Didi's is quiet and small and exactly like the inside of that warehouse behind the Taj in Bombay. Plastic white Formica chairs, plastic white Formica tables, plastic spoons, plastic thalis. A television in the corner pumps out a Bollywood playlist off of YouTube. I bare my teeth at Priyanka and nod my head in time to the beat. She smiles at me.

The smell of the food is fantastic.

My cousin over in England sent me a link to an article recently, about some landlord who refuses to rent to desis because our food smells too much. Lord, I wrote back to him. Curry smells so much better than egg mayo, my god.

Curry smells better than boiling ham, he wrote back.

I laughed for hours about that.

Smelling this food, I'm immediately taken home.

Pops, watching that television, as the girl dances the item number. Mom sitting, one foot up on the chair, her elbow draped over it, smearing gajar pickle into her thepla and eating it in two bites, the smell lingering for hours, me gulping down a salt lime soda as a treat.

Further back, to school, Mom making me get changed out of my school things, into home clothes – a plain kurti, trackies – so that my clothes didn't smell of the food. Us keeping our coats and our outdoor clothes out of the kitchen. The worst thing, she was intimating, would be being told that our clothes stink of curry. The first dish I learned to make myself was pasta with tomato sauce. The care packages she sent to me at college, theplas and parathas wrapped in tin foil, the empty jelly jars now filled with gajar pickle, keree ni chutney, I'd eat 'em on benches in the quad, by myself, knowing that Lindsey, my roommate, would complain if I ate them in our room, because she complained about everything. It made me feel so far away. Like when they served some sort of miscellaneous generic chicken curry in the cafeteria and she put her scarf over her nose, baulking about the smell and looking at me.

Anyway, all of this is undone those first few moments in Didi's.

There are a couple of people eating, dressed in black suits with black shirts. They eat separately but both look up at Priyanka and smile at her. She waves back at them.

'They drive cabs too,' she says.

'What's the worst thing about driving cabs?' I ask.

'People spoiling movies for you,' she says, smiling. 'Or television. Or basketball. Or your seats, with vomit, cum, oily foods. People thinking they know better than satnav. Traffic. DVT. Having to buy things so you can use the bathroom. There's a lot of things.'

'Wow,' I say. 'Is there anything good?'

'I get to listen to a lot of podcasts.'

I laugh as Priyanka leads me towards the counter. Didi is checking her phone, leaning against a wall. I recognise her as one of the people who gave me the nod the other night. I realise now, this is the building I walked past with Spider-Man. I look around – the rest of the nodders are all here, serving food. She has a permanently open mouth, seemingly mostly smiling, and thick-ass glasses. Her hair is pulled tight into a bun. She wears one of those black tees that lists a bunch of names: Hers says *Didi & Masi & Faiba & Ba & Mota Ba & Bhen-a-ji.* I love it. I take a sneaky picture of it, for the Gram. Didi looks up at me as I hit snap.

'Kem cho didi,' Priyanka asks.

'All right, che,' Didi replies, without looking up from her phone. 'Who is your friend?'

'A customer,' Priyanka says. 'She is missing home.'

'Gujarati?' Didi asks me, looking up. I nod. 'You want some khichdi?'

I haven't eaten khichdi since Dada's cremation. I sat in the kitchen with Mom and washed great bowls of brown lentils by hand as everyone sat next door singing prathna. Pops kept popping his head in the door asking if we needed help. He looked so lost. Dada had been such an integral part of our lives. When he had his mind, he dictated our social engagements. When he didn't, we did everything for him. It was all-encompassing. Jesus fuck, the amount of times I had to help Pops lever him out of a bath and Dada got all weird cos his penis was out, like there was anything either vaguely sexual or humiliating about the nudity, and not the fact that this man no longer possessed a mind that could control his own damn body. It was depressing.

At Dada's cremation, relatives turned up with food – samosas, bateta nu shaak, paneer, rotlis, but it was Mom's khichdi that kept us all going. When I asked her how to make it, she said it was her favourite too and she would teach me one day – either peasant food or grief food, she said. I laughed, wolfing down my second bowl of the stuff.

'Yes please,' I say to Didi, as she spoons a mound of

khichdi into a white plastic bowl, handing me a white plastic spoon.

Priyanka asks for some bakri and gajar nu pickle. Didi unwraps some foil and lifts a hard disc onto a plate.

'Together?' Didi asks and Priyanka looks at me.

I'm about to say sure why not, when Priyanka laughs.

'Separate,' she says. 'This is not part of her fare.'

I'm about to bite into my khichdi as I walk towards a table, choosing to sit on my own while Priyanka heads over to catch up with one of the other drivers. The other one disconnects his phone from a phone charger and stands up, ready to leave. He looks familiar, like I've used his cab on Lyft or something. He has a thin, pencil-like beard and moustache and his hair sticks up like he is Guile in *Street Fighter II*. He catches me staring at him. He rubs at his chest, two fingers slip between the buttons under his shirt, and he nods at me as he leaves.

My cheeks burn. I'm embarrassed.

I nod back at the shadow of his departure. He is long gone and part of me feels bereft.

I bite at a huge mound of khichdi, and, too much clove aside, it tastes just like how Mom used to make. I feel like I'm at home.

SIX

I eat leftover khichdi at work the next day. I'm sitting in front of the coffee shop. Maggie told me to eat my smelly food outside.

I joked that it did overpower the smell of avocado on fucking sourdough toast somewhat. She smirked as if to say, I functionally understand this to be a joke but refuse to understand it or honour it with a laugh.

Fuck her, fresh air.

I'm leaning against a bench when a guy approaches wearing a bomber jacket made out of sherwani material and fucking Bata chappals. I smirk at him, except this smirk says 'I am digging the fashion, my friend, and I get it, I get its heritage, but this is not necessarily an invitation to stop and chat, so keep walking'. He nods at me.

'What's up, ma?' he asks in a hoarse voice, like he's been on too many villain auditions in one day. 'You good?'

He talks with such clear familiarity and friendliness that, for a second, I worry that we know each other, even though I can count the number of brown people I know in this city on a thumb, called Rohan.

'Do I know you?' I ask.

'Aren't we all related?' he says, laughing.

'Sorry, we're in an awkward exchange now. I love your chappal-and-sherwani look and you said hey and for a second, I thought I knew you. But I don't. Do I?'

'Naw, but it's good. Always good to see another desi out here. It's like a mayonnaise factory.' I laugh and he laughs too. 'What you eating?'

'Khichdi?' I say, unsure why I'm embarrassed, suddenly, claiming food-authenticity with another brown person, like he might correct me on my pronunciation, or say, actually, that is Gujarati brown-lentil khichdi, it's important to be specific, lest I think it's a Nepalese red-lentil khichdi, mixed with lamb mince and parsley.

'You sure?' he says.

'Yeah, it's delicious. From Didi's,' I say, like a goddamn pro. I coulda lived here my entire life.

'Oh word,' he says. 'I love that place. Gotta get me some oondhwo. Anyways, stay blessed.' He starts to walk away, stops then turns to me again. 'Jay Shree Krishna,' he says, and leaves.

SEVEN

'I cannot believe Didi's is still there,' Mom says.

I'm surprised she has heard of it. It has become an obsession of mine. I've been there three out of five nights, tried pretty much the entire menu, each dish tasting like home. I've eaten alone with a book, I FaceTimed a buddy in London, and I brought Rohan. Who tagged us on Instagram. Which is how Mom knew about it. Since she joined Instagram to share Sanskrit memes and follow Priyanka and Deepika and the hungama of all the other Bollywood stars, she is obsessed with the app. Of course she comments under every one of my Grams. Of course she follows Rohan. Of course it means he tags me into everything every time we see each other. It's his way of ensuring we keep in touch. His mom died four years ago. Since then, he's been ending every episode of his podcast with 'Call your mom. She misses you'.

Every time I hear him say it, I well up.

'How do you know about Didi's?' I say, shoving a pizza slice in my face so Mom can't tell how sad I feel, interacting with her through a screen.

'Darling, we did not always live here. You know you were born in Queens. A few blocks away from Didi's.'

'Yeah, I know. But it was open then?'

'Of course, Didi's is as old as desis in the city themselves.

60

It was a place for all of us to go and be amongst our people. I know my colleagues at the college here call this self-segregation, but they are goras, Rakhee, darling. They do not understand that this was self-preservation. Going to Didi's every Thursday and listening to people read out their letters from home, or on Saturdays when we would move all the tables to one side and listen to mehfils, or the friends Papa made with other taxi drivers. We had a community in the city and that was our central clubhouse.'

'Wow,' I say. 'Well, I love their khichdi.'

'You used to come with us,' Mom tells me.

'Really?' I say, and for the first time in ages, I feel like I'm truly all ears to Mom. Like whenever we talk, I tell her the bits about my week that are palatable to her: the micro-progressions of my career, the micro-aggressions of hipsters, what I've eaten, have I been on any dates. We don't really share stories that count. Everything is a list: a list of meals, a list of names of people I've dated, a list of hipster racist incidents, a list of commissions. There is nothing that makes this conversation easy.

But now, all I want to hear about is the good ol' days of Didi's.

'That place, we called it *the other house*,' she tells me.

'I like that a lot, Mom.'

'Your papa has some good stories, want me to get him on the phone?'

I try to say it as tempered and as plainly as I can. 'I don't want to speak to him,' I say.

'He misses you, beta,' Mom says. 'It was just a vote. It doesn't matter.'

'It does,' I say. 'Anyway, tell me how to make khichdi,' I say, taking the laptop over to my kitchen counter.

'Have you soaked the dhal?' she asks.

I love my mom in this moment. She is firm and clear with instructions, but you can tell, from the smirk on her face, that there is nothing she would rather be doing than telling her only child how to cook her favourite dish over the internet.

She's even put on an apron, even though she's not cooking anything herself.

I want to cry, and tell her I miss her and use any excuse to go home. But she has that determined look on her face, like I will teach this child how to cook like me. I choke back a tear and listen.

EIGHT

Didi's becomes my comfort-food spot.

I eat away bad dates, rejection emails from editors, my silent spat with my pops, Mom's well-intentioned sharing of news of more successful cousins, Spider-Man's death, Rohan's upset, my upset, loneliness, the empty apartment, bad sex, the season finale of a show I would never admit I watch publicly, trolls who seek out women of colour with political opinions on the internet so they can describe to us all the ways they would like us to be raped, a guy I used to hang out with who's now on a pretty successful AMC show ignoring me when I say hello to him at a random bar ...

Didi's becomes where I bask in good news. I only take Rohan if I take anyone. I won't let white people ruin this place for me.

I eat to celebrate a new commission, a published work,

a successful reading, a day at work when I didn't want to spray boiling milk into a customer's eyeball, friends' successes, a guy I used to hang out with getting cast in a pretty successful AMC show, a good conversation with Mom, a care package she sends containing theplas in tin foil and a Hanuman Chalisa book.

I get to know what it's like to know where everybody knows your name.

NINE

It's 4 a.m. and I'm back in the bar cos I know Teddy's working. I'm trying to finish a terrible book I need to review and the only way I can finish it is if I wash it down with two or three beers. I'm at the corner of the bar, leaning against the wall and against the bar, almost squatting over my stool just to stay awake because this book is terrible.

I can feel the man next to me try to get my attention. He flicks a beer mat repeatedly against a knuckle to distract my peripheral vision, he sighs a lot so I'll ask what's wrong, when my mac 'n' cheese arrives he asks the bartender what I ordered, to establish a connection, even though it's just fucking mac 'n' cheese, he makes a phone call to a buddy and says he's doing nothing, just propping up a bar next to the most beautiful tanned lady in Queens.

At which point I put my book down and turn to him. His phone call mysteriously wraps up quickly and he turns to face his entire body at me.

'Brad,' he says, extending his hand.

'Did you just call me tanned?' I ask, curtly.

'Yeah, best tan in Queens. Especially for this time of year.'

'It's my skin colour, buddy.'

I shake my head in disbelief. I hate this, when it's this casual, this normal; it causes my stomach to burn, for me to be that weird kid who never fit in once more.

'So . . . ?' he says, not getting it.

'This is not a tan,' I tell him, slowly, seeing Teddy hover near us, just in case this escalates and he can use his bartender privileges to chuck someone out. 'I'm always this colour.'

'Well, lucky you,' he says. 'Imagine being tanned all year round.'

'Fuck you, asshole.'

'What the fuck did I do?' he says, picking up his phone from the wet bar and then dropping it in beer-spill again. 'It's not like I'm a racist or anything.'

'No,' I say, gathering my things, flaring my nostrils. 'But you said something racist.'

'I'm not a racist,' he says.

I'm out the door.

At Didi's, there's a line; it's Ramadhan and I've come just as people are having their last meal before the fast starts. Priyanka nods at me from three people in front. All the men lining up look tired, haggard. Summer-month fasting must be the toughest.

As I wait, I stare at a collage of pictures, on the wall, near the entrance. I've never noticed them before.

Faded, curled at the corners, almost over-exposed, is a photo of two people I instantly recognise. Beaming, banging dandhiyas together, facing the camera, him in an all-white juba lengha, her in one of her pink floral saree specials.

It's my mom and pops. Doing garba. The inscription reads *Navratri 1989*.

I lean in close.

There I am, almost three, sleeping on two chairs pushed together, wearing a red salwar.

I realise something.

This *other house*, it's always been here for me, home, I just hadn't found it yet. I look at the line of people in front of me, the most brown faces I've been surrounded by since Nadya's shaadi.

This is the *other house*. I snap a photo of the photo on my phone.

I'm ready, I think. It's early, but I'm ready.

I finally feel at home.

I text Pops.

A Quiet Tidy Man

Claire Fuller

Artwork by Luey Graves

A Quiet Tidy Man

Claire Fuller

Before everything changed, my siblings and I liked to canter our horses across the lawn in front of the house. Their hoofs would turn over great clods of turf and my stepfather, Charles Grubb, would follow at a safe distance to stamp the grass back into place. Phyllis, my middle sister, once led her horse into our entrance hall and encouraged it to tackle the stairs. Charles, who happened to be walking past with an un-iced Christmas cake, only raised an eyebrow and returned a few minutes later with a shovel and bucket for the manure which the horse had left along the patterned runner.

Charles accepted us and our house, and the way we lived, because he was in love with our mother, and had been ever since he saw her at the county gymkhana when they were both seventeen. He'd been too shy to declare himself then and so had waited, whilst she married our father, produced first me and my twin sister Joyce, then another child and then two more. Charles's patience paid off, because when our father died unexpectedly, Charles was on hand to step in.

Our mother inhabited an unstructured world where home-schooling was often forgotten for weeks and mess and dirt went unnoticed. But there were six horses and five children to feed, electricity bills to pay, and a stable roof to re-slate, so she married Charles Grubb on the understanding that she didn't have to take his second name, the idea of which caused a scandal amongst our neighbours. When she and I walked into the village post office I was aware of the silence that fell, but my mother was oblivious. She swept her cape around her, taking up more than her share of the available space and dislodging curling postcards of the church font and dusty packets of custard powder.

'I have been Marjorie Bird since my first marriage,' my mother said in her booming voice to the postmistress, Mrs Mardle. 'I may have caught a Grubb, but there is no need to become one.' And she would laugh at her own joke.

As well as trailing after the horses, Charles cleaned up after us in the house, which was old and broken and had a kitchen which was sometimes flooded by the Thames. We children didn't use our own bedrooms, but slept wherever the fancy took us, or sleep overcame us, and consequently all of our clothes, books and toys were left wherever we dropped them. Yet another girl from the village who 'did' for my mother had resigned, this time citing 'feral children, animal droppings trodden into rugs and ducks paddling through the kitchen' as her reasons for leaving. And so our stepfather took to carrying a willow trug he found discarded in the orangery. He picked up single shoes, empty teacups and damp towels as he wandered through the house, placing them in his basket and amiably matching them with their partners or returning them to where they belonged.

Charles had arrived in our house with a portmanteau, a great deal of money and a silver-topped cane engraved with the letters CCG. He allowed my youngest sibling, Clementina, to look at it, and one evening at the dinner table she asked what the C stood for.

'What a ridiculous question,' our mother said. 'C is for Charles.'

'Or cabbages,' said Thomas, one up from Clementina.

'C is for Christ,' said Phyllis who was going through a religious phase.

'Constipation,' said Thomas, laughing and spilling potato from his mouth. 'Cardboard cut-out,' he shouted. 'Curds! Custard face!'

'Thomas!' said our mother. I caught Joyce's eye, and we both looked away, hiding smiles. At fifteen we were supposed to set an example. Charles held his hands up to quieten us.

'You mean my middle name, don't you, my dear? It also begins with a C.' It was Joyce's turn to start laughing.

'Creepy-Crawly Grubb!' she exclaimed. The table was in uproar and we abandoned dinner.

Then, one night when we were least expecting it, our lives changed for ever.

No one discovered what time Charles went into the stables or why – my mother and he had separate bedrooms and she said she'd taken a sleeping draught and didn't hear a thing. It was poor Phyllis who discovered him. She told us she'd been worried her pony might catch a chill in the first January snowfall, so before the sun had even risen she went to the stables with a candle and nearly tripped over Charles lying on the brick floor, his pale face haloed by a dark circle of blood. Her scream pierced the sleeping house, so that we were all awake at once, running in every direction in our night clothes and bare feet.

Finally Joyce put on her shoes and ran to fetch the village doctor who called an ambulance to come and take Charles away. For the whole of that day, with no news from our mother, the five of us huddled around a fire I had lit in the drawing room, eating savoury crackers with apricot jam, going over the events of the previous evening: whose footsteps had crept past Joyce's door just after midnight, what had Thomas heard our mother say to herself in the pantry, and who had been the last person to see Charles. Phyllis – too big for Joyce's lap, but perching there like a cuckoo – could only cling to her sister's neck and sob. Joyce stroked the child's face until she was able to tell us that although all the horses had been locked in their stalls, when she had held the candle aloft over Charles's face she had seen the semi-circular stamp of a horseshoe on his forehead.

Charles lay in a coma for fifty-nine days. Our mother visited him every third day – getting a lift to the hospital in the post van. The passenger seat had been removed, so my mother nestled herself down like a giant tweedy hen among the sacks of letters and parcels. By the time she got home she was too tired to give us much news about how our stepfather was progressing.

On the sixtieth day Charles woke up, although we didn't

learn it from our mother. Joyce had sent me to get gravy browning from the post office where I heard Mrs Mardle talking to a customer. They didn't see me, crouching behind a tall pile of sandbags, listening.

'The poor man opened his eyes and sat straight up. Pulled out his tubes and whatnot and demanded to go home. Just like that.'

'No,' said the customer, sucking her teeth.

'Yes, true as I'm standing here. He's changed, you know.' Mrs Mardle paused for effect and then continued in a loud whisper. 'They say you wouldn't know him. And such a kind man he used to be.' Coins chinked on the glass counter and there was the click of a purse. 'He used to come to the shop to buy his cigarettes. Always happy to pass the time of day.'

'Oh yes,' said the customer in an encouraging tone. 'A lovely man.'

'Well, not any longer. He's been shouting filth at Marjorie Grubb.'

'Marjorie Bird,' corrected the customer, but Mrs Mardle continued talking.

'Demanding to see the doctors at all hours, ordering the nurses about – he's got my Nancy running around after him like he's the only patient on the ward.'

Forgetting the gravy browning, I hurried out and down the lane to tell the news to Joyce. As I looked over my shoulder I saw Mrs Mardle and the customer craning their necks over the fancy goods in the window, their mouths open like hungry fledglings.

Two days later we found out for ourselves how Charles had changed when our mother brought him home. As soon as he limped through the front door we crowded around him, talking at once, asking how he was feeling. He ignored us and pushed through to the hall stand where his cane was resting. He grabbed it by the bottom end, swung it, and like a shot-put, the weight of the handle spun him around. The silver head of the cane struck flesh. Clementina, the nearest to him, got the full force of the blow across the back of her thighs.

'Quiet! All of you,' Charles bellowed. We were so shocked to hear him raise his voice that we were suddenly silent, even Clementina, and in unison took a step backwards. 'I will not have such behaviour in my house.' Charles pointed at me. 'You, boy, help me into the drawing room and you, girl,' he reached forward and prodded Joyce with the cane, 'fetch me my slippers.'

Charles, leaning heavily on my shoulder, limped into the drawing room and indicated that he wished to sit by the fire. As he sagged backwards with a groan, I saw the pink curve of the scar on his forehead and when Joyce came in with his slippers she and I exchanged a look: disbelief and incomprehension.

From that moment on and for the next eight months, Charles dictated and we obeyed. We were all called 'boy' or 'girl' as if there were only two children in the house. We hid from him and for the first time kept to our own rooms and didn't dare leave anything lying around. On rare occasions we were given a glimpse of the old Charles – a quick wink and a smile as if it was all a big joke, but then his face would again turn stony. We whispered in the corners and like ghosts we slunk along the corridors. An apathy came over us and we almost gave up riding altogether – in the mornings we simply turned the horses out into the paddock, where they bunched together, shivering at their sudden change in circumstances.

Our mother, too, was an altered woman. It seemed everything she said or did was to placate Charles. On Saturday evenings she sent me up to the Lamb and Lion for a pint of stout, a few spoonfuls of which she stirred into his Welsh rabbit. But too often melted cheese and slices of toast would be hurled into the drawing-room fire. Once, as she left the room, I saw her uncurl her fists, revealing red crescents which her fingernails had cut into her palms. But the way Charles broke her was to make her change her name. Marjorie Bird became Marjorie Grubb – dumb, passive and infinitely smaller.

If Charles saw us creeping about the house, the best we could hope for was that we would be made to scrub at the tide mark around the kitchen walls, or empty the mouse traps in the attic; worse would be a slap on the back of the head for just passing by, or most terrifying of all – a beating with the cane. My siblings and I often met in the furthest stall in the stables and with the comforting smells of hay and warm horses we compared atrocities and punishments, tended wounds and dried each other's cheeks. One afternoon in early November Clementina ran in crying. She flung herself onto the hay and refused to talk until Thomas, Phyllis and I had gone off for a desultory ride. Eventually, with much cajoling from Joyce, Clem revealed her backside and told all to my twin sister, who later related it to me. Clementina, put in charge of shoe polishing, had forgotten to buff with the soft cloth. She had been summoned by Charles to the drawing room and made to bend over the arm of a wing-backed chair. Clementina, knowing what was coming, shut her eyes, gripped the upholstery and gritted her teeth. Charles pulled down her knickers. Her muscles tensed, waiting for the sting of the cane. It didn't come. Instead she heard him poke at the fire in the grate. Then he was beside her and once again she readied herself for the beating. His hand stroked one of her exposed cheeks, down one leg and then up her inside thigh.

'This is what little girls get for not cleaning shoes properly,' said Charles. And he pressed the end of his silver cane, heated by the fire, into the flesh of her bottom. Joyce told me in the stable that afternoon that she had smoothed horse ointment across Clementina's skin and the clear imprint of the reversed initials, CCG.

It was Joyce who came up with the plan. Younger than me by ten minutes, but sharper and more practical, she told me about it when we were peeling vegetables in the scullery.

'We have to kill him,' she said. Just like that, with a potato in one hand and a knife in the other.

The decision to do it was simple; *how* was the onerous part. Joyce and I discussed the options endlessly – an air-rifle pellet in his head, pushing him off the church tower, drowning him in the river. Phyllis heard us one night arguing in whispers about whether we could steal the post van, run Charles over and get it back in time for the next day's delivery. She told Clementina, who in turn blabbed to Thomas, and so when we all met next in the stables

Joyce's idea had become a plan without any of us really discussing it.

'Cut out his heart,' said Phyllis. 'It's the only way.'

'I could strangulate him,' said Thomas, putting his hands around his own throat and rolling around on the floor making choking noises.

'Don't be silly,' said Phyllis, 'your hands aren't big enough to kill a grown man.'

'They are too.' Thomas sat up and held out his hands. They were remarkably large for an 8-year-old's.

'Suffocation,' whispered Clementina, who had buried herself up to her neck in hay.

'Hanging's too good for him,' I chipped in. It was a phrase I had heard without quite knowing what it meant.

'A sharp blow to the temple might do it,' said Joyce, leaning over the partition to stroke her horse. 'Three bones join at the side of your face. It's a very vulnerable spot.' I wondered where she got her information from.

'Electrocution!' shouted Thomas, falling backwards and jerking his body around.

I laughed, but when Joyce said 'Thomas!' she sounded like our mother used to. We all sat quietly for a while thinking, or in my case thinking about what Joyce might be thinking. 'I know,' she said finally, 'we'll all do all of it, together, all at once. Then they won't know who killed him and none of us will face the long drop.'

'The long drop?' I said, my voice wavering.

'Well of course. There are bound to be consequences. This is murder we're talking about.'

I can honestly say that up until that point I hadn't thought of it in terms of ending someone's life. I had simply seen it as a new beginning. There was silence again whilst we all contemplated our future.

'Children don't get hanged,' said Thomas suddenly, 'they get sent to borstal – the boys anyway. I don't know what they do with the girls.' And then with relief at the one sensible thing Thomas had said that week, we were all talking at once. And so in the afternoon the plan was made and we went in to wash our hands for tea.

Charles liked his household to follow a clear and set routine. We all had our duties; we all knew when breakfast, lunch, tea and dinner were served. And if we weren't already sitting at the table with our fingernails scrubbed and our hair combed when he limped in, there would be trouble. After dinner Charles retired to the drawing room to read his ironed newspaper. Then at a quarter past ten my mother lent him her shoulder and they walked slowly up the stairs; she helped him change into his pyjamas and made him a cup of cocoa, and we children formed a line to peck his whiskered cheek. Thirteen minutes later my mother went back upstairs to help him use the chamber pot, plump his pillows and turn out the light. By quarter past eleven Charles was snoring. I knew this because for two weeks I had watched it through the crack in his bedroom door. His routine was unfailing.

We decided to put our plan into action on the night of 22 December. The five of us went to bed as usual, but I lay in my room listening to every sound the old house made. Each creak and rattle was Charles coming to denounce me as a murderer; every gurgle in the pipes was the rumbling stomach of the policeman pressing his ear against my door.

For hours I lay there, hoping everyone had fallen asleep and wouldn't wake until morning, but at 2.30 the girls tip-toed into my bedroom, followed by Thomas. Clementina perched on a chair.

'I miss the old Charles,' she whispered.

'The old Charles is gone,' said Phyllis coldly.

'Couldn't we knock this one on the head and bring him back?'

'No,' said Joyce. 'This is the only way.' And I knew then we really were going to do it.

In single file we crept along the corridor to Charles's bed-room. Inside it was dark – only a pale moon glowed through the curtains. We tried to be quiet but there were shuffles and bumps as we got into position. Charles didn't stir.

'One, two, three!' hissed Joyce. At once a jumble, tumble, flailing of bodies, of bedclothes, arms and legs and pillows leaking feathers fell upon the man on the bed. And we children pressed a last lungful of breath down and out, and large horse-riding hands squeezed like a stopper, and from a fumble of covers a moonlit hammer flashed, and my paltry stab with a penknife jerked and twitched into a dead man.

It was over much faster than I had anticipated and with much less mess. In no time at all I was back in my own bed, lying in the dark, heart racing. Now, the house's night noises became even more sinister, and Charles's ghost creaked the floorboards and billowed the curtains. All night I lay awake and when the sun rose I steeled myself for our mother's screams. They never came. Instead I heard her voice in Joyce's room, calm and measured, and then a few moments later, shoes clattering down the stairs, the front door opening and slamming. Fifteen minutes later I joined Phyllis, Thomas and Clementina, as we hung over the landing balustrade watching a deathly pale Joyce take the doctor's coat and lead him up the stairs into Charles's room where our mother waited.

After all those dragging night hours everything happened in a rush. Phyllis shut the front door in the face of a police photographer when she thought he was a reporter from the *Oxford Courier*. Two sergeants arrived with moustaches and notebooks, our mother fainted and the doctor brought her round with smelling salts, and finally at lunch time, an ambulance came up the drive.

'But he's dead,' said Thomas.

'It's to take his body to the mortuary for a post-mortem,' said Joyce in a tinny voice.

'So they can look at his insides,' said Phyllis.

Clementina, sitting on the bottom step of the staircase, gave a shudder. Joyce pulled her out of the way as two uni-formed men struggled down with a covered stretcher. We went into the kitchen to make ham sandwiches.

We were questioned of course, individually, and with our mother. No one was arrested and no one seemed to know what to do with us – there was some talk of borstal and the girls being boarded-out, but our mother refused to let us go. If we had expected life to return to how it was before Charles was knocked on the head, we were mistaken. We moped around the house and made a half-hearted attempt to celebrate Christmas. Thomas and I went into the woods and spent an afternoon in the rain hacking at a fir tree with a blunt axe. Eventually, knowing we were beaten, we dragged home a fallen branch which we propped up in the hall and decorated with the five white doves which had stood on last year's Christmas cake. For a week the hall was filled with the woodlice which crawled out from under the branch's rotten bark. We were in limbo, waiting for the inquest – the final outcome which would seal our fate.

Then, when the Christmas holiday was over and a date had been set, we were told that, like much of the county, the court had been flooded and the inquest was postponed. Whilst my siblings and I mopped water from the kitchen floor, our mother took to her bed and refused to see anyone but the doctor. He happened to play bridge with the coroner's cousin and at his intervention the inquest was rearranged to take place in the village hall at the top of our lane.

Phyllis, in a yellow sou'wester, insisted on riding her pony, with the rest of us trudging behind – our mother leaning tiredly on her dead husband's cane.

'Who does Phyllis think she is?' Clementina asked me under our shared umbrella.

'Joan of Arc,' I said. Over the past month Phyllis's studies had focused exclusively on martyrs. As we entered the little balcony that had been reserved for us, the crowd below turned en masse and looked up. Mrs Mardle, sitting in the first row, dabbed at her eyes with a handkerchief and shook her head. On a podium at the front of the stage, the coroner coughed and the audience turned back to face him and were silent. A thin man stepped out from the shadows and started speaking in a monotone:

'An inquest held for our sovereign lady Queen Elizabeth II in the village of Little Wittenham in Wallingford Rural

District, United Kingdom of Great Britain, on the tenth day of January in the year 1957 by the grace of God before William Payne, Coroner at Law of our said lady the Queen, for the county of Oxfordshire on view of the death of Charles Carew Grubb ...'

'Creepy-Crawly Grubb,' said Clementina under her breath as the man droned on.

'Within the jurisdiction of the said coroner ...'

I have to admit my mind wandered and it wasn't until I heard the shuffling of thirty pairs of wellington boots below that I realised the doctor was about to speak. Yes, he had been called to the house where he found the deceased in bed, yes he had telephoned for the police, yes he had signed the death certificate.

'Get on with it,' I whispered. The doctor strode off into the wings.

'I have before me,' the coroner said in a reedy voice, 'the post-mortem report on Charles Grubb, late of this parish.' He splayed his hands over a thick sheaf of papers.

'Although the deceased appears to have received several wounds, the report clearly states these were inflicted after death occurred.' The coroner hacked loudly and wiped his mouth with a grey handkerchief. 'Charles Grubb died from an overdose of tincture of opium, more commonly known as laudanum, likely to have been administered in the cocoa he drank before he retired to bed.' A collective gasp came from the people in the hall. Only our mother was silent. At the front Mrs Mardle stood up and turned towards us.

'Marjorie Grubb!' she exclaimed, pointing her finger at our mother accusingly. Again, all the heads looked around.

Our mother rose unsteadily. 'My name is Marjorie *Bird*,' she bellowed. And the little balcony and the people of our village trembled as one by one – first me, then Clementina, Phyllis, Thomas and lastly Joyce – stood up beside her and stared back.

THE LIGHTING
OF THE LAMP

Ben Okri

Artwork by Marco Palmieri

THE LIGHTING OF THE LAMP

Ben Okri

ONE

The room watched her. It was nine o'clock.

She had been trying to sleep. In the dark her mind seemed a vast space. Sleep seemed only a tiny thing. She was oppressed by the weight of her imaginings. Her body felt heavy in the night.

She stared at the dark shapes of flowers in their pots. She had taken much care in their arrangement round the room. She had wanted the leaves of the potted plants and the trailing vines to catch the street lights and create intriguing patterns on the walls at night. While contemplating the mysterious shapes cast on the walls, she often drifted off in pleasant musings. The shapes reminded her of magic lanterns.

Sometimes in the shapes she saw mountain ranges and

the red horde of warriors on horseback. Sometimes she saw lovers whispering in a glade. Often she glimpsed furtive adultery in a grotto. At times she saw dancing nymphs on Arcadian plains. Once she saw a murderer creeping away in the dark, and she cried out at her own vision.

Every night these forms and figures were different. Every night their narrative grew and changed. She thought of them as the perpetual autobiography of her imagination. They were lives she dreaded, lives she would like to live.

She never dreamt at night. If she had dreams she never remembered them. This was her form of dreaming, eyes wide open in the night. She was not sure if she were normal or a little mad. Maybe a little mad. Yet she had all the good fortune in the world.

Many friends had complimented her on her plants and flowers and their delightful fugal configuration about the room. The compliments had brought her a secret glow and made company more pleasurable. But now, unable to sleep, neither the evocative patterns of the plants, nor the praises they drew, could make the spaces within her any more comfortable.

TWO

In the darkness she watched the patina of the street lights on the goldfish bowl. Earlier she had discovered that one of the fishes had died. She had changed the water. She had given the goldfish a fitting funeral. She washed the slime off its tiny body and took the fish to the bathroom and let it sink to the bottom of her bath water. Perched on the toilet seat, she re-read passages of *Hamlet*. She intrigued herself by thinking that the death of the goldfish somehow illuminated Ophelia's suicide.

She had a herbal bath with the fish in the water. When she finished she dried herself and performed a funeral rite over the dead fish, singing a Lou Reed song. Laughing quietly, she mused at how wonderful it was that in a room of one's own any whim can become a reality. Later she threw the goldfish into the dustbin.

THREE

Staring at the goldfish bowl, she allowed herself to become sentimental. There were two goldfishes and now there was only one. She was slightly afraid.

FOUR

On the wall facing her bed there was an abstract painting. The painting was often a portal into musings. A friend had given it to her. One evening, over a bottle of Muscadet, they had an argument about art and life. The abstract painting was his reply two days later. For her it put an end to the possibility of a refutation. She could not remember what the argument was about, but the painting was its definitive conclusion. She had an acquired awe of art. She believed it conferred meaning on life even if the meaning eluded her. A work of art was not hers to decipher. Three years at university had given her words, classification, and instruments of criticism. But these had only served to deepen her awe, her incomprehension. She liked to think that art was inexhaustible. The fact that her friend, the painter, was now in a mental institution conferred on the work an iconic authenticity, an extreme intelligence.

FIVE

Lying on the bed, she had an illumination of sorts. The meaning of the painting came to her. It invaded her from the fear of sleep, the disembodied footfalls in the street outside, and the demise of her precious goldfish.

Death, she thought. That's why he went mad.

SIX

She felt better now. The understanding brought a sense of security. She could now allow her mind to wander, to experience the aesthetic pleasures of unbridled thinking.

SEVEN

There were footfalls of someone coming down the inside stairs. She tried to give the footfalls a face. The person was silent for a moment and then burped. A door opened and closed.

She listened, waiting.

Somewhere in the distance the shrieking of cats circulated in her mind. They are having orgies, she thought.

Then the shrieks transfigured into shapes on the wall. They became wailing figures of women racked with anguish, their hair streaming wildly about them. They rose in rough waves, rising from the floor, and when they bore down on her she gave an involuntary shriek. She turned over on the bed, shook her head, and changed her mind about the meaning of the painting. It must be anguish, she thought. The anguish of the numberless.

EIGHT

Perturbed, she permitted herself a literary meditation touched with the metaphysical. She allowed herself a combined vision of T. S. Eliot's Eumenides on window panes and fragments of Dante's *Inferno*. And damned sleepless urban nights.

She decided to get up. To act. To do something to dispel the dark mysteries of the mind.

NINE

Her mouth tasted sour. She smelt her breath. It smelt of stale wine and garlic and stale vegetables. The odour of wilting plants and cigarette ash came to her as she made her way to the bathroom. She brushed her teeth and then flossed. By the time she had finished she felt restored to that sense of self-satisfaction that comes from conforming to an ordered, accepted way of living. She felt a little more at ease among her assorted objects and artefacts. She felt she held her place in the modern universe.

She combed her hair, brushing it backwards, and applied a hairspray which kept it tinted in the front. The rest of her hair was artificially blonde. The brilliant light bared her features in the mirror. I am finally beginning to rust, she thought.

On the way back to the living room a mass of air turned in her stomach. With a half-guilty sense of freedom, she modulated its expulsion.

TEN

Across the street people had gathered. They were squabbling about something. She watched them for a moment. As she took her eyes away she made out, in the margin of her vision, that they had begun fighting.

Two women who looked very drunk and two men who were blind drunk were beating up a younger man. The women smashed their handbags on his head repeatedly. The men kicked his ribs and threw wild swinging punches at his face and neck. The younger man doubled up on the floor, screaming and waving his arms uselessly.

When she turned back to see what was happening the scene had changed. The younger man was tearing across the street, zigzagging between parked cars, shouting abuse. The others bounded after him like maddened thugs. A moment later all she could hear was the violence of their voices as they disappeared from view.

A few lights went on in rooms across the street. Timid-looking couples peered out of their windows. They looked up and down the street. Seeing nothing they lowered their windows and their blinds.

She extracted a musing from her observation. The Eumenides on window panes and in the streets and no one notices.

She felt like some wine.

ELEVEN

She brought out a bulbous wine glass and poured herself a full glass of cheap red wine which she bought by the litre from the Italian shop round the corner. She rolled a stick of cigarette, trembling lightly. Gliding about the room, embracing the air, rearranging her work table, she drank steadily.

She made a note in her diary. She fingered the potted plants and turned the lampshades so the light shone more obliquely on the wall. She wanted the dreamy atmosphere of certain movies of the forties. She began to sway. Serenity flowed through her. The wine loosened her and her movements became more elaborate. She lit the stick of tobacco and smoked languidly. The lights touched all she saw with a hint of fantasy. She was getting a bit drunk.

TWELVE

Feeling elated, she went to her wardrobe and changed into a pair of clean silk underwear. The sensation of the material spread a sensual tingle through her body. She toyed with the sensation in her mind. She drank steadily and lit another roll of tobacco. She searched for her address book and rang a few friends. Most of them were out. While talking to the ones who were in, her voice was uneven, with a barely controlled intensity. She was more forward than usual. She made accusations where she might have made barbed comments. Her bristling remarks left the voice on the other side laughing nervously and wishing her goodnight. She was angry that they wouldn't come over. She felt slightly humiliated that she had to resort to jibes at their manhood and that it didn't work anyway. She slammed the phone down on the last one who refused to come and have a drink with her. They were scum anyway. Next time we meet they'll see. They know what a verbal terror I am. They'll see.

THIRTEEN

The bottle was half-finished. She'd been trying to re-read Dante in the OUP translation. It was nitrogen to her sense of life. Reading it brought back her university days. Suddenly the flat filled with gloom. The place seemed to shrink. The tobacco gathered a nauseous taste at the back of her throat and the wine all of a sudden tasted insipid. She felt a wave of panic rise in her.

She moved round the room and touched the kettle, her books, and the newly installed work bench. She washed the dirty plates with yellow plastic gloves on. She cleaned the kitchen table and then she wore the new pair of jeans she bought two days ago and went out.

FOURTEEN

It was cold outside. She tightened her coat about her. The street was quiet and she was not particularly afraid. She had never had any trouble and having lived in the area for so long made her feel safe. There were lights on in isolated rooms. Music pounded the pavement from a basement flat. There was a party on and she didn't know anyone down there.

She passed the block of tenements that was being demolished. Many houses were being torn down. At the road junction she was surprised that the pubs were still open. She never owned a watch. She felt a watch would limit her sense of life, determine her sense of time. It was an attitude she had kept up from her Oxford days.

Strange faces confronted her in the pub: faces of old men with old women, faces crumpled and squeezed. One of the men had a clotted eye. They all stared at her. She had been feeling old but in that moment she was almost wickedly pleased that she would never be as old as any of them.

She bought herself a glass of red wine and sat at a table. She drank and smoked and wandered amongst the memories the jukebox music aroused in her.

Not long afterwards a black man in his late forties came towards her.

FIFTEEN

He came with a pint of lager in his hand. He smiled knowingly, almost cheekily. His overcoat emphasised his swagger. He carried himself well, which was what she expected. Smiling to herself, she sipped from her drink. She was determined not to say a word or make a gesture that might betray her uneasiness.

SIXTEEN

He struck up a conversation which consisted of slurred questions. She could not make out much of what he said and could not bring herself to say pardon so many times. She replied to him from what sense she could make of isolated words. In fact she answered questions she would have liked to have been asked, questions that his words lent themselves to: she answered an echo.

'What do you do?'

For a long time he did not reply.

She filled his silence with many speculations and rather liked his silent occupations. She looked at him. He was broad-shouldered. Though on the short side, he gave the impression of a certain monumentality. His face, revealing little, was of a solid cast, giving way to sharply defined lines. She thought him an abstract sculpture. She thought him full of character. His silences spoke more than the forced wit and the facile conversations of most of her friends.

She found herself laughing for no particular reason; there was something funny about him in an obscure way. She found his presence relaxing, undemanding, comforting.

She still could not make sense of him, but he was like a mountain she had grown up with, that was just there. He seemed to ask nothing of her except that she follow her whim and be herself, whatever that self happened to be. It was a feeling she hadn't experienced before. It was simple and uncomplicated and it made her dreamy.

SEVENTEEN

When the pub finally closed she asked him if he wanted to come back to her place for a drink. This was partly due to her sense of freedom and her cultivated directness. He had been reciting lines of Rimbaud in drunken French which she took to be incantations in a mysterious language.

They staggered out into the street, where she began singing a Leonard Cohen song. Realising her desire for closeness, she urged him to sing with her. He sang too but they were songs she had never heard before. The songs conveyed to her a vision of islands and sun and sea. He was singing a made-up melody to Rimbaud's final words in 'Une Saison en Enfer'. They were Rimbaud's last published words before he set off in exile to a life in Africa: 'Mais pourquoi regretter unéternal soleil, si nous sommes engagés à la découverte *de la clarté divine.'* He had been mixing his own words with the poet's words and was happy in his improvisation. He had found the melody in the company of this friendly, laughing woman.

Somewhere in her mind, as she sang and listened to him singing his ancestral songs, his freedom songs, was the sense of a sanction that to love a black man was an act of imagination, a kind of solidarity. They both seemed happy as they stumbled down the street, singing.

EIGHTEEN

In her room she offered him coffee, to which he said thank you. She brought out her packet of Indian coffee and two tiny coffee cups.

'Do you take it black?'

'Yes,' he said.

He sat in monumental serenity in her sunken cane chair.

'You have a nice room.'

'I painted the walls myself.'

'You painted that?' he asked, pointing at the abstract painting on the wall.

'It was a gift from a friend,' she said proudly.

Then after a moment she said:

'He is now in a madhouse.'

He stared at the painting a long time and said nothing. She was not used to that quality of silence. He looked around the room. As he looked only his eyes moved. His face betrayed nothing. He looked at things as if they had just come into being.

The innocence of his looking fascinated and bothered her.

It seemed so pure. It was as if he looked at things without assigning them words or contexts in his mind.

She tried to fill the silence with words. As she spoke little bogeys of doubt crept up in her mind. Things she had heard. Fears lurking in the whispered rumours of the race. But she shrugged them off. He wasn't her first. The others though had been younger and eager and showy and shallow and she understood what they said.

NINETEEN

He came closer to her by a soft kind of magic. She did not object. They touched hands and she withdrew, not knowing why. She asked about his coat and he took it off. She noticed how interesting his form was underneath. She felt herself becoming dreamy again.

She got up and switched off the lights and was surprised to find that she was undressing herself. She liked her naked-ness in the dark. This was new to her. Something about him made her like her body. It was all silk, all sun-kissed, all cream, all river, all undulating landscape, all the sexy songs she had ever heard.

TWENTY

Her body began to sing. This was new to her. She did not recognise this body of hers. It had felt under-used, under-noticed, under-looked-at, under-desired.

In the dark she saw that he was undressed as well.

His body seemed to give off the pure simple glow of an uncomplicated desire.

She jumped slightly when he touched her breasts. Not

in fear, but in astonishment at how so simple a touch could create so complex a sensation.

TWENTY-ONE

He was experienced. She could tell. It was the little things. It was as if he were a woman, as if he were her, in a way. He had great strength and power and force of personality, but did not use any of it. His restraint almost drove her mad.

The vigour was hers; hers too were the sinuous movements. The depth of contact was her acceptance, the sensations were her awareness.

He moved gently and sensitively and she had to hold her breath to catch the tender stars that opened out of the darkness and rushed past to another darkness in the vast universe in her head. She found herself suspended in a state of pleasure so complicated that she wanted to scream. She was no longer aware of what she was or wasn't doing; and because all this was new to her she felt the need to talk, to think, to rationalise, and to follow a habitual route to her destination.

She wanted to get there quickly and he was delaying her and it was a kind of punishment too sweet and intolerable to her wilful nature.

She told him what to do.

She told him to stop stretching her out this way, that she couldn't bear it, and wanted a swift resolution.

It was her cultivated directness all over again.

Touch me here, she said. I can't get there your way. Touch me like this, in this way, round like this, indirectly, avoiding and yet not avoiding the swelling point. Yes, like that.

Much better. That's it. I'm enjoying myself tremendously. I'm much more used to this, oh, this. What's the matter? You don't think I am a freak, do you? Do go on. Yes, like that. It's perfectly perfectly nor . . . normal you know, and lots lots of wo . . . women feel that way, the only way, yes, yes, yes, no, I mean, heavens, yes.

TWENTY-TWO

Then she lost what she was saying and was slurring in the dark. She was slurring and singing in the silky dark in a body that had passed into the dark, leaving behind only vast empty spaces in which a happy emotion flowed. Her tensions were all gone into the dark. She felt now that she was glowing.

She noticed, a little vaguely, that he wasn't glowing as much as she was. But her glow filled up the bed and she could hear the dark humming and the goldfish swimming.

Moments passed as she swam among the emotions and the memories in the night. When she opened her eyes she was aware that she was smiling.

She could see his face in the dark. His face revealed nothing except a faint sense of misunderstanding.

She stammered on about how lovely it had been. She asked if he wanted another drink. He muttered something about a child of the stars. She thought he said something about his children in cars.

A moment later he was in the bathroom, had come back, was hugging her, then kissing her, then wearing his coat. He said something about the singing of flowers in summertime and she agreed that they should meet again sometime.

Then he went out. She listened to his footfalls down the hall and out into the anonymity of the world.

TWENTY-THREE

She had a wash and pottered about the room. She kept telling herself that she'd had a lovely evening. She had gotten to know a bit more about people. Then she realised with a slight shock that she did not know his name. She stood still as she took in this fact. I expect that he probably doesn't know mine, she thought.

TWENTY-FOUR

Outside in the street a tramp went past. He was urinating on the pavement, zigzagging his liquid on stone. He sang incoherently, but loudly, to himself.

TWENTY-FIVE

She brushed her teeth and flossed. She took two capsules of barbiturates, and climbed into bed.

TWENTY-SIX

The room was quiet. Sleep began to invade her but she wanted to invade herself before she fell into the spaces in her mind. She felt round and round on a moving point. She moved her fingers to the patterns on the wall. She traced abstract lines and the waves came in unstable colours. The Eumenides had risen from the window panes. Her hair waved with theirs. The satisfaction that imploded came on the soft tang of the absurd, which made it all the sweeter. She imagined all of her favourite lovers to be there with her.

When she relaxed on the pillows she found not only sleep waiting for her. She felt that the room, with its potted plants and the flowers and the goldfish bowl, had experienced some kind of meaning with her.

TWENTY-SEVEN

The goldfish wound its ceaseless way in the mysterious membrane of water.

TWENTY-EIGHT

The spaces within her were still large and frightening. But as she fell asleep she constructed a poem in her mind, which she would never write.

Meanwhile, the room watched her.

And then the lighting of the lamp.

THESE SILVER FISH

Anne O'Brien

Artwork by John Robertson

THESE SILVER FISH

Anne O'Brien

'I've got something, Kaj. Big. No. Not big. More than one.'

'I'm coming.' Her son throws down his rod and runs towards her, feet pounding the concrete.

'I can't hold them.'

'Let the line out.'

She passes the rod to Kaj. It bends as the fish dart left and right, leaving trails of bluish light behind them. He reels them in until they are close to the pier. When they come to the surface, it's clear these are no tinkers but three or four pounds each. They flash emerald against darker stripes, silver underbellies glinting.

The rod curves in a moon and up they come, one, two, three, four. Kaj's face is tight with concentration. On the fifth, the rod tip snaps, dangling like a broken arm. With the sudden slack, the last mackerel escapes; the other four lie on the concrete gulping air, tails beating a frantic drum.

As the boy unhooks the fish, she drops the bucket into the

sea to fill it. He grips a mackerel with a bloodied tea towel, raises his hand and brings the brass-topped priest down between its eyes. She sets the dead fish in the bucket; the forks of their tails clear the rim. Their bodies stiffen but for one that continues to twitch long after it is dead. She places the net over the bucket. They'd learnt their lesson at the start of the summer when seagulls stole their catch. Mackerel were scarce then, but now, the rich pickings of late summer have drawn big shoals up the coast of Jutland.

Kaj takes her fishing spot – where there's five there'll be more. She props herself against the wall as he casts again. The heat of the stone is warm on her back. This could be their last long summer with the boy but, as usual, Olaf is back at the holiday house his grandfather built, touching up paint-work and filling holes in the unpaved road with buckets of stones brought back from the beach.

'Who else will do it?' he'd said over breakfast.

It's always about the house. Each generation has borne only one child, a custodian. One day, he reminds her, it will all pass to Kaj.

Olaf is fussing even more than usual. At the beginning of July, the neighbouring house, the last one before the moor, changed hands. The first they knew about it was when they saw the photo in the estate agent's window, a red 'SOLD' slashed across it. There'd been no *For Sale* sign, no visits.

For weeks, he's been pacing his land, prodding the earth with a stick and poking amongst the wild roses, searching for the markers that say *this far and no further*, placed by his father over forty years ago.

Olaf was twelve years old when the neighbouring plot

first sold and a concrete house was built. Before that, their summer house had long views across the moor with its heathers and stunted trees. The heathers are beautiful, but they shelter *hugorme*, whose venom can kill a small animal and even bring a grown man down.

The mackerel gives a final shudder. Though it's sunny, she shivers too, remembering the day at the start of the holiday when a *hugorm* came right up to the back door, past Olaf who was clearing weeds on the patio. As it reached the lintel, it raised its head, its tongue tasting the air. She recognised the male of the species, by the silvery black zigzags running down its back.

She'd shouted, but the snake continued towards her, unafraid, right into the kitchen. She grabbed the broom and flicked it away. It moved through the air landing outside the back door. Olaf split it in two with the blade of his spade. Its wine-red blood stained the patio, as shocking as a human's.

Kaj continues to cast and reel in. He's picking mackerel off a shoal that's come into the harbour to feed. There can be thousands in a shoal but they move as one. She's read that the placing of their eyes helps each fish pace itself against its neighbour. They are born knowing exactly what to do.

Along the pier, men start to arrive on black bikes with buckets hanging from handlebars and rigged rods strapped to the crossbars. Word must have spread. She knows some of them by sight. There's a couple of old fellows, brothers who come on Honda 50s. Next, the tall trawlerman from the vast Hirtshals-registered boat which is berthed on the pier's east side.

The boat's been there for three days. With Kaj, she'd

watched it come in, seen the seagulls shift from their perch on the roof of the fish-processing plant to swoop down and pick at the rolls of net on the back of the boat. The sky filled with flashes of wings and their cries as they tried to get a grip so they could pull at small fish or torn crab claws stuck in the net. As the trawler laboured to the side of the pier, the tall man jumped down. He'd stood, feet apart, ready to take the weight of a thrown rope which he coiled around a bollard. Machinery cranked as nets unfurled. A second man joined him and together they'd pulled until the net stretched the length of the pier, plastic floats thudding the concrete. The spread nets revealed more bits of fish and the seagulls dropped and pulled and rose, fighting mid-air, taking scraps from the beaks of young gulls, whose brown feathers marked them out.

The trawlerman leans his bike by the wall and calls to the boy.

'*Mange?*'

'*Syv hidtil.*'

Seven, too many to eat. Maybe the trawlerman will take some home. It was him who'd shown Kaj how to unhook a fish by pushing the barb down, twisting it and then pulling it back. He doesn't respond to her tentative *Hej* but stands and chats with the boy, talking rigs, and spinners, the merits of psychedelic greens and yellows. She hears him say how the rigs look like the *små fisk* the mackerel devour.

'*Makrel*,' he says. The guttural Danish better suits the feisty fish. He points to a silver arrow streaking across the surface as the boy catches another. The trawlerman carries no spare weight. His hands are large but skilful at tying hooks to lines, at gutting fish. She knows his father fished before him, his grandfather too. Fifty years ago, the town only had fishing and the fish-processing plant. Now it's full of galleries and gift shops which close in the winter, to reopen in May when the leaves unfurl on the branches of birch that they cut and place in tall pots by the doors, ready for the first visitors who come with the late spring.

Over the past three days, the trawlerman's been down to check the nets, lifting them in sections to look for tears. He carries a wooden needle and a ball of nylon; the needle flies faster than any woman's crochet hook as holes are mended and he moves on. The nets are picked clean by the gulls and ready to be winched onto the boat. She's seen how he watches the weather, eyes fixed on the horizon. The catch has been auctioned, now there's only the waiting.

The boy and the trawlerman fish side by side.

She closes her eyes and pictures Olaf with the metal detector, scanning above the wild roses that are too dense to penetrate, alert for the bleeping that will signal the presence of the metal stakes his father drove into the land to mark the boundary in the summer of seventy-two, when the neighbouring house was built. Olaf's told her the story many times; how his father watched the diggers start on the foundations, his rage mounting. The new house was raised quickly, with concrete blocks placed one on the other, like a child building Lego. Somehow that was worse. Not that his father would have accepted any building, but it might have been easier with a house made of wood.

'*Vi behøver ikke at se på det,*' his father had said, the day he took a spade and started to dig, to build a ridge that would obscure the house from their view.

115

There was a heatwave that summer. All the other holiday houses had emptied, their occupants taking to the beach. Olaf told her how his mother stood at the window as the mound grew and the hole on their land deepened. July turned into August and his father continued digging, more urgently now. He'd wanted the new ridge planted before they returned to the city – before autumn winds could blow the soil away. The more he dug, the less sandy the soil, and that was good. The crater deepened and soon all that could be seen was the top of his head.

She hears the trawlerman's voice and opens her eyes.

'*Vi skal smide den i havet,*' he says when her son lands a too-small fish. The seagulls gather, ready to swoop and catch it before it hits the water. But the trawlerman leans over and gently drops the fish into the sea. It floats on its side for a moment, then dives.

A few more casts and the trawlerman lands his first string of mackerel. Sunlight glints off his knife as he deftly unhooks and guts them. The gulls catch the discarded heads he tosses to the sea.

She can't recall a single day when Olaf joined them fishing or lay beside them on the beach. There's only a week left before they'll pack up and head back to the city and still he's at the house, scraping peeling paint on the north-facing facade and picking over the story of his father.

Last night, he told her again how he'd stood by the wheelbarrow as his father filled it from the deepening hole. The skin on his father's back had turned blackish brown and hung loose on his bones. Olaf helped as much as he could, pushing barrow-loads of soil to the new ridge.

For each shovelful he threw on top, more than half slid back down.

The day it happened, his mother had made a jug of *hyldeblomstsaft*, poured a tall glass, and given it to Olaf.

'Take that out to your father and tell him we're off to the beach.'

Olaf told her how he'd held the glass in both hands, his eyes on the swaying liquid, stepping carefully so it wouldn't spill. Then, how his throat and chest burnt as he ran back to the house and, sent by his mother, to the nearby hotel – the only place with a phone. He'd gasped out words, the taste of iron in his mouth.

'Min Far. Jeg tror han er død.'

Seventeen minutes, it took the ambulance to arrive, sixteen minutes too many.

She feels cold, she'd dozed off. The trawlerman has gone and, though his bucket is full, Kaj fishes on. The sea has an oily look, streaked red from the rays of the setting sun, as if some deep-sea creature has bled onto its surface. A small fishing boat passes close to the pier, blue paint flaking on its sides. Seagulls follow in its wake. The yellow-clad fisherman raises his hand to return Kaj's wave. The boat heads out through the arms of the pier, leaving the still waters of the harbour and setting its course for deeper fishing grounds. Kaj's eyes follow it, until it is little more than a blot on the horizon. She watches, sensing him pull away from her, a dragging she feels deep in her belly, like the outgoing tide sucking the sea back over shingle.

The marker at the end of the pier lights up, ghostly green. She gets to her feet and they pack up the fishing gear. In the car, Kaj sits beside her, gripping the bucket between long, skinny legs. Water sloshes as she drives the rough road to the holiday house.

Back at the house, he spreads a newspaper at the kitchen sink and begins gutting the mackerel. At the start of summer, she'd cleaned them. Now Kaj does it alone, gripping his knife and, in a single movement, slitting the belly, right up to the gills. He pulls the innards out and rinses the cavity. The smell of fish is strong. On the third, he stops and calls her over. With the pressure of his hand on its back, the biggest mackerel has disgorged its last meal; a tiny silver fish, perfectly intact, emerges from between its parted lips.

She looks out the window, beyond her son. Across the patio, the spade is propped against the wall of the tool shed. The hips have set on the wild roses, red and firm, like miniature apples. Another summer has been and gone. Once they leave for the city, autumn will be brief and soon winter will come.

Olaf, exhausted, sits in his father's chair by the stove. The skin on his arms is crisscrossed with scratches from his search for the boundary markers amongst the roses. Some run deep.

'The new owners came by today,' he says. 'They plan to build a new house. They only wanted the plot.'

She knows it will be a relief to him when they pull down the concrete house; a relief but not the end.

'I was thinking,' he says. 'There's no reason we shouldn't have a bit more shelter. Now would be the time to build up the ridge; before they start.'

Her heart flips. She slows her breathing, parting her lips

to let the air escape. Words, like the silver fish, work their way up her throat and lodge there.

This far, she wants to say. *This far and no further.* But she doesn't and the only sound is Kaj as he slices and rinses the fish.

PANIC ATTACK

A. L. Kennedy

Artwork by Coco Crampton

Panic Attack

A. L. Kennedy

You can't even touch a woman, not in the slightest. You cannot.
Times have changed and that's what they've changed to, apparently.

Ronnie is not completely happy with the crowd at King's Cross station.

Times . . .

Ronnie is not a large man, not tall. If he raises himself and stands up off his heels he makes it to about five foot seven and his build is slender. He doesn't run to fat, but he doesn't precisely run to muscle, either. Still, when he walks, he seems bigger than is strictly logical. He sways largely with each step – not so's you'd think that he's drunk, but so's you'd definitely notice that he's there. He can't sit, or just placidly wait, or prop his shoulder in against some handy surface and be idle, because the preservation of his bigness lies in motion, his blur of expansion. His shoes are always the heaviest Doc Martens he can find and in mild disarray. They don't – *not quite* – make him look as if he's newly come from a factory floor – *God knows there aren't many of them any more and the ones that are left are pin-clean* – nor climbed out of a coal pit – *none of them left* – but nevertheless his feet can suggest to the world that he's got stamina, inhabits an industrial-grade existence. He maintains a dull finish on his toecaps, treats them with dubbin, not polish – *they are clean, I keep clean* – and has the air, the bearing, of a man who can comprehend sweat, one who can hold things the right ways and put them to craftsmanlike use. His arms maintain an extra bit of bend at the elbow and are braced out from his sides to let him occupy more space in the manner of a tiny, invading army.

You always know that Ronnie's there. He's a one-man bridgehead.

And this isn't an accident – he's been practising being there since he was eight, maybe nine at the latest. He's got it down pat by now and doesn't notice, not often, that his body makes so many efforts additional to the norm, or that – *why not? they probably deserve it* – he leans in on other men during conversations, hovers a grinning breath too close. When he walks, he might be forcing his way through a clumsy gathering, a mob, while also kicking up leaves on a bumpy, country pathway, or else hoofing tin cans down an alley.

That kind of thing.

He occasionally thinks, has this persistent imagining of himself wearing brownish, lived-and-worked-in clothes – thick cloth, simple jacket and trousers and some kind of muffler – *not a scarf, a muffler, an old-timey muffler* – and he is swinging his big boots through leaves and heading down over the rise of a lane.

And there's a house at the foot of the slope, an alone and peaceful house, and it's known to me and a kid's there by the opened kitchen door and he's going to run out in a minute and hug my legs. He's that kind.

Ronnie is jigging on the spot and searching his pockets for nothings, acting out an impatience he doesn't feel, while examining an indicator board that is, as it happens, being quite evasive about his train. There is fulsome information available on a number of other trains scheduled to depart much later than his own: platform numbers, confirmations of timeliness, even instructions to board. His service is simply listed as existing.

So far.

Stuff changes. Add time to anything and it'll change.

And lies – if there's lying, in time all the lies are found out.

Ronnie is so noticeable and apparently ill-at-ease that he has cleared a significant ring in the would-be passengers scattered and gaggled about.

He spins, yet again, to study the figures, the faces behind him. He might almost be at large in a hostile landscape – clinging fronds of alien Viet Cong wetness blocking his view, or expanses of dusty jihadi concealment, Rommelish foxholes . . . so many enemies are available as inspiration. He frowns, his eyes staying calm while his face approaches fury. He's a quandary to those who do not know him, is Ronnie.

Not a woman – you can't – no touching.

Women are present at the station, naturally. There are women standing in the open carelessly, contained in the crowds.

Women, old blokes, a priest who might be a vicar or pastor or

*one of those job titles – you can't differentiate, can you? – then
there's couples, kids, solo bastards with rucksacks. You always get
attitude with a rucksack, you always get smugness about the feats
the rucksack owner could perform. And you can see it's bollocks.
You can see it's just a student taking home washing to his mum.*

*That one's fake military – he's pretending he's a squaddie on
leave, but he's not, he's just a wanker with some army surplus and
a fucking rucksack.*

Over towards the shop which sells shit sandwiches and
pots of other shit that nobody sane would eat – *like you want
to eat everything mixed in a bowl; like you're a cat, or something –*
over that way towards the shop there's a man with a beard
and a woman beside him. The man looks uncomfortable and
Ronnie wants, quite urgently, to be absolutely sure of why.

Because the woman is shaking.

*Not a hipster-bastard beard and not the full I-have-mice-in-here
nonsense, either. Average beard. Not a white bloke trying to show
off being Muslim.*

*Not that. The way he looks – round shoulders and a little
box-set-watcher's belly – he's just slack. The beard is because
he can't be bothered shaving. That's all it is. Laziness growing
across him, springing out plain on his face. Evidence.*

The woman is still shaking.

*I bet he says he's got sensitive skin. Prone to shaving rash
and spots.*

*I bet he keeps ointments round the side of the bath and is full of
weaknesses and talks about them.*

*I bet he hasn't got a bath – shower. Mildew in the curtain and
towels with no colour left in them any more. No self-respect.*

I bet.

The woman is still shaking.

Ronnie does not like the man with the beard, although they haven't met and are not going to.

Fucker. Look at him. Fucker.

The man is wearing beige cargo pants, slung low beneath what will surely become an ever-larger gut. He has additionally a pair of trainers with show-off-complicated laces and a purple t-shirt showing what might be Japanese characters. He is clearly afflicted by reading magazines of the most arsehole sort and then adjusting himself to fit the world they show him.

The woman is still shaking.

He won't know what the words on his t-shirt mean and probably they're 'this dickthistle bought a t-shirt and can't even read that it's calling him a dickthistle ...'

The man has a backpack lolling against his left shin.

Little brother of your rucksack, isn't it ...? Just as bad, but half-hearted.

Ronnie is trying to puzzle out whether the woman beside the fucker is his wife, or girlfriend, or has any other type of connectedness. He is almost decided. The pair are standing over-close if they're strangers.

The woman – she's still shaking.

She is slender in the way that women who shake in public tend to be. Ronnie peers at her and thinks of bones and breaking. He is aware that he shouldn't peer, because he fell asleep in his mum's garden yesterday and has cheeks and a forehead ablaze with sunburn and implied stupidity. He is a redhead. He is visibly someone who should not stay out on a clear day without a hat. But he was tired and relaxed and

his mum has two comfy loungers on the patio and either one
is an invitation to nod off.

It bloody hurts, too. Mum laughing.

*Yeah, well, I'm an idiot, aren't I? Yeah, I know . . . Yeah, go on,
laugh then. I didn't laugh at you when you did the same in Rhyl,
did I? Yeah, go on . . .*

His mum had kept laughing while she smeared calamine
lotion onto him and he wondered how she got a hold of such
a substance. It smelled of his childhood and surely nobody
made it any more and if that were the case might her supply
not be out of date and ineffective?

*Worked, though, didn't it? Dabbing at me like a stain. And then
it felt the way a blessing ought to. Afterwards. Blessed.*

The woman is now beyond shaking, undergoes deeper
disturbances, spasms that rise through her body. Something
seems to be lashing at her while she attempts to simply
weather impacts she can't avoid. In certain moments a
presence, a vile presence, might be holding her by the waist
and tugging, tugging, rattling her, making her teeth meet
in her head. It is forcing her to survive it and, meanwhile,
her expression is an almost unfathomable mix of flittering
emotions: shame, weariness, grief, an angry desire to fight
and an understanding of endless defeat. She is managing to
stand inside this earthquake no one else can see.

*Only they do see. They're blanking her, but she's right here and
can't be missed.*

*You'd think the vicar would do something about her, step in.
That's what men of the cloth are for, isn't it – removing pain, comfort, words? She's in pain. You'd think that he ought to be walking
across to her and consoling.*

The bearded man is the most discomfited by the woman. He edges away from her, then towards and backs off and then heads in again by millimetres, observing her from the tail of his eye as he does so.

Fucker.

There are points when it seems the man might speak to her, interject, but then he says nothing, studies the train indications instead. He looks guilty.

So what did you do to her? What did you do?

Ronnie rubs the tips of his fingers against his temples, up and down, up and down. This will, he realises, leave his hair bristling, disordered and werewolfish. It's something he does; occasionally in front of the bathroom mirror. During that situation, his sink will fill with uprooted red and greying strands. He probably will go bald in a peculiar way as a result. He'll start receding above his ears.

The bearded man does finally mumble some handful of sentences to the woman, while she breathes in short, animal rhythms. He does this during one of the intervals when her body is not assaulting her, betraying her, and she is tiredly still. She makes a reply and – although Ronnie can't hear what's spoken – it's clear to him that the beardyfuck is, in fact, a stranger to her and that she is shamed by his attention and simultaneously concentrating on stating just a few words with considerable force.

Then a station announcement breaks in and the bearded man uses its smugly disembodied female noise – *someone's idea of a chirpy nanny saying where you're meant to go* – as cover for a swift retreat. He steps surprisingly lively with his scrawny, lumpy backpack rapidly uplifted and clutched, as if it's at risk from the woman, as if she will most likely choose to leap after him.

She is, rather, caught by another wave of shuddering, plainly hauled down by it towards somewhere bleak inside herself and harrowed.

Bastards. Everyone's a bastard – ducking their heads and avoiding.

When you see stuff like this you're supposed to help out, aren't you?

Somebody's done something to her. And the bastards must have seen it happen. They'll have stood about and let it, too. That fucker beardman, he'll have seen it and been closest and ignored it.

Everybody in this station would step over you if you were dying, I swear.

At this, the almighty female in the ceiling blared out pressing, if distorted, instructions for Ronnie's, now slightly delayed, departure. He didn't absolutely want to pick up his holdall yet, though.

Can't cut and run – that wouldn't be respectable.

If you want to be a man who's respected you do things other people can respect, are able to respect, you make sure to be respectable.

His substantial footwear gets heavyish with his confusion and is going to give him trouble, root him and force him to miss his train, but then the woman starts up moving. She's off. She lifts her bag, which is over-stuffed and of the flimsy shopping type; jute with pinky flowers printed on it, insecure.

The sort of thing you'd give a kid, a girl, so's she can play at being housewives.

And then she pauses while the weight of it – *which can't*

be that much, Jesus – while the weight of it foxes her, distorts her until she appears to be drawing up a heavy bucket from some deep well and losing, staggering.

Let yourself be lost in a railway station with a little girl's bag that's open-mouthed, that would get your stuff wet if it rains and that isn't suitable – why do that? It's like advertising so robbery will happen.

'Fuck.' Ronnie had intended to think this, but instead delivers it out loud to a space near the right shoulder of a young guy in yet another lousy t-shirt, this one emblazoned with a long quotation in curly script.

Bands. You put the names of bands on t-shirts. You put what music you like on your t-shirt, so people can know who you are. And you only do that when you're a teenager and won't manage to give indications in other ways. It's not complicated, the t-shirt issue. Why make it complicated?

As Ronnie watches, interested, the young guy reacts to being sworn at, snaps through the first few sections of becoming outraged and maybe combative, but then sees Ronnie being Ronnie and being there, Ronnie being Ronnie and being ready, and changes his mind. Ronnie lets the milky whites of his eyes flare feistily, licks his lips and nods as the bloke half-stumbles back and then onto a sideways trajectory, speeding his bastardly self away, bolting as somebody bloody well ought to, if they're wearing quotes from poetry.

The woman has made it a few paces onwards and then buckled, set down her playtime bag as if it contains an impossible burden: compressed hell, a mid-Atlantic chasm, grief.

'Fuck.' This time the syllable emerges only softly and

troubles no one as Ronnie's masculine boots take him forward and forward until he is only as far from the woman
as he would stay from any wild animal, anything trapped.
'I'm ...'

The sound of his voice seems to hit her.

He begins again, feeling watery in his stomach, 'I'm
Ronnie. Is there something wrong?'

The woman slow-turns her head, side to side, in such a
way that it means both 'yes' and 'no'. It also strongly suggests
'go away'.

But Ronnie digs in, because he is the digging sort, 'No, but
there is though, love, and it's okay and you can tell me and
I'll fix it. Just spent all yesterday fixing the mother's bathroom tap and I'm not a plumber, but – you know – I'll try. I
try things.' He cranes himself nearer without moving either
of his feet – looks increasingly like a ski-jumper leaving the
slope, that big downward slide that looks mad when you
see it on the telly. He also finds that his chest is jerking with
these sour, shallow gulps of breath. It's the effort of keeping
generally still, of controlling his limbs so he doesn't threaten,
that's upsetting him.

*But if she's hiding and down and hurt you mustn't move. You
have to make noises that sound like not killing her and you hold
one hand in the other so that neither one of the fingery little sods
breaks out and wrecks the atmosphere of calm. Calm – that's you.
Compulsory soothing.*

Ronnie drives on, low-worded, a driving murmur what
he's aiming for, 'You can say. I don't mind. I don't mind
anything, me. I'll have forgotten tomorrow, I'm a stranger,
where's the harm ...?'

Her mouth twitches and he can't help being angry that she's dressed in these many layers of fawny, rose-spattered, thin cloth that are only ever going to tell the fucking world she's a soft target and she has these halfway-ballet kind of shoes on that won't protect her and the bloody bag – *she bought it herself, for herself, because it's a kid's thing and she wanted to be a happy kid getting a present* – the whole everything of her invites every swine in London to come and have a go. She's broadcasting from all angles. Reckless.

Don't look weak, darling. Never. Not ever. And when you are weak, I mean … It's then that you can't be forgiven if you let it show. You've served yourself up. You're like a spy doing sabotage behind your defences.

Silly cow.

'Only I think you're for the Edinburgh train and so am I and we'll miss it, if you don't come with me.'

She pauses at this. Completely.

She's this entire stillness.

Then her mouth is overwhelmed with the shapes of crying and he gently sets just his one elbow that's closest out even further to be near her, inviting, and then turns his face ahead so his gaze won't intrude, gives her privacy for her decision – looks far off at the distance as if he's about to pull some sledge across the Arctic, or such, and she does, she does, she hooks her arm around into his and lets him take a fraction of her burden.

He begins to walk her. 'What is it though you're doing great lovely what's wrong though must be something it's always something is what I find.'

The unendingness of his talking finally pushes her to

interrupt, 'Panic attacks.' Her notes are a tone lower than he'd expected and something smoky in the vowels and a sense of a heat there, or heat that she might have contained in other days. 'I get I get I get them.'

'Say no more. That's a bastard that is.' She halfway smiles at this.

'A proper bastard, darling. Yeah.'

He leads her along the platform while inconsiderates push past with bloody trolleys that either trip you up as they cross your path, or form roadblocks in narrow spaces.

You take up the room of two people with those things.

He feels as a spasm starts to hurl itself about in her and battles to keep their progress even as a response.

Best not to talk. It's the animal stuff that's useful now, your demeanour and the way you rest your hands.

Through the wool of her sleeve he can feel that she's in a hot sweat. It's the soak of fear.

Turns me over – when anyone stinks of fear that way. It'll stick on me, too. Sinks in for days, that does, curdles your skin.

She attempts to make some adjustment to their balance, her hand colliding with his fingers and tear-wet, anxiety-wet, and this makes them seem warm and familiar, before they leave him.

Reminds you . . .

His shoulder mildly clatters hers and he flinches, doesn't want a reaction, begins his patter again to waylay her alarm, 'But you're okay. You're all right. It's your head, isn't it? Your head is telling you to run off like buggery or hide in a hole, but it's wrong and you can be polite about it, but you can recommend that it should bugger off because it's lying. Because

136

you're okay. This is okay. You're catching a train. People do that every day.'

The woman attempts a full smile, or some close relative to that. Ronnie smiles back and catches her eye and the sunny patch this makes between them lasts for a couple of breaths and then the edge of weeping bangs at her again. 'Thanks.' This appears as a cough of sound.

'Don't mention it my pleasure or not pleasure cos it's horrible for you but I don't mind ... only ...' They are well along the platform now, level with the carriage Ronnie knows contains his seat. Ronnie always makes reservations, otherwise there's bother and uncertainty. Ronnie likes a solo seat and a little table, books early and gets cheap first-class.

Not that cheap. Not that first-class. It's like it was in Ordinary when I was a kid. That and free cups of tea.

Ronnie lets his longing for a seat and some peace drag through him. He halts her. 'See. Here. This is J. This is my carriage.'

She blinks at him.

'But I'll walk you up to where you are. Okay? And you remember – J. Okay? You need anything, you have any bother, then you come and see me in J. Or you tell someone to ask for Ronnie in J and I'll come running. Proper running. Okay?'

She blinks.

'Where are you, love?'

Standing apart from him at this – *kiddy's bag in one hand, holding out her ticket like, like she's my daughter, like she's ...*

He takes the ticket and it is damp and unbelievably crumpled, as if she has been worrying at it in her hand as some

137

kind of token to ward off ills. This has made it almost illegible and no use. He frowns at it. Then he unfrowns, because her whole body reacts to frowning by tensing in a way that he can taste.

Like the smell of those old-fashioned gas fires with the cylinder in the back. Ten quid a cylinder and the dying in your sleep from being poisoned was for free.

'All right . . . E. You're in E. We'll nip along there, then.'

'No. I'm fine.'

'I can go with you.'

'Thanks.'

'I can do more.'

'Thanks.'

And she heads out for her carriage, nibbling at the distance with child steps in those stupid fucking slippers, with that stupid fucking bag and he wants to have coppers go with her, armed guards. Nice ones. Kind ones. He wants.

Her shoulders turn a little as they retreat. She's expecting trouble, but doesn't stay with him.

He wants. 'Fuck.'

But that's the end of it. Unless she needs him and does send a message, or walks through and finds him. That's the end, if she decides it is.

Ronnie climbs aboard, slots his holdall up aloft, sits in his by-itself seat and looks out of the window. A steward passes, on the way probably to fetch the first big pot of tea. Can't keep first-class waiting – it needs its beverages.

'Fuck.'

And Ronnie leans forward and sets his head against the tiny table which is only his and his breath mounts and heaves and struggles and sweat lifts on him and then trickles, crawls at the backs of his legs, makes insect-shivery moves down his spine and his neck locks and his face hurts and he's making these *huff huff huff* noises that bastard strangers will notice and ponder and it seems like someone is slapping his chest and won't stop and it seems like someone is threatening murder and it seems like his mother is there in the kitchen, curled on the floor in the kitchen, curled years ago on the floor in the kitchen and shaking, shaking, shaking and that bastard, that fucker she's married to is gone but Ronnie knows where he's been and Ronnie knows what he wants to do to him – what he wants – and Ronnie lies down and he holds her and he doesn't say a thing, not a letter, he only does what he always does which is to keep his arms around her until all the terrible stuff has passed from her and into him.

Long gone. Huff. Huff. Long gone.

The filthy fucker. Huff. Huff.

Huff. Huff.

We have nice times, we try to. Loungers. Flowers. Sun.

The walls are peeling in at him and the floor is turning nasty – it's making him sick.

Long gone.

And Ronnie sweats and concentrates on not throwing up and showing himself as a fool for everybody. He keeps his head down. He breathes.

He hopes the woman comes and finds him. He would help her if she did. He'd like that. *I would. I always would.*

THE WAY I BREATHED

Anna Stewart

Artwork by Fani Parali

THE WAY I BREATHED

Anna Stewart

I pushed the door and wind blew in my face, blowing my hat aff my heed. I crouched doon tae pick it up, but the hat blew alang the street and I ran tae catch it. I dusted it aff and held it on my heed til the wind died doon. I stood fir a minute catching my breath. I crossed the road at the bank, ootside sat a young lad begging fir money, I looked in my pockets and tried to gie him something but he said, 'Naw, naw, yir awright pal, naw, naw.'

I passed a building I remembered wis part o the university and in the distance I saw the roof o the mosque. There wis a patch o grass across the street, the council musto planted aw those different roses fir men like me, men like me who were on a stroll and wanted something nice tae look at. There were benches there too and a fine view o the river and the rail-and-road bridge, I could see all the way tae Fife. There was a student on one o the benches, sketching. I sat for a minute and hoped she might draw me, but she wis looking the other way. So I turned and watched a bit o plastic instead. It'd been covering a window but had come loose and wis blowing aboot in the wind. Then I heard this man wi a white beard pointing oot local architecture to some auld ladies. I knew aboot architecture, I had white hair. Why not a white beard? I set aff again and passed twa men wi young bodies, but auld faces. They were smoking and walking, looking at the groond and in a hurry. I should follow them to find oot whar they're going, they might be ghosts, they looked like ghosts. There wis excitement in my legs again. But then I remembered they might turn on uz like sometimes happens, I know that sometimes happens. The street was covered in clumps o moss that had fallen aff the roofs wi the rain. I stood on them and felt slippy, I was slidy, I might fall. And if I fell who knows what would happen, I was likely tae break bones. I crossed the road so I could walk under scaffolding. A man walked by uz wi a wheelbarrow and radio noise came blasting fae a giant hole in the wall. There were men in there and they were working. Why had I never done that kind o work when I was young? I'd a body wasted. I could've built a wall couldn't I? But then I remembered I was slow, even back then. No, my life had been best as it was, nae point raking ower auld groond. Across the street wis a door wi wooden panels painted wi pictures o moustached men, a sleeping fella and a standing ane. Blue and white tiles o turbans, covered wi jewels. A big face made up o wee faces. My legs were tired. I passed a pub, then turned back and pushed the door, I was thirsty, I needed a drink, I deserved a drink. I deserved a bloody good drink. There was no one else in the pub, just me and the barman. He reminded me o someone

I used to know ... a familiar face. But time moves on and faces are easy forgot. Everything is easy forgot, in the end.

What?

No, nothing, nothing, I just put one foot in front of the other, me. I just keep walking, nae point turning back.

What time is it? There isnae a clock in the damned place, does naebody hae a clock any mair, what's happened tae aw the clocks? Does it matter, do I need tae ken the time? Is it teatime?

I looked aboot the place; red walls wi a cream roof, three TVs, framed photos o players fae both fitbaw teams:

Jocky Scott
Alan Gilzean
Ian Phillips
Jim Skele
Gordon Smith
Ally Donaldson.

It was comradely, I felt happy. I asked the barman fir a pint o 80 and he asked what I'd been up to, I said, 'Nothing much, I'm just on the lookout.'

He laughed and handed uz my ale, then went on a computer behind the bar. I looked at a photo on the wall o men kissing cheeks and photographers in caps, underneath it said, 'Scotland's Billy Bremner and Jimmy Johnstone celebrate victory over the old enemy, England.' And above the bar was a mirror wi an etching o a bridge.

'Oh,' I said to the barman, 'this must be the Taybrig Bar.'

'Yup.'

'Churchill used to drink here when he was an MP, you know.'

'Up the road.'

I looked at the barman, the barman looked up fae his computer, he pointed a thumb oot the door and for a minute I thought he was asking uz to leave.

'Up the road,' he said. 'Churchill used to drink in Mennies, up the road.'

'Oh did he? I thought it wis here. I'll need to hae a look in that establishment.'

I thought, then, that the barman rolled his eyes. Wis there something wrong wi the way I presented myself? I looked in the bridge mirror, aye I was old, but dishevelled? No! I looked awright. I stood up and headed fir the bog. In the corridor ootside the Men's there's a black-and-white photo o the Tay Bridge, must be a theme. It smells o piss this corridor. The photograph's long, folded and unfolded in twa lines, making three parts. It's o five boys playing in the harbour, climbing the wall that leads to the foot o the bridge; five wee boys, in black and white.

The sink in the Men's wis green wi soap fae a leaky dispenser. I unzipped my fly and stood ower the urinal waiting fir something tae happen. I wis afraid coz I remembered how it sometimes burned. And then it came, that burning again. That made uz stop and drips o piss trailed aff and hit my shoes. My bladder wis still full. I shook and tried again, I needed tae relax, just relax . . . the barman banged the door.

'Oh sorry, Jimmy, just came in tae check that sink.'

'Aye fine.'

I zipped my troosers, there wis a pain in my bladder fae holding the rest in. The barman let the door bang again, it rattled roond my feet, my legs, my chest.

I should try again now he's gone, but there wis the burning, so I decided tae wait. I washed my hands, there wis nae mair soap in the dispenser, it was aw ower the sink, whatever he'd done he'd no fixed it.

I went back oot and there were twa new fowk sitting at the bar. They couldnae have known each other coz they were talking aboot the weather. One o them said it was mild for winter, the other said the last time it had been a mild winter like this he'd seen it snow in spring. They both agreed that the weather was aw back tae front and had gone tae the dogs since their day. Ane of them said, 'And now, here they are blaming it aw on the global warning, and yi ken, they might be right, it's no as cald as it used tae be, I could practically have gone oot in my vest the-day.'

I sat next tae them at the bar, patted the 80-shilling tap and the barman poured uz another. I ordered a wee dram to put in it and sat and supped, and listened to the other men talking. Some o the time I nodded in agreement and they looked ower and nodded back, then mair and mair o the conversation wis directed at me.

The twa men started tae talk aboot the fitbaw, I hadnae focused on a full game fir a long time and I couldnae tell yi any o these new players' names. I agreed wi the men they were paid too much, but I'd nae idea how much they'd been paid.

The thing wis, I couldnae remember who I used to support, the orange anes or the blue anes, I remember something aboot blue, but . . . aye I liked them both, I musto liked them both, that's why.

I ordered another pint o 80 and a nip. Yi hae tae watch if

yiv a shaky hand when yi pour the nip ower yir 80, yi hae tae be very careful pouring it in.

Efter a while the conversation dried up and we focused on the fitbaw, there's only so much men can say tae ane another. There wis music playing fae another TV in the corner wi a woman singing and dancing, it wis aw aboot hips, it's a funny kindo sang tae sing; hips,

hips,

hips,

I remember hips, someone's hips, when? When was it?

In a bed,

a bedroom … skin,

waist,

breast,

arm.

Blonde hair sitting bonny in a hollowed oot space between a shoulder and a neck; a clean neck. A smell o soft.

Aye yi were bonny.

Why do women smell like that, different fae men? How do they get tae be that way, a cushion fir aw the weight o days that seem never ending, ach but they go in so quick.

What could I smell? Oh aye, piss, piss on my shoes, that was it.

I finished my drink and stood up.

'S'that you away, Jimmy?'

'Aye.'

I headed oot the door, up the Perth Road in the same direction.

Och, the hips wouldo been my wife. I did hae a wife yi ken … she's no here, is that awright? I hope nothing bad happened. Am I allowed tae speak aboot her? I covered my mouth just in case.

She wisnae fae Dundee, I remember that, she'd a funny accent. Or was that my mother? It doesnae matter any mair. Had I seen my mother's hips? I must've at one time.

There wis a wee lass as well, I've been meaning tae find.

I came to Mennies, I cannie mind why I caw it that, something aboot a wifey, there's a woman involved in that story. I sat on a stool at the bar. The young lad behind smiled.

That young lad, he knows me, yi ken that.

Then this auld fella patted my back and said, 'Awright Jimmy, how've yi been keeping?'

'Aye fine, fine and yirsel?'

I wis being polite, yiv got tae remember tae be polite. The auld fella got uz a drink, he knew I'd like a pint o 80. I do like a pint o 80, it warms my insides, I like the feeling o creamy bubbles and the sharp watery stuff efter, twa wee layers o goodness fir my mouth tae dwell on.

The auld fella telt uz aw aboot his bad chest, he said he'd likely be going soon what wi his cough, but I didnae ken whar. I supped my pint, pulling thick bubbles past my lips, then the quick stuff slipped across my tongue and doon my throat.

Can I taste it any mair?

Can I taste it like I used to?

I wish that auld fella would shut up, he does nothing but jabber on, it's hard tae keep up.

I'm wantin tae drink my pint in peace.

I dinnae even ken him, what's he on aboot? Och he's tried tae phone his doctors aboot a cough, but every time they said the appointments were full and he should ring at eight in the morning, but he said when he tried tae ring at eight, the phone wis ay engaged.

I've got things tae do though, I cannie sit roond here aw day listening tae this.

I order a nip and let the auld fella pay for it, he seemed happy enough wi that. He started talking aboot his pension and how he couldnae survive on what they'd gien him and how he'd worked aw his life; *real work,* no like the layaboots these days, and what did he get back fir it, how do they repay him? I shake my heed, coz I dinnae ken. I dinnae ken mysel how I live and it isnae in my mind whar I live, but I'll walk and I'll find it, aye I'll walk and I'll find it.

Just one mair pint, and then I'll go.

The auld fella bought uz another pint o 80, but I didnae acknowledge it, his buying me a pint, I just started drinking. He didnae seem tae care and there wis something charming in that, the way he didnae make a fuss o his kindness. I started feeling sorry fir him, coz I kent he wis wanting a drinking buddy and I kent he'd get taken a loan o fae some o the buggers that come in here, once I'd gone.

After I'd finished my 80, I said cheerio.

'S'that you away then is it?'

I said, aye.

'Off to make yir tea then is it?'

And I said, aye, again.

'Awright then, Jimmy, see yi the-morn,' he says, and I gave him a nod and headed fir the door.

I ken a shortcut up Hawkhill way, so I came oot the side door and turned back on mysel. It's quite a steep wee brae up that shortcut, but I took it slow and managed it aw the same.

Then I saw the Campbeltown ower the main road. The cars were busy, it musto been teatime, so I waited fir the green man but when I reached the other side I stumbled and fell back against the wall o the pub. I tried tae get up but I couldnae, and I started greeting; I wis mair angry than anything else, coz I couldnae get up. Then I wis shouting and I got some funny looks fae fowk in cars. A young lad fae inside the pub came oot and saw uz.

'Yi awright, Jimmy? What yi doing doon there? What yi shouting aboot? Come on in here, I'll help yi up.'

The lad grabbed under ma oxters and pulled uz up, I fell back and bumped against the wall but he kept a hud o uz and said, 'It's awright, I've still got yi. C'mon in here and get a seat, what yi greetin aboot?'

The lad took uz by the arm intae the pub and sat uz doon at a table wi other men.

Look at the state o him.

'Ach come here and sit yirsel doon, Jimmy, Eddie, get the man a dram tae settle his nerves.'

'S'that you been oot wandering, Jimmy, getting the exercise is it?'

'Aye he's walked too far yi can see it.'

'Look at his hands, he's shaking.'

'What's he greetin aboot?'

'Jimmy, yi awright pal?'

I picked up my glass and drank, hoping the men wernae talking tae me.

The woman behind the bar brought ower a plate o food and said, 'Here yi are, Jimmy, get some o that doon yi and yi'll feel right as rain.'

I did feel better efter a few mouthfuls I have to admit, and I wis grateful to the bar woman. She wis hefty and had streaky short hair, I wanted tae sit her on my knee, I patted her thigh when she went past and she patted ma heed in return. I felt fine here, fir the time being.

I listened tae the men's banter and the wimen chirruping and laughing coz they were trying tae join in, even though they couldnae coz they'd nae good jokes like the men. I managed tae make it tae the loo and hae a slash in peace, the burning had eased off. That's why I like a pint, it helps yi relax.

The mair yi think, the mair it hurts. But as the night wore on I started getting itchy feet, so I stood up, and put my coat on.

'Aye, off he goes,' ane o the men said. 'See him doon the road, Davey, eh?'

I waved my hand, and walked oot the door.

I thought aboot walking right alang the Perth Road, right through the city, oot intae the country as far as the road would go. I'd done that before. That walk, the sun wis still up even though it wis night-time; gein athin a yella glow. I'd wandered that far, the pavements disappeared. I wis too close to the cars on the motorway, so I crossed a metal barrier and walked in the long grass, dodgin bits o tissue and auld nappies and shite bags. The grass seemed too bright, like it wisnae real, the wind blew in ma face and the cars made giant sounds that floated past uz; I was alive, I was *still* alive!

But I didnae like that feeling fir some reason.

I cannie mind when that wis? It couldnae o been lang ago, coz I've got them grass stains on ma boots. Nae point doing that again though, coz there are very few refreshments the further yi get alang the motorway, apart fae hotels, but the prices in those places are oot o the question. No, I never drink in hotels. Plus, yi dinnae ken wi these teuchter buggers, they ay end up being wee Tories that dinnae put their hand in their pocket. Nah, I like it alang the Perth Road fir the drink.

I was standing ootside the Campbeltown, wondering which way tae turn, when the young lad wha helped uz afore came oot.

'I'll get yi up the road, Jimmy, I'm awa hame.'

I walked wi him, coz it made nae odds tae me.

The young lad was quiet, but every now and then he would ask if I was awright and I'd nod. We reached a tenement block and the young lad said, 'Here wi are, Jimmy.'

We headed intae the stairwell, he walked uz tae a red door and I saw my name on the brass plate: Mr J. Corrigan.

Funny, seeing yir name like that efter forgetting what it wis, makes yi feel yiv been living someone else's life.

But that wis fine, I wis glad I wis hame.

I fiddled in my pockets and found keys. The young lad helped uz open the door then said, Night, Jim! And he headed up the stairwell, he musto lived upstairs.

When I got in the flat, I held ontae the wall aw the way doon the lobby, coz I wis feeling dizzy. Oh aye this is my place, coz here's aw ma things. I went in the kitchen and filled the kettle wi water and lit the stove. I waited till the steam blew across the ceiling and the water bubbled, rattling the metal o the cooker top, then a whistle blew and I kent it wis time.

I put my tea on a wee tray that had a cushion underneath, and I made up a plate o shortie biscuits I found in a tin, some had chocolate on top and some were just in shapes that I like, like the thistle. Aye I like the thistle, it minds me o something.

I went in the living room and sat the tray on my lap. This is comfy, this high-backed chair wis a good buy, I cannie mind when I got this but it must be new, it's half-decent this. And it looks ontae the TV and the windee. Aye I can see aw the goings on fae here. I look aboot the room. Aye here are aw my things, an ashtray o stubbed oot fags, that jigsaw I keep meaning tae finish, a standing lamp wi a pink shade that has tassels hanging doon, some o them are unravelling; that's mine. There's my wooden cabinet wi glass shelves and inside is that brass horse wi carriage whar I keep bits and bobs, the odd match, an elastic band, a pin fir if I need it; there's books too, an encyclopaedia, 1001 beers o the world, a holiday brochure fir Majorca fae 1992 and a book called *Golfing Legends*.

I rub my legs, they're sair fae aw the walking, and I lean my heed back against the chair and close my eyes, hoping fir just a memory in my legs; in my chest.

Just a memory o breathing, the way I breathed before.

Feathers Thick
with Oil

Craig Burnett

Artwork by Murray O'Grady

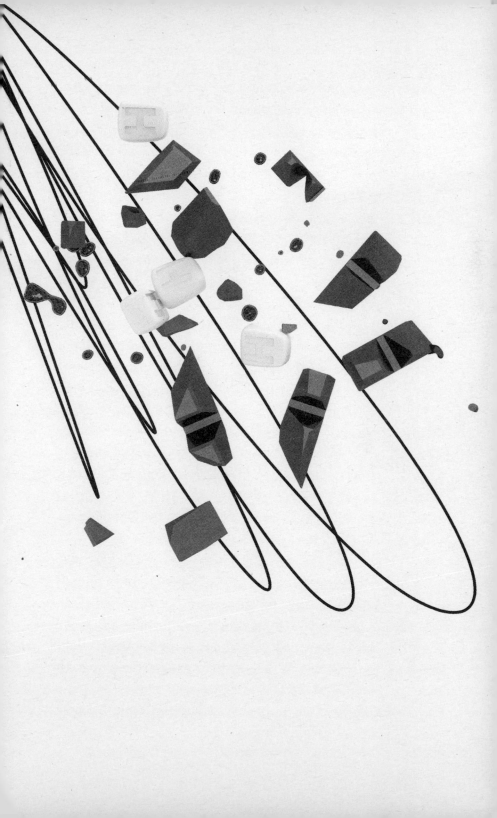

FEATHERS THICK WITH OIL

Craig Burnett

Walking between gates eight and nine, I see a slender woman in a charcoal-grey suit pick up her case and spin around with it, like a hammer thrower about to release her missile. After a few turns of increasing speed she straightens her arms. She's still gripping the case, which is now orbiting her at head height. To keep her balance, the woman sticks her backside out and throws her shoulders forward, setting her body in the shape of a question mark, albeit one revolving a couple of times a second. Sickly yellow light bounces off her patent leather heels. She growls, dredging the sound from the back of her throat. This is going to end very badly indeed.

The case is a Samsonite Neopulse. I think so, anyway – at the speed it's flashing past me I can't really tell. I squeeze the handle of my own Neopulse and smile. A great case, the Neopulse. Sturdy. You'll know this if you've ever had one clattered against your shins or dropped on your foot by a fellow passenger. 'That's a solid case,' you'll have told yourself, as the pain fades away. Pain is only temporary, even in airports. That's something I tell myself before every flight, so that I don't turn into the woman in the charcoal-grey suit.

The case – I'm sure it's a Neopulse, you can tell by the metallic-black finish – clears a circle roughly three metres across. The growl has moved up the woman's throat now, turning into a raw, animal scream. The people on the edge of the circle are frozen, terrified that any movement will cause the case to slip from the woman's hands and fly into the crowd. I'm stood a little further away, next to an elderly man with thick glasses and carefully swept hair. He's wearing a lemon-yellow polo shirt tucked into beige chinos, and mumbling 'oh my, oh my', which seems a fair appraisal of the situation. The whole thing has been going on for less than five seconds, but the absolute certainty of imminent disaster means I already feel voyeuristic.

The man looks about seventy, the same age as most of my patients. Please don't misunderstand what I mean by patients. I don't tap on ribcages, or coax children into showing me their inflamed tonsils. I don't break bad news, I don't ask if you have any questions, I don't leave you alone for a moment so it can all sink in. I fly to European cities and persuade hospital boards and health ministries to buy truckloads of Haxatin, an arthritis pill roughly the size and colour of a child's tooth. Haxatin's popularity means I take more than 150 flights a year, which is wearing for both me and my luggage. But robust defences (my vigorous gym and yoga routine, the Neopulse's 100 per cent Makrolon polycarbonate shell) see us through. The mantra helps, of course.

Everyone near the woman is staring, from cleaners to

business travellers like myself. This woman is one of us, I suppose. We business travellers share a quiet camaraderie, one that belies our reputation. We respect each other for moving through airports with crisp, clean precision, slipping quickly from scanner to passport check, unencumbered by impulse buys of perfume or premium Swiss chocolate. We are self-sufficient, but this doesn't stop us admiring self-sufficiency in others. I notice my peers shuffle a little further away from the spinning woman and her Neopulse. The Neopulse is not just tough, but lightweight too. If this woman releases hers, my peers are thinking, it's going to soar. Their wariness prompts me to step back too. We look out for each other, us business travellers, in a funny kind of way.

But we break sometimes, just as you do. I couldn't tell you what sparked the raging pirouette of the woman in front of me, but I will say that even premium luggage cannot sweeten the bitterness of frequent air travel. Not completely, anyway. So, yes, we can find ourselves slapping, spitting, swinging fists outside just-closed departure gates. But more often we simply want to scream, to fill the dead air of cavernous departure halls with our anger and frustration. That's how I understand this woman's behaviour – a violent occupation of space, a declaration of free will after years of dutifully obeying instructions about shoes and belts and laptops.

I had a similar experience queuing for a latte at Amsterdam Schiphol. The moment it was over – a little girl left cradling the remains of her doll, shocked Korean backpackers wiping frothed milk from their guidebooks – the mantra struck me for the very first time. It was a revelation, a transformation. 'Pain is only temporary!' I shouted joyfully. Then I shouted again, louder, beaming: 'Pain. Is. Only. Temporary.' It still warms me, knowing my moment of rebirth was shared by that little girl, by the backpackers, by the stewardess cowering under a nearby table. Maybe they're using my mantra today. I like to think so.

Rebirth is a theme of the promotional material I carry in my own Neopulse. The leaflets it holds speak rousingly of new dawns and lifted worries, without promising anything too specific. This language – great foghorn blasts of optimism, unburdened by detail – is one I learned on the job, more or less teaching myself. Pharmaceuticals are not a priority for my firm. We mainly trade in cleaning products, synthetic cattle feed, and a thick green slime used in the manufacture of skin lotion, make-up remover and instant noodles. Haxatin was originally sold by its inventor, a global drug company whose products are probably sitting in your kitchen cabinet right now. But then this company realised Haxatin, which had barely scraped through its clinical trials, was having disquieting effects on the people who consumed it. Their blood was thinner than before, and streaks of it began to leave their bodies in unnerving and unpredictable ways.

The company behind Haxatin thought it prudent to withdraw it from the market. But they faced a problem. To suddenly deprive people of the drug would raise embarrassing questions, for its creators and for the doctors and health-board functionaries that had already ordered billions of tablets. The answer was a corporate sleight of hand that began with Haxatin's inventor quietly selling the rights to the drug to a holding company in Belize. Weeks later the

Belize firm was swallowed up by Aristotle Healthcare, a £28 million company run (in a certain legalistic sense) from an empty office above a used-car showroom in Panama City. Aristotle Healthcare awarded the European sales licence for Haxatin to my employer, in a deal brokered by a retired Thai politician and a Danish investment trust. So now, as well as selling detergents and green slime, we ensure a steady supply of Haxatin across the continent. The whole thing will unravel sooner or later, of course, but the mess it leaves behind will be complicated enough for everyone involved to plausibly claim ignorance and blame someone else. In the end, the only person questioned face-to-face will be 33-year-old single mother and used-car dealer Maria Nunez, who knows nothing about pharmaceuticals but can offer you a *sensational* price on a 2005 Toyota Camry.

This shift in supplier is really a formality for our customers, who know full well it's a result of Haxatin's failings. The meetings I arrange could easily take place over the phone. But no emailed factsheet or legal document would reassure these nervous officials like I do. I am an actual flesh-and-blood person, one who will look them in the eye and tell them it's all going to be fine, just fine. I am a guiding hand at the crook of their elbow, a soothing whisper in their ear. I am bait. The meetings tend to be brief – sometimes customers wince at the grubbiness of the pantomime, and the collective amnesia it demands. But most play it straight, nodding thoughtfully and smiling or frowning at appropriate moments. Some even enjoy it. I think they like being taken back to a happier time, before murky water was lapping at their ankles.

I told someone about Haxatin, about its grubbiness and my part in that grubbiness, on the 0715 Lufthansa to Hamburg last week. I get truthy with people I meet on planes, particularly when I've had a few drinks. I think it's because you're sat next to each other, but facing forward. This seating arrangement reminds me of a confession booth, or what I've seen of confession booths on TV. Anyway, I told my neighbour how I'd drifted from the oil business to the cigarette business to the Haxatin business, stoically taking on jobs that would make others retch. She nodded uncomfortably, worried I had noticed her disapproval. Of course I had noticed. But once you've encountered enough disapproval you build up a protective layer against it, like the dead skin on your soles of your feet. You find this sensation odd at first, then fascinating, so fascinating you poke the skin just to see how it feels, or rather how it doesn't feel. The conversation with my neighbour didn't last long. After talking about Haxatin, there seemed little else to say. So we sat in silence for the flight's final hour, two decades of oil-covered birds and scarred lungs and dangerously thin blood hovering between us. We were descending into Hamburg when she mumbled that we all need to get by in an imperfect world, which was very sweet of her. And as we unbuckled our seatbelts, she said: 'Just as long as you help the people around you, I suppose.'

I remember these words when finally, inevitably, the woman with the Neopulse releases her grip and flings her luggage upwards. It glides serenely away from her, trajectory smoothed by the first-class aerodynamics of the case's Makrolon polycarbonate shell. The woman's face is flushed,

166

her hair has fallen loose and she is sucking the air up in great ragged gulps. At its highest point the case nudges the strip lights above, and the sickly yellow glow coating us all shivers just a little. As the case starts to drop I see exactly where it's headed – into the 70-year-old man to my right, who's still rooted to the floor. He seems to be travelling alone. Maybe he takes Haxatin. I picture him crumpled on the floor, his dangerously thin blood washing over the Neopulse's Makrolon polycarbonate shell. I know exactly what to do.

I step in front of the 70-year-old, ready to absorb the impact of the case hurtling towards us, and as I do my heart soars. 'Help the people around you.' It's so simple, so brilliantly simple. This could be my new mantra. I could share it on flights, in departure halls, while queuing for my latte. Why should I limit myself to one rebirth? To quote the promotional leaflets stuffed inside my own Neopulse, 'The day to start your new life is TODAY.' The pills those leaflets promote might be imperfect, or even a 'lethal timebomb', in the words of one regulator, but that shouldn't detract from the underlying truth of the message. The machinations of the pharmaceutical industry are not the *leaflets'* fault. The leaflets are pieces on a chess board, just like me. Until today.

But as I stare at the looming case, my faith in rebirth wavers. Because the Neopulse really is moving incredibly fast. I grab the 70-year-old's polo shirt and dive to the left. As the case whistles a couple of inches past our shoulders, I tell myself that not standing in its path is less overtly heroic than my plan of a few seconds ago. And so, in a sense, an even more heroic course of action. We fall to the floor, me on top of him, and I take the chance to whisper my new mantra in his ear. He's trying to talk; his mouth is flapping, but he can't seem to form any words. I turn and see the case a few metres away. It's lying open – I'm surprised the owner hasn't engaged the Neopulse's integrated three-digit TSA lock, one of the features that really elevates it above its competitors. Next to the case is a small boy. He is shaping his mouth to scream, but just like the man underneath me, he can't coax any sound out. On the scuffed floor in front of him are what at first glance look like dozens of Haxatin tablets, but are more likely his teeth.

HEART'S LAST PASS

Douglas W. Milliken

Artwork by Pio Abad

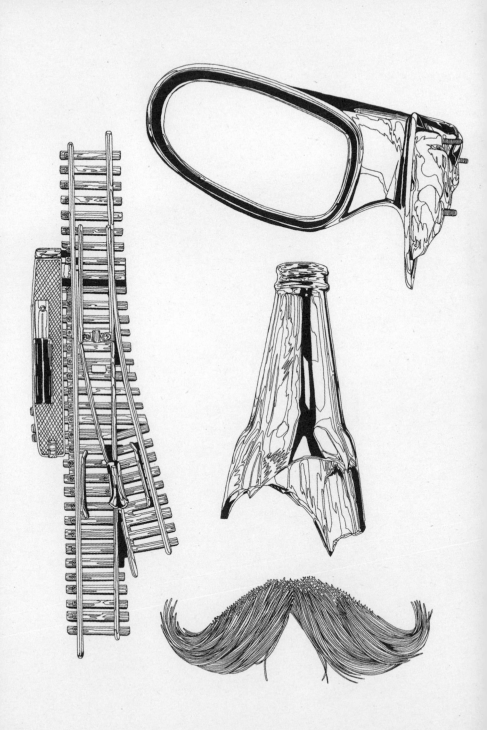

HEART'S LAST PASS

Douglas W. Milliken

The plan hadn't ever been to be in Syracuse at all. Somewhere in Nebraska between nowhere and Lincoln – amid the gliding crop-dusters and their pale mists of drifting poison, along the razor-straight slash of I-80 East – the rides just sort of dried up for me. I was wind-tortured and dark-eyed and strung out in countless small ways and not one blameless soul wanted me inside their car, and though the prospect scared me like some grasping dreamtime horror, I really had no other choice than to try my luck stowing away on freight trains (or staying: I could have just stayed). I did what I thought I needed to do because an urgency was pushing me hard from behind, away from the West's dead plunge into the Pacific and back east to the Atlantic and to you. I took a risk and hopped a train and somehow made it to Chicago, although once there the crust-punk kids I fell in with told me I'd done everything wrong. I shouldn't have legs left, they said. I should've been beaten senseless by bulls. There was a book they showed me, made on a photo-copier and bound with staples, written by some anonymous train-hopping prophet of their generation. His method was a sort of religion. His way was the only true way. On the next train, I followed their lead, but I didn't really see any difference between what I'd intuited and what they had to show me. Which maybe proves just how wrong I was. We rode across Ohio and a little bit of Pennsylvania into New York State and had to change trains in Syracuse. If we stayed on our train, we'd end up in Montreal, which I guess would've been fine for my friends but not so fine for me. Our stowaway car jostled to a stop and we escaped into a railyard that looked halfway haunted by itself. Busted-up train pieces and piled railroad ties, rusting chunks of metal and compressed-fuel tanks and garbage. We bunkered down in the woods until dark. About midnight, we spotted our eastbound train rolling in real slow amid the creosote-stinking gloom. We gathered our stuff and trotted up to the tracks and easily tossed ourselves aboard. The train appeared to be mostly empty cargo cars. We settled in and slid shut the door and a few minutes later, content with our easy berth, we slept.

I remember, I dreamed of the unceasing wind of Nebraska, ripping down across the sky to rake the land like a million pissed-off crows. There was dust in my mouth and snakes in the grass. No evidence of any human anywhere. When we awoke some indeterminate time later, it was impossibly dark outside and raining hard. The train had stopped moving. All this, I was told, was bad.

'If they find us, you realise,' Vale kept saying in a hoarse stage whisper, 'we are totally fucked.' He twirled the ratty fetlock knotting off his chin to add gravity to his point. Vale's tendency when sober was to repeat obvious things as if they were imperceptible truths, things only he could see that we were idiots not to see. He was lordly in his condescensions. But get a few drinks in the kid, and he'd soften right up like Play-Doh in the rain.

Our other companion, Molly, threw him a little pint bottle of MD 20/20 and told him to shut the fuck up. To this day, Molly remains one of the toughest dudes I've ever met. Only about five and a half feet tall, Molly had long black hair and Indian eyes and these beautiful full hips and breasts. It was very confusing to me. Most folks would assume he's a girl, and maybe but for his perfect sweeping black handlebar moustaches, they'd be right. I mean, I'm pretty well convinced that Molly had a vagina. But that didn't make him any less of a man. Perhaps, in some ways, it made him more so. Probably not. Regardless, I was drawn magnetically to Molly and also scared of him and had learned to follow his lead. We passed the bottle of booze around – in the dark, I couldn't be sure of its colour, but it tasted like antifreeze green – and everyone relaxed into our predicament. The rain fell and the train didn't move. We waited.

In my youth, I picked up a wise tip about developing a nervous gesture that would not read as nervous. Like having a pipe to chew on and fuss with, or like an old man wiping his rheumy eyes with a hankie. Give yourself something to do, is the idea, when you've really got nothing else to do. So while we slumped there doing nothing in the train car, I popped out my partial plate and with a rag from my pocket wiped the metalwork clean. It's unlikely you've forgotten how I lost my top front teeth when I was a kid, during one of the most glorious games of H-O-R-S-E ever recorded. But a lot later, after you'd already cut me loose, I lost one of the neighbouring teeth when my mouth caught the tip of an aluminium baseball bat. That time was categorically non-sports-related. All I can say about that is, man, don't *ever* go to Florida. The only good I found while there was a newfound fondness for my teeth, real or otherwise. I rubbed the gunk off my palate and popped the piece back in.

'I wish I still had my uke,' Vale lamented.

'Shut up about your uke already,' Molly said.

Vale's ukulele had fallen off the last train somewhere near Erie, Pennsylvania. It fell off because Molly made it fall.

Given how long we'd slept, Molly assumed we were stopped somewhere out near Albany or maybe further west across the Massachusetts line. I took this as good news: I was that much closer to being home with you and Melanie, that much closer to reclaiming what I'd lost, to putting my life back together. It would be hard work fitting back all the far-flung pieces. But I had faith that I could do it. I could make this work. Vale took out a deck of cards and shuffled. Molly passed his bottle around again.

Our fear was that, with the train stopped, rail workers might be checking the cars or something, that somehow someone might find us, so we played our game of poker as quietly as we could. Molly slid open the train car's door so that we'd have a little light. The rain eased up, then got harder. In a while, we were drunk and didn't care about making noise. Molly took off some clothes. I squirmed. Then

Vale leaned out the cracked-open door to take a piss but instead started yelling.

'Man, what even the fuck, Molly. This ain't Albany.'

'Yeah it is.'

'No. It's not. We never even left the rail yard.'

Molly stood and leaned beside him out the open door.

'Yes we did.'

'No, Molly. We didn't. We hopped aboard a stopped train.'

'Bullshit we did.'

'Bullshit nothing. I can see where we made camp from here. I can see Billy, for Christ's sake.'

Billy was another kid we were supposed to be riding with, but he'd disappeared right around the time our train came chugging through. While Molly and Vale argued, Billy stepped up to our open car door.

'Hey guys,' he said merrily, water streaming through his adolescent fluff of beard. 'What're you all up to? Hiding out from the rain? That's cool.'

'We're going to Albany,' Molly said.

'No,' Vale corrected. 'We're not.'

'How dry is it in there? I've been stuck in this shit for hours.' Billy was a good-natured kid: if he sensed the tension between Molly and Vale, he didn't let it show. He was wearing a tennis visor that must have made everything right now appear to him through a waterfall. While Molly and Vale stood by and didn't help, Billy pulled himself up into our car.

It would be a few days yet – when we finally hopped our actual train east – before Billy lost his grip and got his legs gobbled up beneath a flat-bed train car halfway loaded with fancy sinks. I remember that last flickering moment when

Billy was still holding on to the train but his legs were getting spread for yards and yards behind us. He looked from the decreasing line of his knees back up to where I was still standing, trying to help him aboard. It's like his eyes were saying 'this is bullshit' while his mouth hung open in a silent, disbelieving O. Then he let slip his grip and he was gone in the rail-side cinders. Until that moment, though, no circumstance was going to dictate Billy's mood. Billy plopped down and drew a forty of Budweiser from his tote bag and raised the bottle like it was some sort of offering. He met each set of eyes and in turn, said, 'Meh?'

Though simple, and perhaps even crude, his point was valid and irrefutable. We three gathered around him and drank and resumed our game of cards.

It always amazes me how these kids with no homes and no money somehow always have booze or drugs. I'd just escaped from a California rehab knowing I had no chance of ever getting clean in a place like that. How could anyone possibly stay sober in California? The evidence I'd seen suggested it was impossible. My guess was that being on the road would be my best bet. All my resources – every dime – would be spent on keeping my forward motion moving progressively, incrementally forward. Under such severe restrictions, survival would be my only option. But these kids, living such similarly structured lives, clearly had found a loophole. If you had nowhere to go and were in no rush to get there, why not enjoy the ride? If twenty bucks gets you sober to Boston, won't it also get you fucked up to Springfield? God willing, you'll get to Boston someday.

But where'd they get their money to begin with? Maybe

they just stole. My gig has always been to make bargains with my body. It's probably easier to always just steal.

After another hour, we'd gambled all the same nickels and buttons and drunk all our booze and rain or not, I didn't want to be in that fucking train car any more. I announced that I was heading out on the search for more beer. I told them they could join me or not. But no one else seemed inclined to abandon our immobile train. They were opting for 'not'. Fine. Fuck 'em. I gathered my one pitiful bag and headed for the door, where the rain kept roaring like a panther in the night. I stood in the slick doorway and looked left and right, then slipped when I should've jumped and smashed my face into a railway tie, so now my partial plate was all stove to shit. I found my feet quick and smiled inside towards those guys to let them know I was okay, but with my fake teeth all bent like that, I had to've looked pretty insane. Everyone shouted all at once. I could feel the blood flooding my mouth. Molly started out of the car after me, and with his beautiful eyes and soft bottom lip shining beneath his long moustaches sweeps, he looked appallingly like a mother. I turned tail and split.

In the way the world often presents these things, my memory of the next little while is not entirely reliable. I know I ran for a long time with the blind sense of being chased, and that beyond the train yard, in a gravel lot abutting a warehouse, I met two dudes in tie-dyed sweaters who were smoking dope through a cast-glass steamroller in their battered old Chrysler Reliant. They got me high and gave me a ride but I'm not sure where they took me. That part of my memory is gone. I remember the scent of leather and weed in the dark backseat of their car, then I remember standing soaked in a parking lot that stretched on for ever in every direction, a repeating gridwork of street lamps punctuating the asphalt like giant specimen pins nailing the world into place, and the rain striking unerringly like an eternity of falling bombs, sizzling white sparks under the mercury lamps with each incandescent blooming. I remember thinking, while the world exploded around me, that those boys must've had something more than weed packed in their designer pipe. Or maybe they fed me some pills in exchange for something I could do for them. It was a really bad scene, with bright lights zeroing in rapidly from the darkness, but soon that ended or anyway, *I* ended. I can't remember much more after that until I woke up early the next morning in the bushes behind a truckers' paradise with the nearby highway roaring like a roller rink. The night's rain had stopped but I was soaked and felt punctured, with my pockets turned out and emptied of even the lint. One of my shoes was missing, but then I found it in the flooded parking lot, wedged beneath a semi's front tyre. The inside of my skull felt scraped clean with a spoon. Like a melon. There were tractor trailers parked everywhere in neat military rows, and a million gas pumps stationed over in an island, and a restaurant in between. All at once, I was rubbery and I was stiff. I headed towards the dumpsters to find myself something to eat. But in the impossible flooding distance between, those dudes' Reliant was parked by itself and I could see movement inside. Someone stepped haltingly out from the back. Grey water sluiced around my walking feet and something trickled down my legs and I realised it was Molly stepping out of the dopers' car, dishevelled and blinking and grinning like a baby in the savage wet morning air.

We stood staring at one another like two idiots on a battlefield while Molly pissed next to the car. Then we waved.

'Molly, man, Jesus,' I said as I crossed the wet distance. 'What the fuck happened?' I was asking about his moustaches, which appeared to have fallen off, but he must've thought I meant something else.

'Yeah, some party, right?' He ran a hand through his long black hair and laughed. He wasn't wearing pants, just a long tie-dye that barely covered his junk. His legs looked really pretty in this light. 'Those dudes really know how to have fun.'

Inside the car, I could clearly see a boy's naked butt. I guess Molly must have followed me when I ran, had possibly been with me all night. But everything I remember feels so alone. Like there was no one else in all the world. Not even me. Just unholy rain falling massive in the lights.

But all that rain was gone now. I stared at Molly all soft and full in the blue morning light and felt everything moving inside of me. All backward and strange. It had been years since I'd seen you, but as broken as I was, I still loved your indifferent cat-eyes and hard hands and impossible stretching limbs. I missed you. I missed our daughter. I missed you. But now here was this man, Indian-eyed and half-naked in a truck-stop parking lot. I hated my heart and everything it makes me do.

Lightly around his lips, Molly was pale where his moustaches once hung. It took everything left within me not to touch that soft, once-hidden skin. Meekly, I gestured towards

181

the dumpster and asked Molly if he'd join me, if he wanted something to eat.

Molly smiled, and closed his eyes, and turned his head. When he opened his eyes again, he was looking in at the sleeping boy's butt. Then his grin grew sweeter.

'I think I'm going to hang out here for a while more, Coleman.' And he eased back into the car. 'I'll catch up with you boys later.'

I'd forgotten I'd fucked up my mouth the night before. Now I remembered. I watched Molly cosy down with his boy. I watched traffic burn along the highway. So many people with places to go. But none of those places was for me. A door kicked open at the back of the restaurant and a man in whites tossed a bag in the dumpster. Then he went back inside. Behind me, a semi's airbrakes hissed. I didn't know where the fuck I was or where the train yard might be or what had happened to the rest of my friends. But that didn't feel like it mattered any more. Knowing things didn't matter. Kicking my feet through the grey floodwater sucking my ankles and heels, I pointed myself in any direction, and no direction I chose was home.

CIVILISATION

Will Self

Artwork by Eddie Peake

CIVILISATION

Will Self

I have been confined to my apartments by a condition at once debilitating and embarrassing: at periodic intervals my body disgorges somewhere in the region of a cupful of matter, which is both colloidal and mercurial – quicksilver and stodgy. I never know for more than a few moments in advance when the discharge will come, or where from: eyes, ears, nostrils, mouth, urethra or anus. This gooey stuff smells at once excremental and aseptic – a bouquet of shit and detergent. I am reminded of the time before I was so sequestrated, when I prowled the city with fierce abandon – my quarry all the sensations it has to offer. So I scaled the stepped-back skyscrapers precipitately, ledge-to-ledge – and on one occasion, using a key I bought in an ironmonger's, I opened a manhole and descended into its stygian sewer system. Clambering down, I grabbed the rusty old ladder's rungs with my rubber-gloved hands, palms gripping then slipping on their thick lagging of ancient toilet paper.

I sloshed along the subterranean drains, feeling amorph-
ous blobs sickly vacillate against my toes, shins, thighs,
through my rubber waders. My torch blade struck feeble
beams and gleams from the uvular walls – I swallowed hard.
I heard the chirrups and squeals of the rats – but never saw
one. At length, I reached the confluence of several tunnels:
a chamber, perhaps five storeys high, into which they disgorged liquid sewage that gurgled and swirled in a mephitic
whirlpool as it drained into some yet deeper chasm. I inched
along a slimy walkway projecting out into the putrefying
millrace, intent on confronting the monocular stare of this
great and ineluctable process – the evacuation of everything
humans deem anathema to the civilised life: their bodily
waste, and the residue of their efforts to eradicate its faecal
stain. My torch beam flickered over a greasy-brown boil
that rose up from the morass, capturing a scrap of newsprint poised on its revolting surface tension. Around and
around it went.

As I believe I may've said: I've no way of anticipating
when, or from which orifice, the silvery goo will be voided –
at most, there're a few seconds of plenitude, followed by
a piercing pain which lances through the relevant duct.
Sometimes it's only a few minutes between these episodes –
others, hours. A week or so ago, when nothing had happened
for an entire morning, I risked an outing to the local park.
A child's model yacht caught in pondweed seemed a suitable opportunity for a good deed – but as I dabbled in the
green water, freeing the keel, a cupful slopped down onto its
deck. The child came running and looked on, appalled, as
I submerged the yacht again and again, muttering fervidly,

'The ducks – they did something mucky. Yes ... very mucky.'
I haven't risked a repeat of this sort of thing – the consequences could be disastrous.

Instead, I remain behind the multi-density fibreboard of
my front door – only descending into the corner shop which
is located directly beneath my flat for essential supplies, or
sallying a few hundred yards further to attend the local
doctors' surgery. He's a young man and an old man and a
middle-aged woman. He's Asian and Bulgarian and English.
'You disgust me,' he said, as he analysed the silvery sample
I'd coughed up into a beaker in the adjacent bathroom, 'not
that this is a professional opinion,' he continued, squeezing
the bulb of the pipette so as to add a few drops of reagent.
'You disgust me – but this is a purely aesthetic judgement,
not a moral one.' He swirled the beaker – the gloop instantly
turned a deep mauve. 'What shall I do, Doc?' I wheedled. 'I
can't live like this.'

'You need to concentrate,' he said, his eyes rippling behind
the lenses of his expensive varifocal glasses, 'become more
attuned to your body. That's the trouble with modern life:
our urge to be disembodied – I blame Christianity ... all
those angels.'

'Angels have bodies, too,' I observed, cinching my belt.

'Maybe,' he sighed, 'but theirs don't randomly disgorge
silvery goo from all their orifices at intermittent intervals.'

'What's wrong with me, Doc?' I asked, as we both contemplated the foaming, steaming beaker.

'No bloody idea.' He snapped back, 'Now, if you'll for-
give me. I have patients waiting ... patiently.' His computer
printer chattered out three prescriptions – one for a dietary

supplement, one for a laxative, and the third for an anti-diarrhoeal preparation. In the reception area I felt the by now familiar pained plenitude – and the next moment a cupful spewed on to the worn carpet tiling. The receptionist handed me the kitchen roll as if this was a regular occurrence – and for that I was grateful. I did my best to scrub the stuff up, but still left viscous snail-trails twining the nylon bristles. I handed back the kitchen roll with an abject apology – then headed off to fill my prescriptions.

The best posture for me to adopt when at home has proved to be on hands and knees – and I wear no clothes. Fortunately the floors of my flat are wipeable wood laminate, and I have no rugs or carpets. So long as I'm left to my own devices, and not required to associate with my fellow humans, my exist-ence is bearable enough. When the pained plenitude comes, I either head for the bathroom – or stick it out. Statistically, two out of every nine cupfuls will be decanted via my anus or my urethra. There's no difference I can discern between this silvery goo, and the stuff that splurges from my eyes, ears, mouth and nostrils – but I'd accord myself lacking in all civilised decencies if I didn't experience its evacuation as inherently more disgusting. Wouldn't I? So, I keep a rough mental count, and try to be seated on the commode in time. Of course, often I'll be slumped there, and instead of my back or front passage, the goo will quit the building of my body through my right nostril – or my left lughole. Sod's Law, they used to call it – but they never said who Sod was.

I don't sleep for very long any more. To begin with, unable to acknowledge my comprehensive leakage, I went to bed as usual – but by one or two in the morning, my sheets, my pillowcases, my covers – all would be soaked, smelly and slimy. The first time that you buy nappies as an adult can be a bit of an ordeal. If they're for you, that is. It marks an important stage of accepting one's incontinence – clearly, it isn't going away. Indeed, it may well persist unto … the grave. A cruel and carping farewell, this – a kick in the dying human's bemerded arse as she lurches out the door. I'll spare you the agonies I experienced, bent double in the aisle of the chemist's – I had my reading glasses perched on the end of my nose as I scrutinised the squishy packages. Was I large or small? I hardly knew any more. At the counter they were discussing painkillers – another cruel irony, since, as I attempted to pay for my embarrassing purchase, I felt the familiar pained plenitude. Wiping the counter clean took quite a while – they shut the shop while I completed the task. I offered the manager some money to let me go, but she insisted I mop it all up myself, while the staff all stood on the far side of the sales floor, beside the electric clippers, talking about a television show. I went to bed that night wearing one pair of pull-up absorbent pants (medium), in the normal fashion – and a second pair on my head, leg-holes serving for my weepy eyes. One beneficial consequence of my new absorbent headgear is that it damps down the buzz … a little.

Have you met the buzz? No, really – have you made its acquaintance? Say hello, Buzz, dearest: 'Zzz-zzz! Zzz-zzz!' There's a good buzz – are you purring? It's a marker of my profound isolation, I think, that the ambient noise perme- ating my flat has become personified. He was here when I moved in – the buzz, and to begin with I berated myself as a fool, for renting the place sound unheard. Next I did my

best to track down the infuriating noise and eradicate it –
but to no avail: the buzz comes from a pair of power units
affixed directly to the wall of my flat, and when I confronted
Mr Vairavar, the proprietor of the corner shop, he explained
that they're essential to his business. Anyway, the buzz is, it
transpires, only first among a number of equally madden-
ing noises: the subtle grind of my next-door neighbour's
bruxism – the awkward night-time breathing of the man on
the other side, each inhalation long and shuddering, ever
promising – but never delivering – his surcease. Then there
are the buses that grunt into, and snort out of, the garage
opposite. In the most minuscule hours, when the owl of
Minerva flies on soft and absorbent wings, they pull out of
the garage and stop at the traffic lights next to my block, so
that their rumbling respiration is borne into me along its
exterior walkways, and through its internal ducts, adding to
the general cacophony. If I stand in my kitchenette and draw
myself up to my full height, so that my head is up inside the
stove's extractor hood, I`m plunged into the aural equivalent
of a panopticon. I'm able to hear all the sounds surrounding
the building – from the chattering of the children who gather
outside the corner shop on the far side of the road after
school, to the barking of Wonga, my upstairs neighbour's
dog. One by one I identified these sounds – and in so doing,
neutralised them. Only the buzz remained irrepressible – the
silvery, gooey, insinuating Buzz: a tintinnabulation of my
brain's own electrochemistry, or so it has begun to seem.
The buzz is the buzz of alienation and anomie – it has this
in common with my malady: occult origins and a refusal
to conform to any timetable. The buzz comes each time

unexpectedly, endures beyond reason, then suddenly stops. In its wake arrives a silence at once shocked and profound: a fermata, during which I never fail to contemplate the utter bestiality of my condition – my bare and forked animal existence. Naked and on all fours – at bay, in a bricky thicket I pay an exorbitant rent for, my money contributing – as my landlady gleefully informed me on the sole occasion she visited – to her pension. So she rests – and I labour.

The doctor was right. I was forced to conclude – after a month or so of this awful existence – that I was indeed unclean. A pariah – excluded from all social norms, a mere body, prey to processes over which my mind could exert no control. Even the best and most malleable of wax earplugs only sealed the buzz in: an electric ear worm, vermiculating my very cerebellum. Exhausted, I held myself in readiness for the next sensation of pained plenitude, and when it'd passed I recommenced cleaning – intent on managing at least this much: a goo-free body, and gooless surroundings. To begin with, on my forays to the shop below, I bought copious supplies of cleaning products – bleaches and other reagents, rubber gloves, sponges, mop heads and absorbent cloths. The flat stank of ammonia – I wept. Each day was a smeary, teary progress, as I wiped and wiped again all two hundred square feet of the wood-laminated flooring. Then I bought a steam cleaner which was delivered pronto. With this magic wand, jetting out water vapour at a hundred degrees centigrade, I could reach every nook and cranny, liquefying all dirt and goo, so that its residue might be easily mopped up with some kitchen towelling. I shuffled down to the garbage hopper – once, twice, three times a day – to deposit my black bags full of crumpled waste, the cord of my old dressing gown dragging in the dried-out cherry blossom that lies in drifts on the exterior walkways and staircases of the block.

There's no love lost when you're afflicted in such a way – because there's no love possible. After all, who in their right mind would be able to cope with this: at a singular moment of passion, when kisses and caresses are being bestowed with passion and artistry – a cupful of silvery goo plummeting down onto bare and wanting flesh? Oh, no – oh, God! I howled to the moon – who showed her celestial face, peeking, silvery and discrete, between low and scudding clouds. And then it came to me – came to me as I was actually examining the stains in the rank nappy I'd just torn from my stinking loins. What was this? At the very core of the sodden clout there were small and glittery flecks – as usual. But this time, instead of taking the residuum for granted and discarding the nappy post-haste, I removed the flecks with a pair of tweezers and scrutinised them further under a magnifying glass. The tiny flecks did indeed seem to be metallic – could they actually be silver? From then on I began to assiduously separate out the silvery flecks from the viscous goo in which they were being deposited. To begin with I simply hovered over the latest cupful where it lay on the wood-laminated floor, pecking away with my tweezers – and did the same with the two pairs of nappies I wore overnight, but soon enough, irritated by such inefficiency, I constructed a sort of panning implement, using a sieve and layers of kitchen roll. On feeling the familiar pained plenitude, I would now wave my implement around, holding it beneath first left nostril, then anus, then right eye – a balletic prelude, perhaps, to a devastating backhand tennis return – before, as the pained plenitude reached its inevitable conclusion, deftly position- ing it beneath the right orifice.

In a week or so I'd managed to accumulate a small and glittering pile – which I shovelled into a small velvet draw- string bag. The next time I hobbled down to the shop, I took the bag with me, and when I paid for my purchases – kitchen roll, toilet paper, basic comestibles – I got it out, untied the drawstrings, and tipped a quantity of the silvery flecks onto the counter. Mr Vairavar – who owns the shop, sits all day, hunched at the counter, his eyes on the distant horizon of the top-shelf magazines – immediately straightened up: 'What's this ... what's this ...' he muttered, getting out a jeweller's eyeglass and screwing it into his bilious, bagged eye. 'What's this ... what's this – why!' he exclaimed. 'This is highest grade silver, man – how is it that you knew I was a silversmith back home in Sri Lanka?' I said nothing – the pained plenitude was upon me, so I staggered outside to void in the gutter. Leaf mould. Plastic twists and shreds. A crushed fruit-juice carton. The desiccated and washed-out face of a politician, smiling up at me from a scrap of newsprint. When I returned to the counter Mr Vairavar handed me my velvet bag with a smile, saying: 'Is there more where this came from? Y'know, I've still got a crucible – and my other silversmith's tools. If you've access to more of this – which is the finest grade of silver – then we could go into business together.

And so we did. In the beginning Mr Vairavar simply offset my silver production against my grocery bill. Then, as his own production came on line, in the form of small but intricate pieces – rings, pendants, earrings, animal figurines – which he displayed in a tray by the till, he began to remit me small cash sums. These, after a few weeks' accumulation, I began to invest in more complex sieving equipment: laboratory clamps, to which I could attach more kitchen-roll-lined sieves, so that, whatever strange pose I adopted, in whichever part of the flat, the goo would be caught and filtered. Mr Vairavar took on an apprentice – while the buzz that emanates from the units which power his freezers full of extra-strength lager and full-fat milk became fused in my mind with my own excretory labour. So the buzz ceased to be the buzz of alienation and anomie – and became the warm hum of industry. Now, when I crawl on all fours, or pirouette in a fugue of pained plenitude – or crouch down to squirt, or rise up to piddle, or place both of my hands behind my head as my left nostril jets out silvery spume – or reach for the kettle, only to have it slimed by my gushing eye, I feel nothing but a sort of stupefying pride: for what have I done? Surely, taken a nauseating and repulsive affliction – this smelly, silvery discharge – and turned it into the fount of a new industry? A primary form of extractive industry, which I manage – as I do its refining and preparation. An extractive industry which is in turn linked to a manufactory, a distribution system – wholesale and retail enterprises. The wood-laminated floors of my flat are no longer a terra nullius, but a territory with which human labour and ingenuity has been mixed – I stare now upon scuffed skirting boards and stained bathroom tiling, with all the pride of any self-made industrialist.

As for Mr Vairavar – through him I feel connected to an

entire network of people: makers and doers and buyers and wearers of his and his apprentice's exquisitely made jewellery. I may still feel the intermittent pained plenitude – I may yet experience the randomised splurge. I may even remain in enforced reclusion, yet I know, that were all these folk to be confronted with my naked, straining and smelly form, rather than repulsion – they'd manifest only the sincerest gratitude. The last time I went to see my doctor, I sat in the surgery for a few moments, listening to him patronise me as he riffed on his computer keyboard – then I took out one of my velvet drawstring bags, crammed full of raw silver, and threw it onto his drug-company-gifted vinyl blotter: 'Take that,' I said, 'and buy yourself a new attitude. You, Sigmund Freud, and all the other soul doctors have it wrong – far from coming into being as humans sought to hide the animal reality of their bodies, it is these processes themselves that lie at the very foundation of what we call … civilisation.'

Rough Beasts

Jarred McGinnis

Artwork by Declan Jenkins

ROUGH BEASTS

Jarred McGinnis

The first monster from the sea was a boar. Amongst the cream of waves, a speck of black. The speck grew. A head became visible, then ears discernible, the yellow glint of eye reflecting the bright summer sun. And, tusks. Long, curved crescents that hummed violence. Opalescent with sea water, they cut the waves like the prow of an ancient warship. The beachgoers watched the beast born from the salt water. They held out their phones in selfie-salutes. Mothers gathered babies with nervous anticipation. Children squealed with excitement following potbellied fathers towards the shore. In the hateful pit of me, of us all, we wanted something to happen on this too-safe island.

I was sitting fifty feet from the first victim. I watched the man with the shaved head hike up his orange-and-blue swim trunks before taking a picture of the animal as it emerged. His gold chain and watch sparkled in the sun. His large hairless body gleamed with sunburn. He was typing into

203

his phone when the boar broke left, ran straight towards him and, before he could react, drove the three-foot scimitar of tusk up between his legs, skewering him. It flicked its head and the body bounced and rolled towards the water line.

The animal barrelled through a blue-and-white-striped windbreak, trampling a family, leaving a baby to scream and thrash in the sand at the disruption of her feed. A keening of voices rose as we began to realise what was happening. Bare-chested young men tried to stop the beast with the pointed ends of closed umbrellas and grill tops. The beach was sown with abandoned sandals and flip-flops. Crumpled towels lay everywhere as if the bodies they had wrapped had evaporated, leaving behind the whiff of burned paper and hair.

Most people stood motionless with flat, empty expressions, holding on to each other. Others threaded through the crowd with their phones on record to accuse the dead. Remember that video showing the elderly woman, grey hair in a bun, her grandmotherly roundness tucked into a black one-piece, carefully stepping towards the body of a young girl? In the distance, you could make out the boar as it continued to rampage the beach. I was there, I swear, just out of shot.

Howls of sirens drew closer. Men in tactical gear surrounded the boar as it obliterated an ice-cream van, its tinkling rendition of 'Jerusalem' refusing to succumb. The pop of their handguns felt an inadequate and nervous response. As the men grew familiar with the pleasure of the bright-red daubs bursting amongst the coils of fur, their confidence built. When the beast turned and charged, their fusillade stilled it in seconds.

The boar drew a long, deep breath. Then exhaled. The sand wisped and settled.

Eyes aimed at the animal's chest, waiting for another heave. A hundred fingers curled around the curve of a hundred triggers. The smallest flex of muscle and their mechanism would happily acquiesce a hundred times. But, the monster was dead. One by one the guns relaxed their stances. Radios blathered hisses and commands. A single clap turned into several then shouts and cheers were added. A soldier took off his helmet and handed his phone to have his picture taken next to the vanquished creature.

The boar jerked back to life and bit off his legs, roaring a rusty, throaty squeal. It stumbled to its feet and charged towards a forensics crew who had been spooling out plastic tape. Another roar of gunfire felled the animal. TV-news-production trucks gathered with the flies as flower tributes multiplied in the setting sun.

In the following days, the TV and radio were all tragedy chatter. Hashtags trended. Celebrities made video appeals. There was this one girl who died. I don't remember exactly why she was famous but it really drove home the sense-lessness of it all. I retweeted some stuff about her. Nothing else existed except the personal stories of the victims. We consumed their last minutes with our morning tea and toast. Their tragic ends fortified our bones. It became such that no one questioned who was on the beach that day, because we were all there.

We took the kids down to the beach where the Boar emerged. It seemed the right thing to do. The stench of dying flowers was overwhelming. Tributes piled up until the sand was no longer visible and the beach became a pixelation of red, white, pink and green. A bank of flowers, easily taller than a man, had accumulated beneath the pier for those who couldn't quite be troubled with the dozen or so steps onto the beach. The naked stems of lilies tumbled in the surf. As soon as our youngest boy reached the promenade the smell of perfume and decay turned his insides out. His hysterics had a liturgical air that people seemed to approve of. We stood in reverence with everyone else until he was hollowed out, emptied of bile and tears. When his mother scooped him up, he slept an angel's sleep on her shoulder as we looked for where we parked the car.

Besides fish unwillingly, and wayward whales, obviously, animals have been coming out of the sea for years. It was remarkable but nothing we paid much attention to. Most of them were benign. Sodden cats skulking, eyes darting as they trotted towards a clump of sea grass to hide and groom the brine from their fur. Dormice by the handful. The occasional pangolin might garner a few lines in the local press. I once saw a swarm of bees emerge from the Firth of Clyde. In ones or twos, sometimes in shotgun shot-blasts, they flung themselves into the hovering, swirling, buzzing mist above as it drifted shoreward. Sometimes, the animals that emerged were a welcome wonder. A trained seeing-eye dog, a golden retriever who only understood commands in Albanian, shook itself dry and trotted up to a young boy in a wheelchair. A male passenger pigeon, a species extinct for one hundred years, startled a surfer in Cornwall by resting on his wet-suited shoulder, looking just as bewildered as the young man. The animals that came from the sea had one thing in common. They all had the smell of burned paper and singed hair.

Behind our house lay a strip of forest. Forest is too grand a word; think of it as a hedge with aspirations. A staggered line of old yews, beech and ash with the occasional prickly holly to shelter piles of fly-tipped rubbish. I sat on a discarded bathtub flipped over like a fat poodle soliciting belly rubs. Staring at the house, replaying pointless battles at work fought by email and PowerPoint, I rolled myself a cigarette and blew smoke towards the house. Rollies at my age, who was I trying to fool? Daydreams about affairs with women I knew and didn't floated past my attention without any real conviction. I thought about taking down the bike hanging in the garage. Get myself in shape, finally. No excuses this time. Then, inevitably, I'd think about the cancer. Two years previously, I got breast cancer. Yes, men get it too. Everyone used words like 'fighting' and 'beating', but we knew in this battle I hadn't fought anything. I had been a vessel to be filled with modern medicine's best guess. When my wife drove me to my appointments, and I pretended her kale smoothies played a part in my recovery. To save my life, my participation was optional. That bothered me over and over.

The sour smell of burning hair and paper wrinkled my nose. Dabbing out my cigarette against the tub, I sniffed at it. Does tobacco go off? Even the rustle in the bushes behind me didn't register as I set to roll another. As I took that first lungful, my brain finally did the arithmetic. I spun around and jumped onto the tub. I may have squealed. A two-foot gerbilish beavery kind of creature, a coypu I figured out later, fluffed and nibbled at the innards of a torn bin bag. Its grey eyes made me think of the industrial ball bearings my company made. It was untroubled by my presence. The carbonised stink of the animal between us, I felt all the hate and anger I had been accumulating. My arms ached with the burden of my do-nothing, for my own life, for those people on the beach. I heard the echoes of spray-tanned politicians yelling into bouquets of microphones that something must be done. The animal paused its foraging, as if it had had a revelation of an important affirming truth. It looked up at me as if it was about to reveal this wisdom.

I clubbed in its head with a pipe. Its leg spasmed then stilled but the weight of the galvanised steel against the animal's body was a pleasure. I continued to pound at it. The fatigue in my muscles felt post-coital. I marvelled at how easy it is to unstitch a living creature and that I had done it. In the brush nearby, my eye was drawn to a wriggling of pink. A clutch of coypu babies squirmed and chittered with hunger. Fag ends, packing-peanuts and animal hair padded the shallow hole. The burned stench thick on my tongue, I shoved a mound of dirt over the squiggly, squeaking nest and tamped it down. When I came back into the house, my wife asked me why I was flushed. My shrug was a sufficient answer and she asked me to deal with the kids. I read them their bedtime stories while I thought about what I had done. *Goodnight bears, Goodnight kittens, And goodnight mouse.*

As the sea's animal-attacks became more commonplace, the victims faded from our attention. The newspapers tried to fit all the memorial portraits until the front pages became a tilework where you had a general idea at the hairstyle and maybe could make a guess at the person's ethnicity. Their stories in multitude became as insignificant as our own. Their deaths seemed to be less tragedy and more cautionary tale. What were they doing on the beach anyway? She was out late, a bit drunk, wearing a skirt that made it hard to run – of course a Kamchatka brown bear opened her ribcage like a tin of baked beans.

Instead we became drawn by the large portrait above the fold of the monster that caused the carnage. We all became instant experts in zoology, biology and ethology thanks to twenty-four-hour news and its animated infographics. We quoted the habitat range (not usually including Norwich) of the Florida panther. Wildlife encyclopaedias replaced serial-killer biographies and crime procedurals on bestseller lists. Invasive species (e.g. grey squirrels, crawfish, knotweed) were no longer our fault. The sea had turned against us and sent forth creatures smelling of ash. We wove conspiracies. The smell of burned paper and singed hair that hung over Manhattan for days after 9/11 was no longer a coincidence. We sought answers and as answers are so hard to find, we got angry. Anger felt like the conclusion we were looking for.

A year after the Boar, a wall was being built along the thousands of miles of coast to keep out the animals from the sea. The whole family, wife too, did its part. We stalked the forest behind the house to stove in the heads of crea-tures great and small. Afterwards, we settled in around the television to cheer our military and the lurid night-vision silhouettes of apex predators with unspooling innards.

*

I pulled the car over to laugh at the chimpanzees. They moved in an infantrymen's file formation through the thick mud of a tidal causeway. Their absurd arms, though sensible for African forest canopies, flopped and splashed in cold British muck. They floundered, their fur caked and matted, but they doggedly processed towards the shore. Two chimps dragged a motionless third, its bowed legs dragging pitifully behind. Tourists left their idling rentals to watch. The falling pound and the novelty of the sea animals had been a boon to the tourist industry. Police cars and Support Unit vans arrived as the apes collected at the shore visibly exhausted. I told my wife to stay in the car with the youngest while the older boys and I went for a better look.

The chimps huddled to pick mud and seaweed from each other with a meditative patience. More police gathered. More tourists gathered. The apes chattered into each other's ears as the crowd churned and grew restless. The boys and I got caught up with the excitement. I felt happy-drunk, watching their ridiculous grimacing heads swivel, big monkey-ears flopping, stupid brown eyes wide with fear. We cursed the chimpanzees. The police told the crowd to get back in our cars and leave. So, we cursed the police. News vans appeared as if by precognition and their antennae rose towards heaven.

We pushed forward and the police formed into a line of black batons and chartreuse hi-viz jackets. My oldest – he's fifteen – with his shirt pulled over his nose ran forward and launched a rock over the shouting crowd and police. As soon as the missile was launched, he did a victorious fist pump and swaggered away. He's always been my favourite. It fell short of the animals, but they scattered. On the packed earth and asphalt the comedy gait of the creatures became sinister. The chimps moved with purpose. They bared their teeth and screeched at the crowd. They banged driftwood on the ground. The animals returned to their huddle only to be interrupted by another stone thudding to earth nearby. Every human, tourist and police, was yelling. Teeth bared and brows furrowed, spit flew from our snarled mouths. My middle boy, barely ten but tall for his age, searched about for rocks so the oldest and I could sling them at the animals. It felt great to be doing something as a family again. The line of police burst into a flurry of batons to push us back. Behind them, the chimps darted back and forth as if pacing a cage. Someone got a direct hit. The crowd exploded into cheers. The animal, screaming and thrashing, held its broken arm.

The next rock smashed through the window of a blue Ford Fiesta on our right. Everyone flinched and looked around confused until we realised the chimps were throwing the rocks back. They rushed the line of police. Their howling screeches seemed to be everywhere at once. Black fur and teeth flashed. A grey-muzzled chimpanzee was jumping on the chest of a fallen riot cop as it bashed wildly at his face with a chunk of driftwood. I gathered the boys and legged it.

We got into the car and sped away. The boys and I laughing, talking a million miles a minute. Still out of breath, I tried to explain to my wife what happened and my oldest was re-enacting his beautiful first throw. My youngest looked between his brothers, glowing with admiration. My wife picked something from my hair. I examined the pink chunk of curd, maybe it was brains. I put down the window and tossed it out.

'Who wants fish and chips?' I asked.

The car erupted in cheers and clapping.

From the great gleaming white wall, we ate our takeaway and watched the continuing melee below until the sun set. From this height, the dead bodies were insignificant, black, punctuation marks. Tiny toy cars burned and popped black smoke. Helicopter gunships strafed the beach. How much it all looked like a video game and one that we were winning. Afterwards we drove along the coast and marvelled at the serene moonscapes of our coastal towns.

Under the Waves

Barney Walsh

Artwork by Mary Ramsden

Under the Waves

Barney Walsh

Abigail died when she was a little girl, just six years old – died and came back, clever trick if you can do it. Like something out of the Bible, not exactly. She drowned. Her lungs filled with water and she sank under the waves, into the depths, as if for ever. Now, loads of years later, she can still feel it happening (she tells Bex) – as if it were yesterday, as if it were *now*. She can *see* it: a young father and his little daughter walking by the sea one dull summer's afternoon. The sandy beach stretching endlessly empty before and behind them, low weedy cliffs walling off the world. A few gulls wheel overhead, darker smudges on the sky's grey. The man's dead skinny, wears a baseball cap; his face is wisped with a patchy attempt at beard. The girl's bright-yellow coat is all zipped up, the hood's drawstring yanked tight around her face. A harsh northern wind slices at her pink cheeks. They ignore each other, this man and this girl, as if they are strangers, together only by chance. Alone in their the headland. Tiny seashells crunch under his unlaced boots, under her little white trainers. The waters twist darkly into the distance.

The man lights a cigarette, but it's soon finished. He flicks it towards the sea; the wind snaps it inland. The girl, Abbie, skips along the water's edge, dancing in and out of the waves' grasp. Tiny lights blink in her heels at every step, red for port and green for starboard. The sea scares her, a bit, the choppy grey masses of it heaving over one another. She's *being brave*, by getting so close – but *God*, just the sheer *weight* of all that water, can you imagine? ('I've seen the sea before,' sniffs Bex.)

Abbie kicks at the pebbles scattered about the beach, looking for one she likes. Of all the many, many stones stuck in the sand here, washed by the sea, *one* of them will have magic powers. She's making it up but she *knows*. If she can only be the girl who finds it. Like in a story. It's here somewhere – telling fibs, pretending to be just normal stone, smooth-worn rock – but Abbie's not fooled. Somewhere there'll be one you can rub to make a genie appear; or one you can squeeze in your hand while making a wish to pop you into some next-door universe, more dangerous than this one but less scary and loads more fun. Or there'll at least be one you can put in your mouth to turn yourself invisible, something like that. Something to make the bullies go away, maybe. She just has to find it. There's lots of different colours and patterns, but nothing that really looks magical. The pebbles are brighter when they're wet; they go faded and disappointing as they dry. They click together under your feet. Abbie keeps looking, ignored by the man, till at last she spies one that's interesting, and picks it up: a translucent jade disc, an almost perfect circle. It's a lens, an eye, of clouded green crystal. Uncut emerald. A crystal ball, a scrying stone. She holds it up to her own eye, but can't see much through it yet: a few dim misty shapes, maybe, a vague swirling. Blurry images of the future, or the past. But she'll have time to practise later, to see better. She zips it for now into her coat pocket.

And just then from nowhere a huge dream of a wave rolls in, catching Abbie unawares, reaching far across the sand. Grey as ash, it lifts her from her feet. She gives a cry and topples into the surf; her tiny fingers claw at the sand, at the shingle, but as it withdraws the wave pulls her with it, its strength astonishing, stealing her little body away – and she's *gone*. Only empty beach remains, as if she never existed; even her footprints washed to nothing. The man, the girl's father, safely above the tideline, takes one hesitant pace towards the sea, and stops. He stands there blinking, clenching and unclenching his fists. He doesn't know what to do. No one else is in sight. After that one freak wave, the water has gone back to its normal, choppy sanity. He twists around to scan the grassy line of little cliffs behind him: there's nobody. No one's seen a thing. He looks again at the sea: the slate waves swell and fall, break at the edges, slide up the sand, cloudy liquid glass, and out again – but there's no sign of his kid. As if he'd only ever imagined that he had a daughter. He has no idea what to do. He thinks of the pub, of the way the evening's or afternoon's first pint begins to drown all a day's bad thoughts. Maybe he'd dive in, if he could see anything to swim for, any hint of Abbie's shiny yellow coat splashing amid the waves – but she's gone. And maybe he wouldn't have bothered, anyway. ('You *know* he wouldn't,' says Bex. 'He *didn't*, the selfish cowardly bastard.' 'Don't,' says Abigail.)

She's gone. Her father tries to light another cigarette, but his hands shake; he tries again, and manages it. He empties his head ('Can't have been much to be rid of,' says Bex), turns and walks back the way they came. Along the crumbling sea, over the whispering sand. The wind beating at his ears, gusts of it shoving him onwards, away from Abbie, little pushes to stop him changing his mind. A path of splintering wooden planks breaks off from the beach, cuts steeply up through the rocks and back towards the caravan site. At the top he pauses, turns back to look one final time at the sea – feels like he'll never see it, or something, ever again. Is it just the sea or is it ocean? He can't think any more. His thoughts hollowed out. His little girl lost somewhere under those waves? – it's just not a thing he can believe in. She must've run off back to the caravan, to the playground or wherever. Can't just be *gone*. He'd been her dad but he'd never actually done much for her. Never even, like, tied her shoelaces. Left all that to her mother. 'Cause the foot's *backwards* when it's someone else's, must make it tricky, what if he got it wrong and she laughed at him? Couldn't stand that. ('Seriously?' says Bex.)

But he's back at the caravan site now, hundreds of identical boxes arranged over a few sloping fields. Each like a child's tiny white coffin ('Yeah, like he'd have thought of *that*,' says Bex), till he gets in among them and they're just plastic rooms on bricks again. He counts the rows to find his: up two steps and the door squeaks as it opens.

The girl's mother is sitting sideways on the couch in the

caravan's end window, hugging her legs to herself and staring out at the little patch of sea that's visible from here. Last night at the caravan site's bar has given her a bit of a fragile head. She lifts her cheek from her bare knees as the man flicks the door locked. He tosses his baseball cap into the corner.

'I saw a seal, I think,' the woman says. 'Even from way up here. A little sleek dark head, I think it was a seal. Or maybe it was just a buoy. A buoy, or a boy. Or a sea lion, what's the difference? Oh my head. Where's our Abbie?'

'What?' says the man.

'Where's Abbie?'

'Oh, right. Out playing, we've got ages.'

'Ages for what?'

'What do you reckon?'

He comes over and kisses her. The back of her head bumps against the glass behind her, not helping her hangover. He puts his hands on her breasts and kisses her. It's kind of unexpected. When's the last time he touched her properly, like this, like he actually means it? Ages since. The only spark of life he's shown in God knows how long; it can't last but what's even brought it on? Whatever, her vodka-stained brain's in no fit state.

'Hey, not right now, no,' she says, pulling back her head from his. 'Get off me.'

'Just shut up, okay?' he says.

The couch is too narrow, he drags her to the floor, uses his knee to part her legs. Cheap scratchy carpet. Anyone passing could just look in, couldn't he at least shut the curtains? He yanks her top up, squeezes her breast, it *hurts*, the other hand's pushing itself down the front of her denim shorts. She almost tells him *okay fine whatever just get it over with*, as the simplest way to make this not be happening, but then instead she goes *no* – for once properly *no* – says, 'I'm telling you *don't*', and when he takes no notice she shoves hard at his chest, trying to push him off, scratches at his face with her nails. It doesn't do much, she's not really got any nails to speak of, chews them too much, but she does sort of catch with a fingertip at the soft skin under his eye – it makes him go 'Ow!' He backs off. Muttering to himself, he slides back across the carpet and up onto the couch again. He gets a squashed cigarette from his pocket, lights it, and sits there, forearms on knees, looking down at her. His mouth opens to speak; he changes his mind.

'You got something to say?' she asks him.

He stares at the carpet instead.

'Or are you just going to sulk?'

She stays lying on the floor. She'd ask him for a cigarette, but it'd mean talking to him again, plus she's meant to be quitting. Smoking, not talking. Her shorts unbuttoned, her top hiked up – God, what if Abbie were to walk in right now, what would she think? But he'd locked the door, hadn't he? From down here she can see sky instead of sea: the grey's a bit lighter, that's all. The clouds have waves too. Drizzle set in for *ever*, it seems; on and off for the rest of the week, at least. Rain ruining poor little Abbie's holiday. No, Abbie doesn't let stuff like that put her off – she'll be out there anyway, running about playing, bossing the other kids, that's if she's not off wandering in her own imagination. Not bothered by a bit of water.

The woman straightens her top and fastens her shorts. She dressed this morning as if it were sunny, not miserable; as if the weather might change just to suit her. But stuff like that never happens. She stands, glares at the man; his head still hangs forwards but he's watching her now from under one cocked eyebrow.

'What?' she says, a hand on the caravan door.

One last chance for him to say something, but he's still not got a word.

'Fine,' she says, opens the door and steps out into the wintry wet summer. She tries to slam the door but it doesn't catch, bounces and slowly swings out again. She has to go back and shut it properly, listening for him laughing at her but hearing nothing.

Arms folded, she walks off down the hill, needing to get away. Barefoot through soggy grass. The wind cold on her skin, a few fine pinpricks of rain touching her bare limbs. This holiday was a bad idea, but she's known that all along. There's nowhere else to go: she follows the path down to the bay, a dent in the rocky coastline, where a few sad families have gathered, doing their best in awful weather. If this summer had any sun, if it weren't for the water lacing the air, it'd probably actually be *nice* here. Maybe. She could go in the little cafe, one of the camp's plasticky log-cabin-type buildings, have a cup of tea. Get out of this drizzle that's threatening to get worse. If she sits there long enough Abbie will materialise, wanting ice cream or something. They can share a dish. But as she gets closer she sees the place is full – miserable people escaping miserable weather – and she can't stand to be in a crowd right now, not if she looks half as bad as she feels. Plus she might have disgraced herself a bit the night before. Women would frown, men would smirk, and she can't be dealing with it right now.

She veers off instead in the other direction, heading uphill to the top of the lumpy cliffs that line the coast. There's a bench up there, usually it's empty, facing the sea, where she's come to sit a couple of times before, just to gaze out at the waves, not thinking anything at all, letting her mind be empty, her hangover drain away. If you can call them cliffs, which you can't really. Low, sandy hills, heaps of brown boulders with little tufts of grass on top. She holds on to the rock with her toes, high enough to see pretty far in all directions: the thin beach curving out from the bay, north and south; the caravan-studded fields behind her, woods rising beyond them; and the sea stretching away for ever before her. She thinks vaguely of her own childhood holidays. Her parents always took her to some godforsaken seaside town, all bleating amusement arcades and elderly candyfloss, tacky gift shops and the smell of fish; whether it was somewhere new or the same dump every year, they all blurred into one. If there were ever days it didn't rain, they've not stayed in her head. She'd promised herself, then and lots of times since, that if she ever had kids she'd take them abroad every year – off into the sun – but that isn't what's happened.

She gets to the bench; it's all hers but kind of damp. She sits anyway, hugging herself, leaning towards the sea, her bare knees pressed together and feet apart, toes pointed in like a child's. She lets her thoughts, memories, all the other bits of her head, all pour into the water, disappear under the waves to be washed away, as if for ever. But once when she was a girl, on holiday, there'd been a ship wrecked on the beach. She sees it again. Where? She can't remember, it could even have been *here*. The wreck looked like it'd been there always. It stood tilted, hull stuck deep in the sand, tall and black and monstrous, dead, a great jagged wound in its flank to let the water in and its guts out. Maybe her memory's exaggerating, maybe it was only a little trawler or something, but she'd crept past the warning notices – *being brave* – to have a better look. It was like a huge dead animal; she'd wanted to stroke its ancient skin, as if she could comfort it. But then when she'd got near it'd been all barnacled and spiky with rust, too ugly to touch. It'd towered over her, its echoey metal creaking high in the wind. Her feet sinking ankle-deep in watery sand, she'd got a bit scared and backed off – what if it was *haunted*? Maybe it set sail in the night, a ghost ship, doing whatever weird and wicked stuff. She walked away, and as soon as the sand got firm enough she started to run.

Now there's no wreck, no ships at all, only a lifeboat, skipping across the water – bringing someone safely home, she guesses, or probably just practising. Though now she's finally wondering, rising to her feet, where's our Abbie got to? It's not that she's looking, particularly, but only that she just sort of notices – as if by accident, as if it weren't anything to do with her, even as she starts again to run – that there's no one in sight, among all the children she can see on the beach, or messing about in the little playground there, who could be her daughter.

*

225

It's fifteen-plus years later and there's no way of knowing it – the bench has long rotted away, and not been replaced – but Abigail has found the spot, the exact spot, where her mother was when she realised she'd lost her daughter. When she'd slowly turned to gaze at the sea and knew what had happened to her little girl, her Abbie. That she'd drowned. Known she'd drowned and couldn't imagine she'd ever come back, the stuff in the Bible or other fairy tales never happening in real life. This is the place. Abigail – grown up now, soon to be a mother herself – has brought her girlfriend to see. Her leather jacket draped over Abigail's shoulders, Bex's hand rests protectively – it seems always to be there, lately – on Abigail's huge, baby-rounded tummy, slowing swelling like the rise of a morning's tide.

The caravan site closed down years ago, leaving no trace; a new development, posh flats it looks like, is under construction in the little bay. Abigail remembers these – what are they, hillocks? – these rocky heaps that run along the coast here, grassy piles of sandy rock, though predictably they're smaller than she recalls: in her head she sees looming cliffs – *beetling* cliffs, maybe, if she could remember what the word meant. It's silly, but she doesn't want to go down to the beach itself, where the waves might try to get her again. As if she were still only little, as if she didn't have Bex to anchor her. This rainy autumn feels strangely like it could be the rainy summer she drowned in, those fifteen-and-more years ago.

Bex is only half-listening to Abigail talk now, she's fiddling with her mobile instead – and if they'd had them back then, would little Abbie's father have called someone for help?

'Come on,' says Abigail. 'Put that away, can't you? This is where I died when I was a kid.'

'I know. I'm tweeting that you're visiting your own grave.'

'I drowned.'

'Your watery grave.'

'You can laugh, but I was clinically dead for like twenty minutes. My mum told me.'

'Yeah but *clinically dead* doesn't mean *very dead*, like people pretend it does. It means *kind-of-but-not-necessarily dead*, otherwise you'd be in the ground. *Ob*viously. Or fed on by fishes.'

'God, you just have to argue with everything I say, don't you?'

'Fine, fine – you were dead. So tell me, what'd you see? On the other side, like? Beyond the light at the end of the tunnel.'

Abigail smiles at last. 'Don't take the piss.'

Nothing magical under these waves. The water is grey, opaque, stone turned liquid but colder than any stone. The weight of it unimaginable, pressing on her from all directions. Her mind nothing but blank terror as implacable currents tugged her into still deeper darkness, as she knew for the first time in her life – just six years old – that she was going to die. That it was happening *right now*, in fact—

'You're, like, romanticising it or whatever,' says Bex. She runs a hand over her head's gelled spikes; they spring back perfectly into place. 'I mean, *blank terror* – cliché much? Plus, *implacable currents*? Come off it. It was just a stupid accident. You're all right now.'

All right? She was dead. Though it's true her head did break water at last – must've done, or else she couldn't be standing here now, growing a new life inside her – her little arm had flailed into the air and been distantly spotted by kindly strangers. An elderly couple walking their dog on the sand had seen her hand's drowning wave, amid the sea's greater waves, and her coat's small splash of colour. But out there in the water she'd been so tiny, so helpless. The vastness of the sky deranging. Her head barely above the surface, she'd kept dipping under again, swallowing more water. Even now she can't have salt on her food (Bex snorts a laugh at that). The land had disappeared, as if it'd never existed. The whole world was sky and water, each as grey as the other, the emptiness infinite, and she felt – she *swears* she felt – her soul being pulled out into it, out of her body and into the air.

'What, so is all this childhood trauma why you're a wee bit mad?' says Bex.

'No,' says Abigail, snuggling her face into her girlfriend's neck, the leather jacket around her creaking like a ship's rigging. 'It's *you* drives me mental.'

How long she'd been in the water was difficult to guess. It might've been an eternity, or two.

'Feels like I'm still in there, sometimes,' she tells Bex, her unborn baby's other mother. 'Under the waves.'

'Don't be daft. It must've been – what, a few minutes, tops.'

'It's like I'm looking at all the world through thick grey walls of water.'

'Don't know who you're talking about but it's not you.'

Because of course she was saved eventually. The lifeboat came, strong hands pulled her from the sea and brought her briskly, professionally back to life. She puked out seawater, gulped in air; her heart thudded again, louder than ever. An ambulance was waiting for her at the dock – no rescue helicopter winching her from the waves, to Bex's disappointment – to hurry her to hospital. She was treated for hypothermia and shock, stuff like that, though she's no memory of this part; there's only a vague vision of waking up in a perfectly white, rainbow-laced dream of a room ('What?' says Bex. 'The kids' ward in the hospital,' says Abigail, 'had loads of cartoon characters and clowns and colourful stuff painted on the walls. It was kind of freaky, actually'), with her mother by her bedside and her father nowhere to be seen, not ever again.

'All this just before my dad ran off.'

'That bastard.'

'No, don't say that. You didn't know him.'

'Neither did you,' says Bex, ''cause he fucked off – that's the *point*.'

'Oh, *whatever*. But listen, they told me I'd been dead, clinically dead, and I remember wondering if that made me a ghost. I should've just asked my mum, so she could tell me *no*, but I was too scared of what the answer might be. I bottled it up, I guess. I was only a little girl, remember. And so I can't help but keep thinking, am I still one? A ghost, I mean. Because you can figure out the medical view of it, it's in the textbooks, but how does a soul reattach itself once you've died and it's been torn from its flesh? So am I a ghost, or what? Or am I, like, just an empty shell – my soul already off God knows where?'

'Don't be daft,' says Bex. 'You're just being weird for the sake of being weird, and you're no good at it. Come on, it's getting cold. Let's get back to the hotel, so I can screw your pregnant brains out all over again.'

'Yeah, okay.'

But first from her pocket Abigail draws a dark disc of translucent green. A crystal ball, only not exactly crystal. A circle of misted emerald. An eye. A magician's scrying stone, like from olden days. She holds it up to her face, looks deeply into it, but can't see a thing – no images of the future, or of the past. It's just a bit of glass, really – the base of a bottle, worn smooth by the sea. She draws back her arm, Bex watching her, and throws it back into the water.

PAPER CHAINS

Rebecca F. John

Artwork by Carla Busuttil

Paper Chains

Rebecca F. John

I remember asking my grandmother why she was bald. It was the summer Trevor Mason went missing and, though I was already too big for it at six, I was tucked in her lap, staring deep into her furrowed face. Grandma Small had eyes like amber beads: the honey irises speckled with deepest brown. Her lips, thin and faded by then, were forever painted a rich cardinal red.

'Because,' she answered, 'one of my hairs fell out for every good memory I ever made.'

'But,' I said, running my hand over her smooth skull. It was warm to the touch. 'How many hairs did you have?'

'Oh, thousands and thousands, I'd imagine,' Grandma Small replied. 'Far too many to count.'

'And they came out one by one?'

'Of course. Sometimes as many as twenty in one morning.'

'That many?'

'Yes.' She tapped my leg; it was time to stand up and get

on with the day. Grandma Small never could tolerate sitting idle for long.

'But,' I pushed as we unfolded ourselves from the chair. 'What if your hairs hadn't fallen out? How would you have kept track of your memories then?'

Grandma Small smiled and huffed and looked sad all at once. 'Then ...' she replied. 'I'd have put them all in a jar on the windowsill, where the sunlight could catch them.'

'And the bad ones?'

She scrunched up her nose and flipped a hand over her shoulder. Rose-petal perfume pulsed from her wrist. 'The bad ones aren't for keeping.'

Grandma Small and I made paper chains. Hundreds of them. People, ducks, ghosts, trees, witches – Grandma Small knew how to cut them all. There didn't need to be a reason. On heavy summer days, we'd sit out on the garden bench and chop and snick, stopping occasionally to rearrange the sun umbrella or take a sip of lemonade. In winter, we'd kneel near the fire and push our chins over our scarves to better see our designs, our cheeks crisping from leaning too close to the flames.

I don't know where any of those paper chains went – into the fire, probably. But each time my mother took me to Grandma Small's, the ones we'd made would have vanished, and we'd have to start again. It became a ritual. Grandma Small would begin the cutting and I, unable to endure the beating silence of the house, would talk and talk.

'Where's Grandpa Small?' I asked as we began a long line of top-hatted men one cloud-greyed day.

'There was no Grandpa Small,' Grandma Small answered.

'My surname isn't Small. You only call me Small because I am small, remember.'

'Then what was Grandpa's surname?'

'Hopkins. Same as yours.'

'Then where is Grandpa Hopkins?'

'He died, before you were born. A long while before.'

'Did you have hair then?'

It became an obsession for me, her hair. My own was thick and gold and corkscrew-curled. My mother's, too. I didn't understand why Grandma Small's was different. All the other grandmas on the street had white cotton-puffs of hair, which they pressed under rain hats before venturing outside, whether it was raining or not.

'Yes,' Grandma Small replied. 'I had hair then. I was pretty then.'

I snipped at the arm of our figure, leaving him lopsided, and stopped. 'What did you look like?' I asked.

'An awful lot like you,' Grandma Small answered.

'Does that mean, one day, *I'll* look an awful lot like *you*?'

Grandma Small laughed. 'I hope not, child.'

'Why?'

'Because,' she said, 'I'm nothing to aspire to.' And I hadn't understood the words then, but if I had, I would have told her that I wanted nothing more than to be like her. My Grandma Small was brave. She didn't need anyone but herself.

When the cold-punch winter thawed and my seventh summer pink-skied in, Trevor Mason was still missing. My mother and I walked past talk of it on our way to Grandma Small's house on Sydney Street, where everyone knew everyone else's name. Grandma Small did not join in with their doorstep tattling. It was morbid, she said; the boy was long gone.

Besides, Grandma Small did not venture through the front door of number five Sydney Street. In all my life, I only ever knew her within those narrow walls where, when we tired of making paper chains, we played dress-up with her old clothes and jewellery.

'What do you think of me?' Grandma Small asked, sweeping out of her bedroom in a black dress so long it dragged across the carpet. With a flick of her hand, she swung a fur stole over her shoulder and tossed back her head.

I laughed and fiddled with the pearls dangling down to my knees.

'I think we look like a pair of film starlets,' she said, grabbing a cloche hat from the shelf and plopping it over my head. I pushed it back so I could see past the brim and, peering up, caught Grandma Small admiring herself in the mirror.

She'd glimpsed someone, I'm sure, who she used to be.

I was just nine when a storm tore in so recklessly that the schools were closed and the shops shut up and the whole town rushed inside, pulled on an extra jumper, and locked the doors to wait it out. I stayed at Grandma Small's and we cradled mugs of hot chocolate and watched snowflakes pile up on the windowsills, the pavements, the shoulders of men returning from work. Everything was black or white, and I wanted it to stay that way.

'Ah, but what would the world be without some colour?' Grandma Small asked.

'Clearer,' I replied. I wasn't sure what I meant, but it was the only way to describe what I saw through the glass. It was all crisper, now the snow had chalk-written the night.

'Is there nothing you don't understand?' Grandma Small said, grinning.

'Hundreds of things.'

'Name one.'

'I don't understand why you only smile when you're looking straight at people.'

Grandma Small raised the bumps of her hairless eyebrows, set down her mug and, hooking a hand around my shoulders, pulled me towards her. I was nearing her height by then and when she spoke the words blew into my hair.

'Oh, you clever girl,' she said. 'I always knew you were clever. Now, what are we going to cut our paper chains into tonight?'

'Snowmen, of course.'

'Of course,' Grandma Small answered and, turning, she disappeared in search of the paper and scissors. Her hot chocolate went cold at the window. She'd forgotten to pick up her mug.

Trevor Mason had transformed into legend by my tenth jelly-and-ice-cream birthday. At school, children taunted each other with sworn sightings of his ghost. In the streets, those people who'd run short of gossip steered their words back towards 'the trouble'. They remembered and mis-remembered his freckled nose, his gap-toothed grin, his wayward hair.

Grandma Small and I cut paper chains in the shape of galloping horses and ignored them.

'Horses,' I told her, 'are my favourite animal.'

239

'Why?'

'Because they're the most graceful. It's like they're always dancing.'

Grandma Small leaned close to whisper. 'They're my favourite animal, too, you know.'

I smiled. Perhaps, given this similarity, I would grow up to be as patient and funny and bold as my Grandma Small. 'Why?'

'Because when I had my little boy, I gave him a stuffed horse, and it was the only present I ever gave him.'

'You don't have a little boy,' I said, levelling the hooves of the paper horses with a long-considered snip.

'Not any more,' Grandma Small answered.

'Then where did he go?'

Grandma Small sighed. 'He went with your Grandpa Hopkins. He just went first.'

I kept my eyes on my hands. I was suddenly desperate to get the horses shaped right. Somehow, at that precocious age, I knew that she was finally telling me the truth.

'And was it him who made your hair fall out?' I asked, cutting carefully, carefully.

Grandma Small nodded.

'Then ...'

'Then what?'

'Then he must have been your happiest memory,' I said.

And Grandma Small gave a little laugh. 'Yes,' she said. 'I think he must.'

I was slicking on a stolen flamingo lipstick, to match the dress I'd discovered in Grandma Small's wardrobe, when my mother returned early from work to collect me. The dress

240

was high-necked and fastened down the spine by a line of buttons, and suddenly I was a grown-up in the mirror. Grandma Small had fallen asleep in her cup of sweet tea.

She woke only when my mother splashed inside and shook off her umbrella. There was news, she breathed, relating to the trouble. The whole village was out, combing the woodlands, the rattling river, the blackened smirches at the mouths of the old mines. A scrabbling dog had unearthed a child's shoe on the riverbank, and the owner had presented it directly to Trevor's mother, seeking confirmation of her worst fears. Four years on, she'd said – or so my mother claimed – and she was as certain as her soul that the shoe was his.

'And why should it be his?' Grandma Small asked.

'Why not?' my mother replied.

Grandma Small pressed her cardinal lips together. 'I'll bet it's not.'

And, staring as I was at her amber-bead eyes, I saw that as she spoke, they turned to coal. It was as if a cloud had passed over and cooled their speckled warmth. I wasn't sure how, but I knew then that Grandma Small didn't want that shoe to belong to Trevor Mason.

The next night, when I asked if we could cut our paper chains into shoes, Grandma Small shook her head and, creaking up the stairs, gathered herself into bed without another word.

The last time Grandma Small and I cut paper chains, we trimmed them into bobbing ships.

'Why ships?' I asked, since it had been Grandma Small's turn to choose the shape.

'So we can sail away on them,' Grandma Small answered.

'We could hang them in the window,' I suggested, 'and the reflection of the rain can be like the waves.'

'That's a clever idea.' Grandma Small tried to crinkle into a smile, but it flopped short of her eyes. 'There you go again, being so clever.'

'Isn't it good to be clever?'

'Oh, yes. Sometimes. But not, perhaps, when there are too many secrets flitting about.'

I laid my paper ships over my knees and looked up. 'Secrets like what happened to Trevor Mason?' I asked. There had been an article in the newspaper about Trevor. I'd read it off my mother's lap one night after she'd sewed herself to sleep. I didn't know whether I remembered the 'talented sportsman' who had sat two desks behind me at school, or whether I only remembered the words people used to describe him, but it didn't seem to matter now. They'd found a skeleton that day the village had stepped the mountains small. They'd called it Trevor Mason and promised to bury it next Monday morning.

I wanted to be able to tell them the skeleton didn't share Trevor's gap-toothed grin, but I couldn't. I hadn't seen it. And they wouldn't listen to a 10-year-old even if I had. 'Perhaps tomorrow we could make some paper chains for Trevor's funeral,' I said.

'We'll do no such thing,' Grandma Small replied. 'Put the idea out of your mind.'

'But—'

'Don't,' Grandma Small warned.

I watched in silence as she made a show of surveying her half-empty tea cup. I stayed silent when she stood to go to the kettle, and her slippered toes snagged in my chain of ships, and they set sail across the carpet torn in two. I wondered if Trevor's bared skull shone as pale as Grandma Small's skin did. I wondered what it would look like under the moon.

The summer after they buried Trevor Mason's skeleton, my mother and I kneeled on the damp cemetery grass and pushed roses stem by stem into the vase on Grandma Small's polished gravestone. The day was daisy-white and we had on our best coats. Mine was too heavy. I wanted to change it for one of Grandma Small's silky dresses.

'What did Grandma Small die of?' I asked.

'A broken heart,' my mother answered.

I leaned forward and traced the indented inscription with my fingertip. It felt like frost on a pavement. *Here lies Millicent Hopkins*, it read. *Reunited with her beloved Edmund.*

'Was that Grandpa Small's name?' I asked. 'Edmund?'

'No,' my mother replied. 'Edmund was the name of Grandma's first baby.'

'Then where's Grandpa Small's grave?'

My mother frowned, and from the ruts surrounding her eyelashes, a sliver of Grandma Small looked out at me. 'Grandpa Hopkins didn't die,' she said. 'What made you think that?'

'Grandma Small told me.'

My mother sighed and put her hand to my back. I could feel its hard cold through my black wool coat. 'Grandpa Hopkins went away,' she said. 'He had to go away. He did something so bad that he was never allowed to come back.'

'What did he do?' I asked, though I was sure I knew by then. I was eleven. I wasn't a fool.

'I'll tell you when you're older,' my mother answered.

I lifted my face to the wind and let it tug tears from the wrong corners of my eyes. 'What happened to Trevor Mason reminded Grandma of Grandpa Hopkins and Edmund, didn't it?'

My mother cupped one of her hands around her knee and pushed herself to stand upright. She could not find her full height; she might as well have stayed slumped on the ground. 'Yes. Yes, it did,' she said. 'Is there nothing you don't understand, miss?'

'Hundreds of things.' I smiled, remembering the way Grandma Small's bumpy eyebrows climbed her forehead when she asked me that same question. And when she wriggled her spectacles on; or took a too-hot sip of tea; and those times we played dress-up and Grandma Small paraded around, swinging her fur stole and tossing back her head and acting herself back to the person she was before she met Grandpa Hopkins.

'She was fun, wasn't she?' I said.

'Yes, she was,' my mother agreed. 'Fun and colourful.'

'Yes. Fun and colourful and brave.'

My mother's lips twitched, brightening her cheeks for a tick. 'So, what are you going to cut your paper chains into?' she asked.

I sat down and crossed my legs, ready to begin. 'Lions,' I said.

'Lions?'

'Yes. Lions. Because lions, I think, are almost as brave as Grandma Small.'

BRAD'S ROOSTER FOOD

Joanna Campbell

Artwork by Jessy Jetpacks

Brad's Rooster Food

Joanna Campbell

Even before Diane enters Brad's driveway, before her shoes embed in his deep, shifting gravel, his rooster is crowing. She walks faster, drawn by the plaintive sound, by the tug connecting the lonely.

In the back garden, inside an enclosure encircled by barbed wire, the rooster is throwing back his head. The nervous gesture vibrates the knobbly, scarlet wig he appears to wear, as if it is made of sun-warmed India rubber.

His beak jabs at the empty water container.

'Oh dear,' Diane says, uncoiling the hose.

The rooster stands erect, listening. He struts alongside the wire, watching.

When Brad knocked on Diane's door last week, he wore his open-necked sports shirt patterned with tropical leaves in bright greens and yellows. Parrots were peering at her, beaks protruding from the foliage. When the sun glinted on the medallion dangling from Brad's neck, Diane could not help imagining the blue-white disc of skin beneath, where the sun could not venture.

Brad, pink-faced and hearty, asked her to visit his rooster while he and Wendy were in Littlehampton, as though he and Diane exchanged favours all the time. But his words came stuttering out, rehearsed. Like her, he suffered the quiet pain of shyness.

Diane never travels further than the parade of shops. She doesn't need to make a cup of tea for anyone other than herself. If she were to take a holiday, nothing would require tending in her absence.

But today she is wearing Brad's shed key on a string around her neck.

Brad and Wendy live in a pale-red house stuck to a primrose house, the builders having strived for a seaside-rock effect. Diane's home, left from the long-ago air-raid that killed her parents, is decaying. Soon it will reach the top of the demolition list.

She finds a plastic tub full of muesli with *Brad's Rooster Food* written on the lid. The food is not, as Diane expected, dry or cheerless, but golden and glorious.

Brad has toasted the cereals, adding fat Australian sultanas, apricot gems and slivers of coconut. Diane plunges her hands into fruits and grains, into pared almonds and crumbly hazelnuts, Brad's mixture tumbling through her fingers.

Pineapple nuggets catch the sunlight, reminiscent of the hundreds of sequins her mother sewed onto the plain muslin frock Diane used to wear to birthday parties when she was a child.

*

'That old thing *again*?' one girl used to scoff.

The dress was specially made with inserts to accommo-date Diane's back-brace, a contraption of buckled straps for supporting weak muscles.

When the scoffing girl issued her own invitations, a glint of anticipation in her eyes indicated the scorn she planned to mete out again. But once bejewelled with glittering spangles, Diane's dress dazzled the birthday girl into silence.

Twenty years ago, when she unfastened the brace for the last time, it was as if she were reaching inside her body and taking out an essential organ. The brace watched her, reproachful, from the corner of her bedroom. The advantages of discarding it ought to have outweighed the unexpected sense of loss, but the confidence she had hoped to acquire after shedding its bulk never arrived.

Diane pushes the metal scoop through Brad's oats and barley and bran, pours the soft rush of flakes into the metal feeding container and fits on the steel lid, a sort of Chinese hat which protects the food from rain.

Brad chose her because the neighbours with cats or dogs or well-groomed herbaceous borders have voiced complaints about his rooster. Or perhaps because quiet people are gentle. She is trusted, a thought which releases a small shaft of light on twenty years of living alone.

When Diane passed by one day on her way to the butcher, a deputation of neighbours from the pastel-washed houses were forming a semicircle, their heels drilling dents in Brad's gravel.

'Now you've sent your hens away, why keep it?'

'You only needed it to protect them from foxes.'

'Not as if it does anything. It can't lay eggs, you know.'

'It's a brute,' said Joy, the woman from the greying prim-rose house. 'Damn thing jumped on our fence. Jogged across the patio. Puffing up its chest, preening itself. One of its massive great wings gashed my leg.'

'It drew blood,' her husband, Ray, added with pride. He was pigeon-chested and the soles of his shoes had metal taps nailed onto them. He wrapped an arm around his injured wife, but she shrugged it off.

While the coterie surrounded her husband, Brad's wife, Wendy, stayed inside the pale-red house, the smooth curve of her hair evident among the tasselled edging of the curtains.

Diane frowned to express sympathy for Brad. She remained on the pavement to demonstrate her refusal to join the rooster eviction mission. After everyone else clumped out of the gravel and marched back to their own houses, the wind blew through her empty basket, a small, brittle sound. Brad looked across at her, red-faced and silent like a withered balloon, and gave her a grateful smile.

She did not go to the butcher's shop. She opted instead for an individual cheese pie from the supermarket, instead of the succulent chicken pieces she had planned to buy.

She asks the rooster to calm down, her voice a surprise. Days can pass without hearing it.

It startles the rooster too. He back-pedals his feet in a mound of straw.

'Look at your sumptuous meal. You can have it once you are less excited.'

Diane holds the container high and steels herself to stand close to him, accepting the risk of a pecked ankle. Any trace of her own fear might engender distrust. His nervy swagger suggests he is terrified too, and yet he is listening.

'I'm celebrating an anniversary today,' she tells him. 'Twenty years without something, instead of twenty years with someone.'

The rooster stands still, intrigued.

'But let's talk about you. You're a magnificent fellow.'

He steps towards her without aggression and she repeats the compliment, stretching out the syllables in the same way each time because he appears to enjoy the rhythm.

When he understands that Diane is admiring his splendour, the rooster settles. He watches her lilac scarf fluttering, tilting his head to one side.

In the next-door garden, Ray switches on his electric leaf-blower. Its raucous racket makes the rooster run wildly about, changing direction every second. With furious wingbeats he propels himself onto the top of his wire, drops to the lawn, hurdles over a wheelbarrow and flaps over the fence, disappearing into Ray's delphiniums.

Diane creates a trail of crumbs from the enclosure to the fence and flings a handful over, taken aback by the velocity and length of her throw, not to mention the speed and wisdom of her strategy.

Ray switches off the tool with an irritated snap.

'That *ruddy* cock,' he shouts, standing aghast among the fallen blossoms waiting for his torrent of air to redistribute them into a pyre.

'I'm afraid he's tempted by your mauve rose bush. I think

it's his favourite colour,' Diane says, her voice travelling further than it has for years. 'I'm so sorry, but I've no guidelines on recapture. Perhaps it might be best if you could just rake up the rest.'

Ray clenches his fists around his blower. The rooster's beak pokes through the foliage, snatching at the crumbs. Then he struts along the trail to the fence and pecks at the wooden planks.

Ray glares at Diane. 'It'll destroy my larch-lap. Can't you come and pick it up?'

'Hand him up to me first then,' Diane says, shocked at her use of the imperative. 'My arms won't stretch over your fence.'

'I'll go nowhere near the blasted thing,' Ray says. 'It'll draw blood. You'll have to come over here.'

The prospect of her footfall damaging his striped lawn is apparently distasteful because he picks up a rake as if aiming a harpoon.

'Just flap a bit, sweetheart,' Diane tells the rooster. 'Jump! Here's my scarf, look. You love that.'

He responds, fluffing his feathers and pumping his wings. Diane has never called anyone sweetheart before. She repeats the endearment.

Joy raps on the kitchen window, signalling that Ray should gee up the debris-collecting and sort out some cocktails. Quite miraculous, Diane thinks, how a wife communicates with such efficiency with a few curt gestures behind glass.

'Expecting her bridge party,' Ray mumbles. 'She wants the garden tidy first.'

'Look, I'll do it,' Diane tells him. 'You go and pour the drinks for her guests.'

Is this her voice, infused with authority, issuing instructions which people – albeit a sad little man and a renegade fowl – are about to obey?

The rooster clambers up and thuds down beside her, his feathers brushing her leg. As he follows the trail to the wire, Diane shadows him, lifting him into his enclosure while taking care to avoid his primitive-looking feet catching on the barbs.

'Hush, hush,' she keeps saying.

His plump body rests in her hands without a struggle, softer than old suede between her fingers. When she sets him down, he stays in the same spot, huddled on top of his own shadow.

Next door, Diane rakes Ray's leaves into a pyramid, working at a swift pace. She always tears through tasks with needless urgency, oddly expectant when the work comes to an end, although her telephone never rings with invitations to tea, or cocktails.

When she props the rake against the fence, Ray and Joy are busy arguing in the kitchen, framed by their double-glazed window, Diane's presence in the garden forgotten. Joy's lips move without a sound, her face contorted. Ray lowers his head and folds his arms, already defeated, even before Joy raises her arm and hurls a cocktail shaker at him, their new glass silencing the moment of impact.

Diane winces. When she opens her eyes, Ray is pacing back and forth, a packet of frozen broad beans clamped to his forehead.

She goes back to the rooster, now striding through fresh straw, his red comb fully erect.

'You must miss those speckled hens you once pro-tected,' she says.

He tips his head to one side, alert and hopeful, as if she might know how to bring them back.

'How do you think the holiday in Littlehampton is going?'

In reply, he pecks at an empty snail shell.

'Between you and me,' she whispers, 'I think it might be a difficult fortnight for Brad.'

Some Saturdays, when Joy has driven off to one of her bridge parties, and if Ray is not at one of his clay-pigeon shoots, Brad's Wendy can be spotted strutting next door. Ray opens his door before she has reached it and ushers her inside. If his hall window is open, the metallic crescents nailed to his shoe soles rap all the way up his oak-effect staircase, closely followed by the click-click of stiletto heels. The echoes resonate all around Diane's garden.

Wendy told the driver who loaded Brad's hens into a van that she thanked God they were going. Apart from ruining her grass, their inexhaustible fertility had forced her to make daily Spanish omelettes and Floating Islands. She would rather sun herself on a Spanish island, thank you very much. Her next mission was to get rid of the puffed-up little Hitler still strutting about the garden, she said, and the van driver glanced at Brad.

It was the day after the hens departed when Brad asked Diane to look after his rooster and, in apparent dispute with the flamboyance of his shirt, his eyes were the colour of sea in heavy rain.

*

The sun is sinking as Diane says goodnight to the rooster and promises to return early in the morning. Although he hops into his coop and up to his perch without protest, his worried face presses against the slot of his window. His farewell squawk follows her all the way to the corner, through her front door and into every tall, echoing room.

Later, when she is halfway up the stairs on her way to bed, an ear-splitting gunshot fires.

Diane grips the banister.

A second shot. A third.

She must be practical. Stay calm. Switch off the lights. Hide under the stairs.

A volley of furious banging roots her to the spot.

There follows a prolonged, raucous crowing.

She pelts downstairs, wrenches the front door open and flies to Brad's house, stumbling in the shift of his gravel. At the back, Ray's patio lantern is flooding his garden with light.

Ray is inside his house, beating his hands on the kitchen window.

In their garden, a fur coat slung over her nightdress, stands Joy, grim-faced, clutching Ray's shotgun.

'Stand still, you cocky little bastard!' she yells.

Diane freezes, her heart drumming out of rhythm.

The door of the coop has been shot open, the latch hanging loose. In the enclosure, the rooster is darting back and forth, Joy's aim apparently skewed by a surfeit of cocktails.

Diane takes a deep breath. Come on, she tells herself. You're *needed* here.

She breathes out hard.

Another shot.

Silence.

She has always lived at close quarters to the lives of others, on the sidelines of their existence, and of her own. The shadow cast by Diane's house spreads further than theirs. But now, her proficiency in solitude offers an advantage.

She is hidden from view, rigid against Brad's wall, beside his garden tap. She reaches down and twists it. The water fizzes inside. She gathers up his garden hose and takes aim.

A posse of neighbours arrives, scattering gravel in all directions, as the blast of cold water reaches its target, soaking the glossy mink and penetrating to the ruffles of turquoise nylon beneath.

The rescue party retrieves Ray's keys from the grass and escorts Joy back inside while she shouts, 'I told him. I said it's not clay pigeons you should be shooting. Not when there's a real live bird fouling up our lives.'

Diane waits until the noise dies down, then walks across Brad's cooling grass, aware for the first time that her feet are bare. She climbs over the wire into the enclosure.

The rooster creeps towards her, his comb trembling. Some of the shot has damaged one wing. She holds out a handful of *Brad's Rooster Food* and as he pecks at it, she pats him. His small heart is thumping beneath his glorious breast, the russet, gold and azure feathers reminiscent of the sun sinking into an ocean.

Diane lies down in the straw, the breeze fanning her hair and fostering the perfume of Brad's night-scented stocks. With the sheen of moonlight on the pinkish pebbledash, his house becomes a Turkish palace.

Remembering he can trust her, the rooster settles next to

Diane. Not once in her life has she fallen asleep with the beat of another heart beside her own.

As she closes her eyes, the breeze picks up, whipping next-door's tower of crisp blossoms into a frenzy, their faded plumes and ashen stars littering Ray's garden. The jubilant rustle keeps Diane awake, smiling.

In the morning, when the rooster discovers he is not alone, the ruby cluster on his head will unfold from sleep to stand upright for the day ahead. He will share his breakfast muesli with Diane and she will stay in the enclosure to protect him until Brad comes home.

Brad will bring a box of holiday fudge to thank her and she will be sporting a nut-brown tan.

'Your rooster is quite safe,' she will say. 'And I think I'd like some poultry of my own now.'

She will track down Brad's hens and ask the van driver to bring them to her. Brad will help her build an enclosure in her own garden, which his rooster can visit, day or night, to keep them in order and protect them from foxes. Brad will wear her shed key around his neck.

They will allow their eggs to hatch. And when they are admiring their brood, she will tell Brad about the click-click of Wendy's stilettos on Ray's stairs.

Brad will keep his recipe for rooster food a secret until their first anniversary, when they will celebrate by making it together, their hands plunging into silky nut splinters and gritty grains.

And one day, when bulldozers are rolling down the avenue to crush her tired house to a mound of chippings, Diane will bring her hens to Brad's house and stand in his kitchen while he disperses their grain across the lawn, and she will knock on their window and make gestures to show she needs him inside.

While the rooster's beak stabs at a sultana which refuses to stay still, she holds her euphoria close. She continues to cling to it for most of the night, but by the time the rooster emits his four o'clock crow, it has faded, as fleeting as her custodianship of Brad's key. The lives of others do not belong to quiet people.

Before dawn, she takes out the shotgun she has hidden in the straw and leaves the enclosure. At the fence, she drops it into Ray's chrysanthemum bed. It was perfect while it lasted, the brief fantasy that she would not need sequins to silence Wendy this time.

FRESHWATER

Emily Bullock

Artwork by Nick Goss

Freshwater

Emily Bullock

The second time our mother left, we packed the car with deflated beach balls, rolled-up lilos, towels and booze, and Dad drove us to Freshwater. The clapperboard chalet had belonged to our maternal grandmother. A signboard tilted out onto the pavement: *For Sale*. And that's when we knew our mother wasn't coming back.

By the time we unloaded, the sun was setting behind the reeds at the back of the garden. We sat on the concrete patio, yellowing plastic chairs creaking, watching the horizon burn. There were four of us kids: Aaron the oldest at nineteen; us middle ones, Ben and Carrie, at eighteen and sixteen; and Diane the youngest at thirteen. We held out the blue plastic beakers, Dad topped them up with gin. A carton of Marlboro Reds lay open on the table.

We smoked and we drank.

There wasn't any ice but a breeze wormed its way up from

the baked mud of the riverbed, wriggling through the humid July evening. The gin tasted sharp like tears.

We didn't talk much, we drank more.

Ben dug out an old board game from a cupboard in the living room. *Game of Life*. It was bowed with water damage but we picked up the plastic car counters anyway, forcing them uphill at times, sticking in pin-people, working our way through the game. We played until the light failed us.

A bulb hanging in the kitchen behind us wasn't bright enough to hold back darkness, swallowing up even the outline of our toes. Pheasants cried for their mates, stalking the reeds at the edge of the grass. No stars, but the moon appeared from the clouds every now and again, bringing the molehills, the cracked angles of the plastic chairs, into focus. The green glow of Dad's Casio watch pulsed, beeping to some agenda we didn't know about.

Time stretched around the chalet. Peeling white paint, small leaded windows like a cricket hut from one of those Sunday-night dramas our mother used to watch. Diane began to hum the *Miss Marple* theme music, dropping notes until it was tuneless as the buzz of gnats about our ears. Ben threw a packet of fags at her. She reached in, stuck a cigarette between her lips. The blue lighter lay on the patio table beside the abandoned game. Dad was nearest to it. Diane eased herself up, kneeling in the grass, stretching for the lighter. No one stopped her.

Five red tips glowed in the grey gloom. Gnats feasted on us. No one swatted them away.

Dad was the first to leave the garden, calling from the

doorway, 'See you in the morning.' But his voice rose at the end as though it was a question he wanted to ask.

Us kids took the bedroom; a double, and a single with another mattress that slid out from underneath. Candlewick bedspreads, in shades of pink and green, lay across our feet and we sweated through the winceyette sheets. Our mother must have slept in the same bed when she was a girl, younger than Diane was now. Our mother was an only child; maybe back then she longed for company. She used to tell us about this place, but somehow we'd never got round to visiting.

The ceiling sloped towards our heads. The blue flowered wallpaper felt hairy, damp like an old flannel. It was a bit like camping.

Dad slept on a lilo pressed against the wall in the lounge; no settee, only those wingback chairs old folks have. We heard the squelch of the plastic all night. He turned and turned, turned and turned.

The next morning we found Dad on the floor, the sheets twisted about his legs. The lilo gave one last dying gasp. He sat up, opened a can of Heineken. We followed ants marching down the corridor, stepping over them to get to the kitchen. Sand under the orange lino crackled, making us notice the itchy gnat-bites on our arms and legs. We scratched, shedding ashy flakes of skin.

No one remembered to bring milk so we had cornflakes with water, and a couple of beers each for breakfast. We carried the rest of the beers, the lilos, beach balls, and some towels, through the gravel car park, across the road, and over the seawall to Freshwater beach.

'I don't need any help,' Dad shouted.

He blew up two lilos and two rainbow-coloured beach balls. We lay on the towels, waiting for him to be done. Diane burned cigarettes into the plastic castle-shaped bucket. There wasn't any sand on the beach, only smooth pebbles that felt like Murray Mints when grasped in your hand.

Dad slapped the lilos on the water. Spray splashed over his rolled-up jeans and bare chest. We all hobbled over the shingle to the shoreline, except Aaron, who didn't want to leave his can of beer. Despite the heat of the day the water nipped at our ankles. Dad steadied the red lilo with his hands. Us girls struggled on, slipping against the hard plastic. It made farting noises as we tried to find a balance, its ridged and wrinkled edges scratching our legs.

Ben tried to clamber on next.

'You're too big,' Dad said.

Ben stood belly-deep in the water, arms over his chest, watching us get hauled away. He sat astride the other lilo but the waves kept pushing him back towards shore. He dragged the yellow lilo up the beach, weighed it down with pebbles and beach towels. The wind was too strong for the beach balls. They rolled away, disappearing over the seawall, off to find some other kid in some other place.

Dad dragged us girls through the waves. We laughed and screamed until holidaymakers tutted and shook their heads. We shouted louder after that. He ran parallel with the beach, twisting, then pushing us out to sea. Our legs, hanging over the sides, grew numb. Behind us, life on the beach shrank and shrank. Dad's chin dipped under the level of the waves. If he let go, slipped and sank out of sight, would anyone notice? How far would we drift?

Diane began to rock, pitching forward. She puked; swallowing too much sea water will do that to you. It frothed like lager, running between the plastic grooves. We wriggled, ready to abandon ship.

'It's too deep,' Dad said.

He half-swam, half-dragged us through the cold water. We reached the shallows. Dad collapsed on top of the red plastic. We rolled off, banging our knees on the shelf of pebbles. Waves buffeted him but the inflatable kept him afloat. We staggered out of the sea, shivering; watched him from further up the beach. Hunched, raw from the sun and the salt, he looked like a deflating beach ball.

'Want a beer, Dad?' Aaron called.

Dad waved a limp hand, signalling he'd be right back. Aaron screwed the spare can into the stones, shielding it from the sun. The pebbles were stacked on top of each other, crevices and holes all around. We dropped cigarette butts, ring pulls, straws. It was possible to lose so many things between the cracks.

'I'm hungry,' Diane said.

She sat herself on my outstretched legs, the warmth of skin on skin took us both by surprise. I opened my knees, she dropped down onto the beach, bum-shuffling away. She wrapped herself tighter in the towel. Against the backdrop of the sea she looked so small.

Other families went to the tearooms, the chip shop, or unwrapped cling-film-cosseted sandwiches, unscrewed tartan flasks of steaming tea, when lunchtime came. We drank the rest of the beer, smoked a packet of cigarettes, chewed our nails. The sun overhead so bright that it ate up all the shadows. After lunch, the tide came in, pushing the beach-goers closer together; jostling with their chairs and windbreakers. Dad lay in the sun, eyes hidden behind a pair of plastic Mickey Mouse sunglasses he'd found on the promenade; the small arms stretched to snapping point. Mums applied sun lotion. Fathers read newspapers. Pensioners sucked on Mr Whippy soft-whip. Kids paddled. The slick, the rustle, the slurp, the splash. The sweet and salty smell of the seaside crowded about us.

The steps under the corner of the seawall were empty. We went there instead. Dad couldn't be moved.

Waves bashed against the top, feathering us with foam. We took it in turns to launch ourselves onto the lilo, cresting the surf, getting washed back onto the steps.

A man with a Labrador, up on the promenade, said, 'Shouldn't be jumping off there. You kids will do yourself some damage.'

Ben laughed, took another dive.

The square-edged bruise on his thigh lingered for weeks, dark and angry.

The next day even the cornflake packet sat empty. We went to the Spar.

The shop smelled of iced buns and the vents over the aisles puffed out hot breath. Every corner of the ceiling had a security mirror, distorting us as though we were walking through a hall of mirrors. We shared the last of the Heineken, passing the can from hand to hand until it was warm as tea. We picked up a cauliflower and a sachet of cheese sauce, chucked it in the basket. The powder inside the packet was set like concrete. When we add water to it later (because we'll forget the milk again) it won't turn out much better. The rest of the basket was taken up with beer, a bottle of own-brand vodka, and a loaf of Mother's Pride. From the running total Ben kept calling out, we were twenty pence away from nothing when we reached the counter.

The old woman on the till rang up the food but her hand hovered over the booze. She twisted the gold rings on her swollen fingers. Ben put the tenner on the counter.

The woman said, 'I haven't got change. Maybe you should come back later with your parents.'

Aaron picked a postcard from the wire rack, a hand-written sticker poked out the top: *20 pence each*. 'Who needs change?' he said.

The woman pushed her glasses high up on her nose, peered at each of us. 'I believe you're going to supply alcohol to a minor.'

Aaron shrugged. 'What's it to you?'

The wrinkle-faced woman didn't offer us a bag and we didn't ask. We cradled the stuff in our arms, walking through the car park, stopping outside the Anchor to collect Dad. An old bloke, in a black suit and white vest, sat opposite him on the picnic bench. A dried yellow stain on his lapel was shaped like a heart.

He smiled at Diane. 'What you got there, missy?'

She held out the postcard. A banner across the middle read *Seven Wonders of the Isle of Wight*.

Diane read them out. 'Ryde where you can walk. Cowes you can't milk—'

Dad flicked the back of the card. 'Who you sending it to?'

Diane shrugged. She put the postcard on the bench as if it weighed too much to hold.

Dad slammed down his pint glass. 'You kids know where your mother is?'

We shook our heads.

The old bloke leaned across, tapped the postcard. 'This place is one of them wonders. "Freshwater you can't drink".' The same rocky outcrop and pebble beach could be seen if you looked over the road. 'But they got it wrong,' he said. 'Freshwater bubbles up through the salt. Brings good luck to those that see it. Looks like smoke out in those rock pools. Cools you down like ice cubes dropped in your drink. It's a wonder all right.'

We left the shopping with Dad, ran all the way.

Skidding over the seaweed-covered rocks. Other kids looked up from their beach-fun, heads turning. We held out our arms, lending each other balance. We were a blur like low-skimming seagulls. One of us laughed and we bounced that call between us.

The pools were clustered under the chalk rock-face at the far end of the beach. The tide eased itself out leaving pools exposed, ringed with emerald weeds and bristling red anemones. We crouched around the deepest one.

We waited for the smoky mist to show us that fresh water was coming. We waited for the sweet scent of it. Maybe salt would harden on the drying rocks, pushed out by the springing of fresh water. Maybe sunlight reflecting off those crystals would dazzle planes in the sky. We waited, knees aching, jagged edges of the rocks biting into our pumps.

We waited.

Diane was the first to leave, and somehow with her gone there was no need for us older ones to stay. But we didn't look at each other as we walked away. Perhaps things would have been different if we had glanced up, seen our own pain staring back. I suppose we'll never really know.

That holiday was over twenty years ago. The last time we were together. Diane and Dad stay in touch sometimes, the boys not so much. Being all together would only make it easier to see what was missing. The chalet must have sold, our mother must have kept the cash; can't blame her for that. We've never been back, but I believe we're all still there: standing on the rocks, staring into the pool, waiting for fresh water that will never spring.

MORELIA SPILOTA

Cherise Saywell

Artwork by Tim Ellis

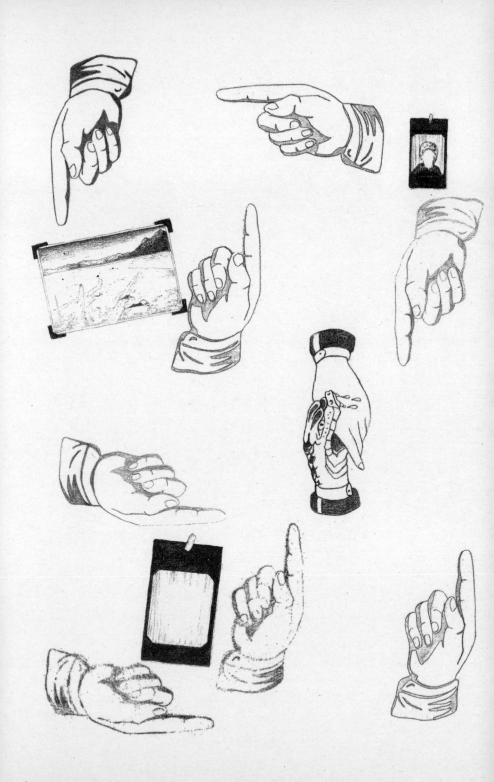

Morelia Spilota

Cherise Saywell

It was dark when we stopped and, though it wasn't yet late, already the road felt endless. I suppose I was grateful for the snake, at first. It lay on the gravel near the edge of a field, and the priest braked hard as soon as he saw it. He shut off the engine and got out, and I got out too, wondering if now was the time to run. We'd been driving for nearly an hour. By my estimation, we should have reached town but I couldn't tell where we were. In the light of the headlamps you could see the neat wheel-shape of the snake, the terrible coils fat and still. There was blood on its side and I was surprised it was red. I expected, I don't know, green or yellow – something more reptilian.

The priest scratched his head. He had a beaky nose and rounded shoulders and although he wasn't old, I couldn't tell his age. In the dim-lit dirt our footprints were visible, trailing among some roadside litter – shredded plastic; glint of broken glass.

'Dead, do you reckon?' he said.

'Maybe,' I said, checking for cars. Nothing at all. Not since we turned off the main highway and onto this quiet road. I'd been looking for signs but there were none.

'Doesn't smell like it,' he said.

'Not yet.'

'It'd rot fast in this heat. Might be fresh dead.'

He'd spoken so little on the road. He'd not even asked my name. Now he talked like he was playing a part. I was hitching on my own again and it was taking some getting used to. Until recently I'd gone about with a man called Lester who was older than me and drank a lot. He took quite a bit of managing but for a while it was worth it, not having to get into cars on my own. I was the kind of girl who could disappear and no one would notice.

There was a lot of arable along these roads, wheat and sugar cane, beans. Inland for cotton. North for soft fruit. There was plenty of work for someone like me, and for cash too – you didn't need an address to get paid.

I'd noticed, coming through the year before, how the people around here liked to observe the roadkill. They'd pull over and get out, check if the animal was dead. They might turn it over with the end of their shoe. If it had a pouch, they'd see if anything was in it. You'd get this list of things they'd seen: a wallaby with its skull crushed flat; a wombat with a bloodied snout; an echidna with half its spines plucked away, taken for souvenirs most likely.

'Looks like roadkill,' I said. I waited for the details of his roadside finds. But there was a strange empty pause, and when I looked the priest was tapping his forehead, watching the ground.

'Not necessarily,' he said. 'It might have come through the field.' He pointed into the darkness. 'In which case it wouldn't have got as far as the road.' He indicated the dirt around where the snake lay. 'You can't tell,' he said. 'No trail.' He leaned right in, examining his own fresh footprints. 'The strangest thing – it's like it came from nowhere.' He scanned the area around the snake and then he looked up into the black sky, as if assessing the likelihood of its arrival by that route.

I was probably relieved at the attention the priest was giving that snake. Had he ill intentions towards me he'd likely have been getting on with things by now. Still, I was nervous. 'I wonder what kind it is,' I said.

'*Morelia spilota*,' he said with some authority. 'Carpet snake,' he clarified. 'They don't bite.'

I knew this. But it didn't mean the creature was harmless. And in any case, a snake could be a great pretender. The elaborate patterns of a poisonous kind might be perilously close to one much more benign. It was safer to be afraid of the lot of them.

'We should just leave it be,' I said.

But the priest continued to study the dirt around the snake. He was muttering, his lips moving silently around something I couldn't make out and I wondered if he was a little crazy. When you're hitching alone and you get in a car, you learn what to look for. Only I'd been with Lester too long; I was out of practice. I'd seen black cloth, a cross, a square white collar. But maybe this man's collar was cut out of card, his shirt adapted from something plain and black from Woolworths. It was about thirty miles back that I got in his car. My bag still lay on the backseat where I'd flung it.

The priest knelt near the snake and pressed his hand in the dirt. He examined the indentation it left. He placed both hands there and looked again. Then he stood and checked the trail his shoes had left between the edge of the gravel, where the car was parked, and the loose dry dirt where the snake lay.

He brushed his hands together and turned to me. 'We are going to take this snake with us,' he announced.

I tried to read his face, to see what game he might be playing, or if he genuinely believed in a sane reason to load a snake into the back of his car. After all, it might not even be dead. The blood on it could be a surface wound from sliding over something sharp – a farm tool or the curled-over lid of a can. And venomous or not, many a snake will draw its coils tight around a person's neck.

'Open the boot,' said the priest.

There's nearly always somewhere to run to so long as you're safe out of the car. But you need to know if running alone into those aching miles of darkness is the better risk. I stood there half-decided until the priest came over and opened the boot himself. He was thin and not especially tall and I thought I could probably escape him if necessary, though you can't always judge a man's strength by his size. He went back now, and he bent down and he took that snake in his arms. Its coils seemed to loosen and I wondered if it was dead after all. A neat round depression remained in the soft dirt where it had lain.

The priest deposited the snake in the boot of the car. The interior light made its patterns uncertain, its colours sallow and strange.

I turned and searched in the direction from which we'd come. The rough forms of ragged-edged hills pitched up from the flatness. The uncertain horizon dissolved in places into an inky sky. I wanted a set of headlamps or any kind of light that might indicate I wasn't marooned out here with a deranged priest and a snake in questionable health. I half-lifted my arm, as if by doing so I might conjure a vehicle.

The priest must have noticed. His arms still rested against the lid of the boot. 'There'll be nothing along this stretch of road,' he said with some authority. 'Not at this time of night.' He turned and smiled blandly. In the low light he appeared quite young, perhaps not even thirty. 'I'm afraid I'm your best bet,' he added. 'Go on. Get in.'

But I wouldn't do it. 'Not with that snake,' I said.

The priest checked his cargo. 'Python,' he corrected me. 'Carpet python. *Morelia spilota.*' He closed the boot. 'Not venomous,' he said.

I chewed on the inside of my lip for a moment, considering. 'But you're not sure,' I said. 'You're no expert. In fact, I'd bet that's the only kind of snake you know.'

There was a pause, only a brief one, but it was pause enough for me. Then the priest said, 'That's not true.'

'Go on then,' I challenged him. 'Name another.'

He didn't hesitate. '*Pseudechis porphyriacus*,' he said. 'Red-bellied black snake. Venomous. *Pseudonaja textilis* – eastern brown snake – poisonous, but rather plain-looking. *Acanthophis antarcticus*,' (he hissed the 's') – 'common death adder.' He turned his head a little, raising his eyebrows. I still couldn't tell if he was mad or just weird – or if this whole thing was a prelude to something else altogether. He folded his arms. Chanted: '*Notechis scutatus* – mainland tiger snake. Extremely venomous,' he said, like he was making a promise. He clicked open the boot again. 'Beautifully patterned,' he added, looking a little too long at the snake lying in his car, perhaps making sure, 'but differently marked to this creature.' He checked the place where the snake had lain, as if to reassure himself. 'Shall I continue?'

I kept my voice level. 'No,' I said. 'You could go on and on; they're all just snakes as far as I'm concerned.' I measured the distance between us. 'And I'm not getting in a car with one. I'm just not,' I said.

The priest held himself perfectly still for a moment. Then he opened the passenger door and reached into the glove compartment and my legs went to jelly. But it was just cigarettes he was after. He offered me one. I shook my head, and he frowned and took one for himself, then tossed the pack through the window into the front of the car. Only he did this awkwardly, as if he was aware of his brain sending each individual signal to his limbs and did not trust that they would obey. He lit his cigarette and inhaled. I observed how deeply he drew back and I saw that he needed it.

Scrutinising his half-lit face, I said, 'You don't behave like any priest I ever met.'

'I've no idea what you're talking about,' he huffed.

'Well,' I said. 'Picking up girls like me, for one thing.'

'I didn't pick you up,' he said hotly. 'I offered you a lift.'

'Call it what you like,' I said.

'I've done nothing wrong,' the priest protested.

'But you want to,' I said. 'And you're a long way out of

town to be alone with a girl like me.' I folded my arms. 'People around here might be interested to hear about your night rides with hitchhikers.'

The priest held himself perfectly still.

'Can I have a cigarette now?' I asked.

For a moment, he didn't move. His face was shrouded and I couldn't tell what he might do. But then he went back into the car and fussed about in the semi-darkness, retrieving the packet. He held it out to me. His hand was shaking. I took one and he offered me a light. But I said no thank you and I put my cigarette in the pocket of my t-shirt. I didn't want a smoke. I just wanted to watch him fetch me one and I wanted him to understand this.

Something came over him then and I did not anticipate the speed of it. He seized the back of my t-shirt. The thin fabric, and my bra strap too, were bunched tightly in his grip. He handled me around to the back of the car and when I was before the snake he prodded the air above it with the fingers that still held his cigarette. 'It will only hurt us if we let it,' he said. 'Touch it. Go on.'

The snake lay perfectly still and the priest's grip on me did not loosen. It seemed best simply to do as I'd been told. So I put my hand out and I touched that snake, and although it felt slippery it was not smooth in the way I expected. The patterns on the animal's skin were like something embossed in cool polished leather. My fingers came away dusty and I wiped them on my shorts. But right then, at the very moment I did this, the snake flicked its tongue and gently, almost imperceptibly, it drew its coils into itself.

The priest about jumped out of his body.

'You can let go of me now,' I said. I wasn't sure if he would, but he did. 'So,' I said. 'Now it's your turn.'

'But I've already touched it,' he protested. 'I just carried it to the car.'

He was unsettled, but it wasn't enough for me. I wanted the pleasure of making him do something he didn't want to. 'When you thought it was dead,' I taunted. 'Are you afraid? A man of God shouldn't be afraid.' I said 'man of God' like someone who knew better.

At this, the priest threw down his spent cigarette. 'I have nothing to fear,' he announced and he swished a hand along the length of the snake. It was done with a flourish – like a performance – to demonstrate fearlessness, I suppose. Though he might simply have wished to better my tentative prod. In any case, he must have moved too quickly because at the very moment he swept his hand over the snake, suddenly and without warning, it lifted its head and, in a brief darting movement, it speared itself at his fingers then sank back into its own safe shape. It may have even hissed. The whole thing was so fleeting I'd have wondered if it'd happened at all, except that the priest screamed, clutching his hand.

'Oh God,' he moaned.

His face was like wax. A fine, dark lacework of blood patterned the skin of his finger. He sank to the dirt at the back of the vehicle.

The still air seemed to massage the darkness. The outline of a nearby ridge leaked into the sky. I stood over the priest and moved my sandalled feet about in the loose gravel at the edge of the tarmac. I was caught somewhere between triumph and contempt.

'I thought you said it wasn't venomous,' I smirked.

The priest didn't answer. His breath came fast and shallow in the hot still night.

I prodded him with my foot. 'If it's not venomous how come you're poisoned.'

He cradled his injured hand. His eyes moved but nothing else. He raised them to mine. 'There was no trail,' he said. 'How could that be?' He lowered his eyes.

I was merciless. 'Are we far from town?' I demanded.

'Half an hour, maybe,' he murmured.

'It was half an hour from where you picked me up,' I said. 'And we've been driving a good deal longer than that.'

The priest seemed to tip a little to the side. His head drooped. 'Yes,' he said. 'I know. I shouldn't have brought you this way.'

A drop of blood fell to the dirt and in the flat, strained light it was the wrong colour. I squatted beside him. I smoothed my hand over the fine hairs on my arms and I watched him.

'I just can't work out how it got there,' he said.

'It doesn't really matter now, does it?' I folded my arms.

He sniffed and angled his bony shoulder so he could scratch at his cheek with it. 'But did you see the size of it?' he said weakly. 'And no trail. No trail. It's not possible.'

'But that's not why you stopped, is it?' I said.

'I don't know why I stopped,' the priest replied. And I saw that this was true.

'Well,' I said, drily. 'You shouldn't have put that snake in your car.'

'I just wanted someone to see,' he said.

'Who?'

'Anyone.' He slumped. 'They like to look at things like that around here.'

'They like to look at roadkill,' I said. 'They don't care what it's called in Latin.'

The priest leaned back and closed his eyes slowly, as if he was shutting them to everything he'd ever hoped for. His forehead and his neck were damp with perspiration – the light that leaked from the interior of the car caught the shine of it. Without opening his eyes, he whispered, 'They probably wouldn't look at anything I showed them anyway.'

My stomach did a sort of flip-flop. How young he looked. Not thirty – not that old. At this moment he didn't even look twenty. He seemed younger than me, his hair damp and curled around his forehead. He plucked at the white rectangle of his collar as if he might stop pretending if he could only take it off, but he was shaking too much, so he gave up and let his hand rest in his lap. He tipped his head back and swallowed, and shadows shifted over his skin. I imagined him propped against the bumper, skin blue and marbled. Or maybe he'd tip over in the dirt as his strength drained away. I wondered who would stop for him, or if anyone would. Where might I be by then?

I heard myself speak and I could have been someone else my voice was so thin and so cautious. 'You were probably right though,' I said. 'It doesn't look deadly. Maybe I could draw off some of the venom.'

The priest seemed to have sunk even further into himself. 'I don't know how,' he said. He waited a moment. 'You don't see many snakes where I'm from,' he added.

'Where I'm from,' I told him, 'there are plenty but we don't pick them up.'

I got onto my knees and I put his finger in my mouth, tasting the tang of the blood and the tar of the fag. I thought I should taste something else too. Something poisonous. Sour-bright yellow, I imagined, or milky and bitter. But when I drew from the wound, there was only blood and an angled edge, sharp and foreign.

I released his hand. 'Ow!' I ran my tongue along the roof of my mouth. Then I ran my finger over his injury, and I felt it again – long enough to pinch out easily. Glass. It must have been lodged in the skin of the snake. Gently I prised it loose. 'Look!' I said, holding the fragment up in the light. 'You've not been bitten at all!' I lifted the hem of my shirt and used it to clean his finger and then I held that up too. 'See?'

I can't explain what happened next, except that colour returned to his face, and there was something in his expression, like he'd found a thing he'd given up for lost. And I wanted a bit of that too. He laughed, and I laughed with him, and then without missing a beat, without even thinking, I put his finger back in my mouth.

The priest shifted abruptly, straightening his legs. Pressing his knees together, he pushed me away. Then he was on his feet. He turned and was wiping his hands on his trousers, brushing dust off his shirt, and I felt as if he was already far away from me, accelerating along a slip road that would take him fast into his future. Whatever he might have wanted when he picked me up, he no longer did. Whatever he had hoped for, or not admitted he wanted but half-hoped for anyway, something had shifted and a new kind of something had replaced it. And I felt inside me an absence, an emptiness, the same as when Lester had fallen, rotten with drink, by the roadside – his vodka-meth scent, the heat of the sun. I'd hoped we'd be on our way north where there were mangoes waiting to be picked and wrapped in squares of tissue, then gently laid in flat wooden crates and shipped south. I'd hoped we'd get there quick enough to bag the better accommodation. I'd imagined us in a room, not a tent, with a bed and a cotton sheet to go over us both, and a window that looked away from the road, maybe onto some trees. But it had been a foolish thing to hope for.

Right then, out of the darkness came bright lights. A heavy rising rumble and a semi-trailer hefted past. The car rocked with the force of the air the truck took with it, and the night whirled around us. The priest coughed as dust flew about and he adjusted his collar. He put his hand up, perhaps to acknowledge that everything was okay, that we hadn't broken down, that we had merely been observing some roadkill. I watched the silty cloud billowing into our footprints and sinking into the place where the snake must have lain while vehicles passed and dust rose and fell, erasing the trail that the creature had left. I thought about how that priest had pushed me off him, and how, soon, I would be getting in and out of cars with people who might want to talk to me, or who might want to hurt me, or who might not even notice me, just let me out again twenty miles later and forget I ever existed.

I wrapped my arms around myself.

The priest was pressing at his finger where the glass had pierced him. He sighed and walked over to me, and maybe he noticed what the dust had done to the prints in the dirt, I don't know, but he leaned in and he touched my face and he stroked my hair and I saw that he didn't want to take his hand away, but he did. After that, he went to the boot of his car and placed both arms beneath the snake and lifting it gently, almost tenderly, he carried it over the gravel and through the dirt, beyond the place where we'd found it, to the edge of the field, where he set it down.

'We should go,' he said, when he was done.

'Yes,' I replied.

We got in the car. He spoke little, though at one point he asked my name and I told him, and he told me his. He whistled as he drove us through the night until we reached a cotton farm where I'd heard there was work. There, he thanked me for my company and gave me a crisp new banknote before we parted and he said to save it so I could travel by bus when I was ready to move on.

How They
Turned Out

Lionel Shriver

Artwork by Adam Shield

How They Turned Out

Lionel Shriver

Whatever Became of Whatsherface had doubtless become a national preoccupation (if not also an exercise in self-abasement; as a rule, the subject of your web sleuthing would never in a million years do a search on you). But she'd long been one of the looked-for, so tracking down an old class-mate was a brand-new game for Sloozie Twitch.

So far, poking around another person's digital residue felt defiling, as if she were rifling someone else's under-wear drawer. Getting the scuttlebutt on the long lost in the analogue era would have entailed, say, chatting with the mother on the phone, and only after proving bona fides. The target would hear about the call. By contrast, prying by search engine seemed cowardly. You weren't required to declare yourself. You didn't have to confess to a curiosity that granted this person an unacceptably large place in your history – worse, that allowed them a place on a rainy winter evening in your very present. These searches felt sneaky, underhanded, and strangely invasive, however ignorant of the impertinence the victim would remain. The violation recalled assault cases in which dentists felt up patients who were under general anaesthesia.

Except maybe the real revelation of these enquiries (with reading glasses, magnification two-point-five, and wine) was less the lowdown itself than what you hoped to find.

Thus before inputting *Grier Finleyson* into Firefox, when the surprising or simply boring results had yet to contaminate her virgin mindset, Slooz missed a valuable and currently rather rare opportunity for soul searching. Did she want to discover that her old suitemate from senior year in college had done spectacularly well for herself, or was she looking to crow over a shockingly poor showing? Surely the spirit in which she began this idle research might have testified to whether or not she was a Good Person.

Sloozie Twitch was getting too old to care about being a Good Person. (Even the handle contrived in her twenties exuded a youthful zing no longer fitting, but she was used to it, and still savoured the way the first name's amalgamation of *floozy* and *sleazy* conveyed an indefinite dirtiness. Besides, there was no fucking way she was reverting to *Susan Twitchel*, who in her mind's eye, being mousy and no-account, was a completely different woman.) Sixty this coming April, she'd risen and fallen in the public eye well before the advent of Instagram and Facebook, and decency was a social consideration. Although she didn't conceive of herself as a recluse, the income from her recordings in the Eighties and Nineties (along with chunky annual cheques of forty-nine cents from Spotify thereafter) had been prudently socked away, thereby affording her the usual curse of what she thought she wanted: a cosy, solidly built cedar-shingled house on the Finger Lakes, with land attached and outbuildings. She had a powerful router and solitude up the ass.

Having naturally feared the inroads of decay, she was pleased to ascertain that having largely lived your life was restful. And it was interesting. She seemed to have arrived at precisely the age at which it was possible to assess matters – to make summary pronouncements, to step far enough back to see a life as a conclusive whole, as an object. Let's face it: by sixty, the votes were in. You'd done what you were going to, and at best you would do a bit more of it. The centre-cut of her career had been too frenetic to provide for looking backwards – at the two ex-husbands and all the impractical foreign boyfriends, at the long graph of triumphs and setbacks like a jag of mountains against the sky: a Grammy nomination one year, a solo gig at the Sydney Opera House crushingly fallen through the next. But now the accumulation of all that messy history, a cranial form of hoarding, made her feel accomplished in an avocational sense. At last she possessed a big, fat past to examine, and its accrual had been work.

Which was not to say that Sloozie Twitch was retired – though she'd have accepted the label of has-been without rancour. She still gave occasional one-off concerts to die-hard fans, most of whom were at least as old as she was, though gigs in Asia or Down Under were no longer worth the plane journey. She granted an interview to *Elle* only last year. She continued to compose songs here – hopped up at first, eventually conceding that the new one sounded awfully like the last ten – if only to justify her purchase of the sleek black electric piano in the den.

Indeed, what had kicked off this digital hugger-mugger into the fate of a bygone acquaintance (*friend* being too strong a word) was keeping a hand in, however limply. This morning, she received an email approach from the producers of a heavily syndicated NPR programme called *Injudicious Journals*, in which celebrities of her second-rate ilk would read aloud confidential outpourings from their sapling years. Slooz possessed the requisite documents (several tear-spattered spiral notebooks, dense with tight scrawl in red cartridge pen). Yet it was one thing to court humiliation to a professional purpose on the radio – to advertise your self-confidence in your very willingness to expose your frailty. It was a much grimmer matter to grow privately chag-rined, and perhaps permanently to destroy your cherished illusions about having been remotely bearable as a college student. So to decide on how to respond to the invitation that afternoon, she'd seated herself cross-legged in the attic under a dangling bare bulb and flipped open the damp cardboard covers with no little trepidation.

There were discoveries.

Her thoughts were often lame and clichéd, and not nearly as well expressed as she expected, given that Sloozie Twitch was renowned for her lyrics. This record was historically sloppy, too: few entries were dated, and one long, paranoid section was written in a code she could no longer crack. Worst of all, her younger self had faithfully chronicled her every *feeling*, but almost never the event that gave rise to it. So the notebooks were margin-to-margin anguish, fury, and pining, but the source of the anguish, the object of the fury, and whatever or whomever she'd been pining *for* were nowhere to be found.

The entry that inspired this evening's Mickey Mouse espionage online was as weak on detail as any other. But something about the opening line – *I have never before in my life been accused of any such thing, and I am stricken, mystified, groping for whether there is possibly any truth to it* – dislodged a lost memory, which plopped into her lap as if a volume whose author's name began with *C*, misfiled under *F*, had toppled from a high shelf. How odd, too, that the memory had ever gone missing in the first place.

After three years of ineffably disappointing higher education, admission to an Ivy League school already seemed a little chicken-shit, and by middle age Slooz would dismiss the imprimatur as meaningless. But that indifference was only possible by dint of having got in. If, annoyingly, an all-girls school, Barnard College was at least located in New York City (an ideal jumping-off place for the pre-famous), and the school further leveraged its muted prestige by institutional association with Columbia across the street. Still, in the latter 1970s, most of Barnard's student housing was bleak and stingy, so it was a relief to have at last been awarded a room in a top-floor suite on West 116th Street for senior year. The more spacious residential arrangement had only one drawback: other people.

In any hothouse of five young women sharing dormitory accommodation, the casting was strict. There was firstly the Prima Donna – the luminary, the centre of all the action, the superstar. Secondly, a requirement for any proper leading lady, the Sidekick – the egger-on, the whisperer, the golem. Then the Mediator – the neutral party, who listened sympathetically and without judgement as indignant petitioners put their cases, and who as the custodian of much tantalising tittle-tattle would have held the most enviable position, barring the obligatory humility that manifestly disqualified the other four for the job. The Defector – the opt-out, above the fray, who spent most nights with an older boyfriend. Lastly, the Also-Ran. The Also-Ran played wannabe to the starlet's authenticity. Her purpose was to play second fiddle to the genuine article. Her purpose was to be shown up.

Susan Twitchel was the Also-Ran. She was at least slim, but not tall. Her clear, accurate singing voice wasn't thin, but it was small. It required amplification – which in due course it would obtain, albeit not when overheard seeping meekly out from under her bedroom door. Back then she dressed to be ignored, in oversize men's button-downs and slumped jeans, and college classmates needed little excuse to overlook you. It would take her a few more years to accept that her face would never turn heads without make-up. The hair, too: more merely pale than blonde, it hung fine, lank, and lifeless, in lieu of Slooz's subsequent discovery of *products*. At that time, her energy ran inward in a destructive churn. She was unsure of herself in a way that made her wary, which isn't an attractive aspect, and she had a tendency to check and recheck what she was about to say until by the time she made the remark the others had moved on and had no idea what she was referring to. It was a timing problem that, with deft, syncopated pauses on stage, she would later turn to her advantage; the double-taking hesitations would be funny.

Besides, most artists began as socially maladroit. Inadequacy in one medium drove you to another.

Secretly, beneath the dreary shirts, flat hair, and anxious mental editing, Susan Twitchel was ambitious, to a degree that astonished her now; the Slooz she'd grow into would marvel at the fire and ferocity of her younger self with a bitter envy she never aimed at other people. It would have been precisely the detection of this light burning under a bushel that made her suitemates leery – the two who were players, that is. The other two didn't count.

The Also-Ran was lucky enough to bunk with Elsa the Defector, she who was never there, and therefore enjoyed a de facto single – which made both roommates lucky, because filtering off to her mysterious boyfriend, Elsa didn't have to put up with Susan's oboe practice. (For a young woman with an eye on pop music to have pursued a chiefly classical proficiency struck most people as incoherent. Foreseeing the wailing interludes that brought Sloozie Twitch's debut album to the attention of the critics would have required more imagination than even Susan could marshal in those days, and the choice of instrument struck her as incoherent, too.)

Grier Finlayson – not *Finleyson*, an initial misspelling that would confound online searches for evidence of her later life until Slooz swapped the *E* for an *A* – was the Prima Donna. She was full-chested, and built on a grand scale in every respect. Grier was beautiful in that slightly odd manner that makes a woman stand out. Her eyes were too wide – not widely set, but too high, almost circular. Her hands flew widely also; dark and gesticulating, a tumbling, rapid talker, she should have been Italian. Freshman year, she'd suffered a bout of anorexia, a term only just entering the popular lexicon in the late 1970s that still seemed exotic. Evidence that the condition had been not only legitimate but had been allowed to become dangerously advanced, she'd lost much of her black hair, which had only partially grown back. It fuzzed from her scalp in an ethereal afro, touching in its sparseness, fuzzing delicately around her head as if drawn in charcoal softened by the smudge of a forefinger. The premature alopecia lent her a hint of tragedy. Somehow when *Grier Finlayson* devotedly followed Weight Watchers, sawing off slices of skinless, too-plump chicken breasts until they weighed in to the quarter ounce and wolfing gallons of programmatically permissible string beans straight from the can, the ritual didn't seem quotidian, daytime-TV, but hallowed, ecclesiastical.

The suite they shared senior year was more commodious than the housing for lower classmen. But this was well before the client-based crowd-pleasing of modern universities, with their convection ovens, massage chairs, and dining-hall sushi bars. So while the bedrooms were larger than linen cupboards, the only common living space was the kitchen – where swabbing the spatter-patterned linoleum was fruitless because the flooring was manufactured to look dirty already, and where the windows wouldn't completely close, so that mildew speckled their rattling wooden frames, and in winter the room was overheated and draughty at the same time. Yet five female seniors sharing vastly more capacious digs would still have allowed room for only one talent.

Grier secured that designation without a fight. With a round, enormous voice, she swooned over a keyboard in the same rolling, frenetic crescendos in which she talked. No amplification necessary. The songs she wrote were tumbling, too: confessional, anguished, accelerating. Her lyrics used the kind of imagery that on paper would have looked silly but that sounded inexplicably poetic when set to music – you know, *the broken etching of my whole-winged soul* or something. It went without saying if you knew the type that she was also an actress, scoring the leads in school productions of Gilbert and Sullivan – and Ibsen, too. From the September in which the five young women first convened, consensus reigned that it was Grier who had the goods, that Grier was the original, that Grier was the one who would go places.

Slooz couldn't remember ever discussing with Grier why a piano powerhouse with a voice the size of the great outdoors hadn't gone straight to Manhattan School of Music, but maybe the explanation was similar to her own. The Twitchels had been adamant that their daughter get a solid liberal-arts education, in their day believed to pave any life path. If she then continued to chase a kooky pop-music pipedream, at least she'd have a reputable degree to fall back on. (As a teenager, Susan took their demand for a Plan B as an insult. Only once she achieved them did Slooz regard her youthful aspirations as preposterous. Her parents' real mistake was not forcing her to get a BA in engineering.) This parental insistence on educational breadth explained why Susan wasn't even a student in the music department, but was enrolled in the recently contrived Interdisciplinary Arts. The programme was ramshackle – poorly conceived, poorly run, poorly taught, and thus anything but reputable, but it was too late to warn her parents that they were squandering their money on a travesty.

Perhaps because it was so transparently tinker-toy, IA was a small department. Amongst the five students concentrating in music, only Susan and Grier were focusing on composition, both with an eye to becoming singer-songwriters. Anyone assuming that this would make the two suitemates natural allies would have to be an idiot.

Instead, enter the Sidekick. Myra Haas must have been an English major, because these people always were. Her intelligence thrived within circumscribed boundaries, where the rules were clear and there was such a thing as a right answer. In other words, she was a good student, in the sense that made so many good students flail in dismay once outside the comforting confines of a curriculum. Accordingly, her vague career ambitions were academic; when you flourish in a university setting, you want to stay there. She wielded a generous Latinate vocabulary. She had mastered proper footnote form. She invested in flashy plastic binders for her assignments, and always waited for the Liquid Paper to fully dry before correcting a typo. She was skilful at regurgitating a professor's lecture in that gently rearranged fashion that flattered the teacher while fostering the infeasible illusion that the paper also included innovative content. Higher education's ideal, Myra was a supremely competent synthesiser, but she could not come up with anything indisputably new if her life depended on it. To be fair, most people couldn't – which was why the reinvention 'Sloozie Twitch' would eventually own an estate on the Finger Lakes, a slate-grey Audi A5, and a bolt-hole on the coast of Belgium.

Myra's appearance mirrored her mind. Everything was functional and in the right place. She was what you would draw when depicting a pretty girl if you had never been in love. It was perplexing why so many pleasantly symmetrical young women still left something to be desired, unless that very expression nailed it. What was missing was something – something intriguing, unknowable, elusive, out of reach – to be desired. Myra's looks were too available.

Yet she did have a sidling slyness about her. Often mocking and unashamedly superior, she was the mistress of the unsubstantiated anecdote. Cracking a grin, she'd perch on that high stool in the kitchen and peer up through her lashes with, *Well, I know I shouldn't tell you this, but* … That facial expression always reminded Susan of the daggered posters for Stanley Kubrick's *A Clockwork Orange*. Myra seduced through collusion. She was conspicuously vain about her IQ, so that those she befriended were complimented by the implication that they must be intelligent, too. She enticed confederates with the prospect of protection from the pointy end of her derision.

Myra surely attached herself to Grier, not the other way around. By instinct or calculation, the Sidekick sensed that Grier's passion and panache provided cachet by association. So they were inseparable – Myra made sure of that. And what better to cement the tie than a common adversary.

A pool of three candidates could be quickly narrowed to one.

Elsa was a poor prospect for the fulltime position of antagonist if she was chronically AWOL; you could only get so much mileage from despairing behind the absentee's back that to squander senior year on a *boyfriend* was politically retrograde, vocationally self-destructive, and criminally wasteful of what, in those days, was hilariously considered high tuition ($6,000 per year! Upper-end refrigerators cost more than that). Pam the Mediator (her surname was now irretrievable, for Pam not only had the kind of name one forgot; she was the kind of person whose name one forgot) made an even more farcical target. Quiet, sexless, and made of straight lines, Pam wore glasses with big, brightly coloured frames that would become all the rage in the following century, but were not fashionable in 1977. She did all the reading for her courses and avoided conflict. She was probably studying social work, and if she wasn't then she should have been. Pam was not in the game.

That left guess-who. As if there were ever any question.

Regarding the vast majority of both semesters – right up until relations grew overtly unpleasant – it would have been self-pitying in the extreme for Slooz to remember that duo as having been cruel to her. Even at the time, whatever injury Susan did experience was mild enough to make her worry about being oversensitive. She'd mistrusted her sense of exclusion from the central life of the suite as perhaps the inevitable consequence of herself having been stand-offish. Still, those two did seem to take turns dropping by the Friday-night Columbia Student Union jam sessions whenever Susan was taking part – as if trading off during a stakeout so that one of them could go for coffee. For they appeared to be keeping tabs on her, a mission quite distinct from providing sisterly support, a popular if optimistic fiction during the flowering of 'women's lib'.

Myra was a master of damning with faint praise. She'd describe Susan's new song as 'really *tuneful*', and what did that mean? That it had a tune? Or she'd commend Susan's intonation for 'getting a lot better'. As for Grier, the Prima Donna was seldom critical. With others, her specialty was effusion, and (if with a touch of melodrama) she primarily disparaged herself. But she would fall into anguished throes of sympathy with Susan over whatever was she going to do with this oboe business, when she spent more time shaving reeds than actually playing the thing, so that maybe she should think about taking up a different instrument but gosh which one would that be, and she'd grow so hyperventilated about this matter that Susan would forget for minutes at a go that it was her problem.

In retrospect, Susan's college compositions truly were uneven. Much of her experimentation flopped, and her voice, both instrument and style, hadn't settled. For female vocalists back then, the cultural atmosphere was still dank with the drippy despondency of Janis Ian, and Sloozie Twitch would later find her stride among the fiercer, more ragged ranks of Kate Bush and Tori Amos, while sometimes falling into sassy step with Rickie Lee Jones. Susan's early songs were too depressing.

Yet few young women would have come into their own by the age of twenty-one, and the predictable hit-and-miss of this period still didn't explain why her suitemates greeted even her most confident performances with a penultimate enthusiasm. By contrast, when bundling back to the dorm in a posse after attending opening night of *My Fair Lady*, at which the promising Miss Finlayson as Eliza had drawn a standing ovation, the superlatives flew, and Susan's confederates *could have danced all night* in the glow of their idol's reflected glory. Susan Twitchel made a soldierly effort, but Grier Finlayson – now, Grier Finlayson was the real deal.

Indeed, so irrefutably had this hierarchy been established that both the Susan of that era and the Slooz of Christmas Future would grow equally confounded why at the end of that year it would still seem necessary to put the Also-Ran in her place one last time.

The pressure-cooker competition on a college campus was wont to suggest that students who distinguished themselves within its grounds – impressed the professors, led the clubs, copped the grades and Phi Beta Kappa keys – were streaking across a finish line at the head of the pack. Only senior year did it dawn dimly on some students – if only on the smart ones, and not the book-smart, but the biologically smart ones: the real race hadn't even started.

It was this very creeping awareness that how well or badly they performed on their senior projects was of *no earthly importance whatsoever* that inevitably drove even the animal-smart kids like Susan to focus exclusively on that project with redoubled ferocity. The intolerable alternative was to face the fact that on the other side of graduation they had accomplished nothing, they were nothing, and they were lost.

To substitute for a senior thesis, IA students with music concentrations were required to deliver full-length recitals to live audiences. Susan planned a contemporary programme of original songs, and put together a cabaret to be performed in a dark, sticky campus bar at Columbia called the Culvert. Subtly worn down by her suitemates' too-moderate approval all year, she was private about her line-up, and rehearsed only in a music-department practice room with the door closed. She mixed up the running order so that the few heavier tunes would never drag the mood of a set to morose. For this second semester, something had started to flow. She'd finally discovered rhythm, so this tranche of new work had drive. Yet the untried tunes felt vulnerable. She was still polishing the lyrics, more personally exposing than her earlier songs, which had hidden under a cloak of nonspecific glumness. She even dared a number called 'Under the Radar' that hinted at the experience of feeling underestimated, of cultivating a rising, unobserved excellence by stealth. In an attic nearly four decades later, she'd discover the first verse and refrain in red cartridge pen:

> *I broadcast on frequencies between your stations.*
> *I lurk on tiny islands unclaimed by other nations.*
> *I wail in registers only dogs and deer detect.*
> *You're colour blind and I glow candy-apple red.*
> *Watch your back! I'm coming up under the radar.*
> *Watch your back! I'm coming up under the radar . . .*

Susan drafted a pianist a year behind her in the programme as an accompanist, who could duet with the oboe cadenzas that she incorporated into her tunes for the first time. Considering how the whole evening ended up making her feel, it was a testimony to the force pulsing through 'Under the Radar' that thereafter she continued to play around with oboe interludes, refining what would at length become her signature sound.

Make no mistake: the cabaret went swimmingly. Pulling out all the stops, she'd bullied friends, family, and fellow IA students into showing up. Once the first set was underway, the full house left off looking at watches, too. Anyone who appears in public will tell you that it's wildly obvious from the stage how a performance is going down, and Susan led this crowd by the leash.

She was tapping into something, a presence. Finally at ease before an audience, she didn't apologise in the intros, or resort to self-deprecation. She seemed to have expanded to fill out a wider perimeter, as if the mic amplified not merely her voice but her very being. This iteration of Susan Twitchel was just as true as the regular-sized one. She was acting all right, but the role she was performing was herself – not a fraud or simulacrum, but her real self. The more searing her vocals, the more vaulting her reedy intervals, the wittier her patter between songs, the bigger and more bona fide she grew. She finally grasped why some people crave live performance like a drug, and it wasn't from a need for love, but from a lust for scale. There was an interior *magnitude* you could never achieve on your lonesome.

The quantity of new material being limited, it was fortunate that she'd reserved a couple of songs for encores. The other thing you can always tell from the stage is the difference between wholehearted and merely compulsory applause, and this clapping bounced off the low ceiling of the bar with a spanking resonance and rapid tempo that you never got from duty.

Down from Connecticut for the occasion, her parents took her out for a congratulatory dinner, so she didn't get back to the suite until nearly midnight. When she entered the kitchen, Pam mumbled an anodyne 'nice job tonight' and fled to bed. Grier was pacing in her quilted magenta bathrobe. The Sidekick was perched upright on the high stool, eyes shiny and darting, like a bird of prey on an outstretched arm.

'How was dinner with your parents?' Myra asked.

'A cut above okay,' Susan said. 'You know, the Indian place. They put the same sauce on everything, but it's a good sauce.' She didn't want to talk about dinner. None of her suitemates had come up to her after the show, which she excused in the magnanimity of her success as their allowing fans who'd a distance to travel home to monopolise the star. Obviously they'd have plenty of opportunity to wax eloquent about Susan's tour de force back at the dorm.

This was that opportunity.

'Do you want to change?' Myra solicited.

'Not really,' Susan said quizzically. 'This is pretty comfortable.' Wearing all black was hackneyed, but she'd varied the textures with a silk shirt and leather vest. The jeans fit for once, and she'd bought the boots especially for the cabaret. With a slim red scarf at her neck as a snazzy accent, in Susan's terms this was dressing up. She was reluctant to swap the hip duds for a bathrobe, thereby resigning herself that the highlight of her undergraduate education was officially over.

'Because I'm afraid we're going to have to talk,' Myra said, clasping her hands on her knee.

Susan didn't get it. 'Has something happened?'

'We think so, yes.'

'Myra, will you stop being coy?' Grier exploded at last, raking her fingers through the ethereal fluff of hair. 'You copied me! You copied me, okay?'

'... Ho-ow?' Susan asked carefully, having trouble adjusting to a very different encounter than the *Aw, shucks* bow-taking she'd anticipated.

'Well, let us count the ways.' Myra curved her elbow atop her knee, rested her chin on her knuckles, and slid a forefinger alongside her cheek. The motion was feline, the pose inquisitional. 'Style, delivery, content. If someone had led me into the Culvert blindfolded, I'd have bet the farm that I was at Grier Finlayson's senior recital.'

'You don't have a farm.' It was the sort of stalling crack one concocted in a state of stupefaction. 'And maybe the reason you don't have a farm,' Susan added, 'is you've made lousy bets like that with it.'

'I'm not saying the imitation was necessarily intentional,' Grier said.

'No?' Myra said. 'Then why was she so secretive about all this new material? Scuttling off to a rehearsal room, when usually she fishes for compliments by practising here?' They must have conducted this conversation in Susan's absence, and were repeating it for her benefit.

'I can see how just being around someone else's work all the time, it could get into your head,' Grier said.

'You mean the way women start menstruating together,' Susan said sourly.

'But at a certain point, you have to step back and realise you've been *influenced*,' Grier said. 'Or worse. That you've been channelling someone else's voice. You step back and realise that – that what you're writing doesn't belong to you!'

'It's called stealing,' Myra said.

'It's also called the sincerest form of flattery,' Grier said. 'But Susan, I just can't . . . I really don't need that kind of compliment right now. I'm under a lot of pressure. My stepmom's gone back to drinking, I just gained another two pounds on a diet of canned green beans, that essay on Joyce is due at the end of this week and I haven't even started it, and *my* senior recital is twelve days from now and I just don't need this!'

'Don't need *what*?' Susan cried. 'I don't know what you're talking about!' Yet she was about to discover that the more she denied the charge, the more valid it would appear. Later she'd puzzle over how one ever proclaimed one's innocence without sounding guilty. *I did not!* perfectly translated *Oh, shit, you caught me.*

'Seriously,' Myra said. 'That stuff you sang tonight didn't sound, even to your own ears, strangely *familiar*?'

'It sounded *familiar* because I've been working my ass off on these tunes since mid-term break, and when you sing your own work over and over, yes, it starts to sound fucking familiar!'

'That little dying fall at the end of the line?' Myra needled. 'The deliberate breaking on the high notes? You could have taken a *course* in Grier's vocals. Congratulations, you aced the final.'

'Our voices don't sound the same in the least,' Susan protested. 'Grier's projection is way better, and she's got, I don't know, more – mass.'

She'd meant to disarm by sucking up, but the choice

of noun, amongst women, was unfortunate. 'Thanks,' Grier said.

'Your voices sound similar enough when you shove the mic down your throat,' Myra said sweetly.

'It wasn't only the colouration,' Grier said. 'It was the lyrics, too. Bringing in whales in the second number, and then you mention an egg timer in the refrain, which is exactly the same as "Kerosene", which I wrote in December—'

'So we're *both* suggestible!' Susan cried, waving her hand at the egg timer on the counter between them. 'The rest of the lyrics don't overlap at all!'

'If it were only the once,' Grier went on, 'maybe it would be a coincidence, but once you throw in several dozen *coincidences* it's not called coincidence any more, it's called a pattern! A consistent, relentless, and yes, for all I know purposeful pattern, and I just feel robbed! The way you used all those slant rhymes—'

'Practically every songwriter on earth uses slant rhymes!'

'And the juxtapositions – the "rancorous cherry blossom" and the "tedious joy" and the "woolly wine"—'

'That was *wooden wine*—'

'Oh, who cares, it's the same technique! The same jarring, dissociative, apples-with-oranges, slightly surreal fish-on-an-operating-table technique, and where do you think you got it? The "glittering sorrow" and "gushy belligerence" and "angry relaxation" ... The "careful daring" and "brave cowardice" and "idiotic intelligence" – all that good badness and evil virtue ... I mean, I was too embarrassed to take notes in the Culvert, but it was like – it was like *you* weren't, *you* weren't too embarrassed, almost like you *had* been taking notes!'

Susan didn't recognise any of these citations. But when Grier was on a roll, Susan had learned early in the academic year not to interrupt.

'Taking notes in more than one sense,' Myra chimed in. 'Taking Grier's notes. The melodies. Like, that fourth song, what you called "Gangrene" or something—'

'"Gargoyle",' Susan corrected, but her voice was starting to catch.

'Hmm-hmm-hmm,' Myra hummed in an ascending arpeggio. 'That's straight out of Grier's "Rock Covers Paper".'

'Three notes? You can't accuse someone of musical plagiarism on the basis of three notes!'

'It was a lot more than three notes, Susan,' Myra chided, looking away as if out of decorum.

There were two of them, and they corroborated each other, while Susan's lonely refutation was subjective and self-interested. She was beginning to feel crazy. Was there something to the allegation after all? Had she subconsciously absorbed lines and riffs and whole phrases to which she'd only half-listened in the dorm, and then unwittingly parroted back that background noise in the guise of new compositions? But how could that be? That hadn't been what it felt like to write them!

'I—' Susan floundered. 'I don't know, I – I really just don't see it, I – I was so excited because the tunes finally started to tick over, and I could hear them unspool in the back of my head almost like they were playing themselves, and I was at long last able to really say something, express what I feel and stop hiding behind the, you know, mopey vagueness of the earlier stuff ... To be more heartfelt, like the songs I made up as a kid and sang to my little brother ... I thought the new material was pretty good, I ... thought it sounded like me, the real me for once, and now you ... I don't see it, I ... I wasn't trying, I wasn't trying to ...' To her horror, Susan had started to cry.

'Typical,' Myra remarked under her breath. 'Turning around who's really the injured party.'

Grier put a hand on Susan's shoulder as the 'thief' crumpled into an aluminium frame chair at the dining table. 'Okay, I believe you, I believe you can't hear it, or at least that you don't want to hear it, and why would you? I believe you didn't do it on purpose exactly but you also have to understand how it makes me feel. I mean, I'm glad you like my stuff and I'm even kind of touched you like my stuff but I can't help it, I'm also upset, all right? I feel a little – a little abused, taken advantage of, like you think you can just help yourself to me. Like I'm some smorgasbord, and there will always be enough to go around. But I don't have anything extra to give away right now, you understand? This stuff with my stepmom, it's left me wrung out, and school's almost over and I have no idea where I'm even living this summer and that kind of anxiety always makes me eat – and then you come along and ... take the one thing I have to protect me, my only solace, the one thing that's mine, the very centre, the core, the essence of what's *mine*.'

'I don't see it.' Susan had dropped her head and was shaking it back and forth so that her hair got stuck in her snot.

'I've heard apologies before,' Myra said. 'And honey lamb, that didn't sound like one.'

Grier broke away. 'Look, this is pointless,' she told Myra.

'I told you, what's done is done. She may not "see it", but the committee will, which means I've got twelve days to come up with a whole new programme. I'm damned if I'm graduating from this dump with the faculty claiming that *I* copied *her*.'

Little remained of the semester, and Susan made herself scarce at the suite. But she still had to return to sleep, which meant that she couldn't altogether miss out on what had become the dominant drama of their quintet: the composition of completely new songs for Grier's recital. The Prima Donna pulled multiple all-nighters, which required a handful of illicit uppers, a steady stream of caffeine, and countless cans of string beans.

Shortly after the already-celebrated showdown over alleged copycatting, on an afternoon Grier had crashed catatonically to bed and Myra was out, Susan corralled Pam against a countertop with a mug of malted milk. 'Okay, you were there,' Susan said. 'Was I doing some kleptomaniacal imitation of Grier – *channelling* her – or are those two out to lunch?'

Pam's plain face constricted. 'Well, I can see, from some perspectives, how they might have interpreted it that way ... But I can also see how you might not recognise the similarities, or maybe even how, for you, there wasn't much to recognise ...'

'You just said exactly nothing.'

'I don't want to get caught in the middle.'

'What a shock.'

Pam's eyes flashed with a flintiness that Susan didn't know was in her. 'What I do think is that this is a terrible way to end senior year, and you and Myra and Grier should try to reconcile and put this behind you. If you don't, I think you'll all regret it.'

'You can't "reconcile" if you're living in alternative universes. I'm not apologising for something I didn't do, and they're the ones, in my view, who owe *me* an apology. Which won't be forthcoming either. So I repeat: off the record, if that makes it easier. Was there anything to that accusation? You're the only one without a dog in this race.' At the time, it still seemed a stylish expression.

'Only you know.' With that, Pam slipped between the counter and Susan's malted milk and pronounced no more on the matter.

Call it ungenerous, but grace is rare at barely twenty-two, and Susan declined to attend Grier's recital. Presumably after all the theatrics, the young woman the suite had nominated as their one true wunderkind did fill out her concert with entirely fresh material, though if the snatches escaping Grier's bedroom were any indication the new songs sounded pretty much like the old ones.

Barring an exchange of phone numbers on graduation day that Susan interpreted as an empty exercise of social form, that would have been it, save for a postscript near the end of the ensuing summer. Out of the blue, Myra called Susan at her sublet and asked her to come by for a drink. (Unsurprisingly, she and Grier had found an apartment together, and they, too, had stayed on the Upper West Side.) Intrigued, and coming to realise that all along she'd been hoping that the doyens of 12C would eventually come to like her, Susan accepted the olive branch.

Yet rather than providing for a halting truce, the occasion was jittery and superficial, discussion mostly centring on home décor, until those two got to the point – pulling out a case of potions and an order form. Grier started chattering about how much more fully her hair was growing in now, and she wasn't being confiding. Obviously desperate for income to cover their rent, these newly matriculated liberal-arts graduates had signed up to sell supplements for a nutritional company that conformed to the personalised-harassment-cum-blackmail model of Amway and Tupperware. Susan Twitchel wouldn't have got her invitation to submit to this sales pitch until late August, because clearly the doyens had already run through their genuine friends, first cousins, and neighbours in the building, and were now down to the long-shot B-list. Mortified for all concerned, Susan didn't buy anything, and left most of her Chablis.

These days Slooz preferred Malbec, of which she took a few contemplative sips in her messy Finger Lakes study. The chill from hunkering over that clammy carton of woe in the unheated attic all afternoon still hadn't ebbed, even after a hot dinner and an hour at this computer. The shiver seemed emotional. Perhaps she had too vividly summoned the experience of being out in the cold in a larger sense – of being so disgracefully young, so hideously hopeful, so inanely certain that baselessly high expectations were fated to be met.

From this vantage point, the confrontation over her purported musical imposture was absurd. At that age, none of them would have developed a voice distinctive enough to emulate. Those two had merely been miffed that Susan

Twitchel was better received in the Culvert than she had licence to be and was getting ideas above her station. Besides which, mimicry was a gift at which Slooz had never excelled. Sit her down and order up an Elvis Costello song, it would come out sounding like one more cut from *Short Walk on a Long Pier*, and nine out of ten of her fans would identify the artist on the first guess. Critics hadn't been universally admiring, but she was fairly sure that the word *derivative* had made no appearance in reviews. In the big picture anyway, everyone derived from everyone else, since they all emerged from the same cultural primordial soup, in which Grier, Slooz *and* Elvis were fungible chunks of carrot.

Yet if she'd forgotten about the altercation altogether until flipping to that journal entry, the trauma couldn't have left her irreparably scarred. Sure, she'd felt wounded at the time, but the incident no more fazed her in the present than did boo-boos from tumbling to the sidewalk at the age of four.

So why on earth had she initiated this half-hearted investigation into Whatever Became of Grier Finlayson? The you-copied-me thing was nugatory. What did cling was the memory of having been cast as second string – of living in the shadow of the Chosen One, and fearing that her own role of Also-Ran was well deserved. Of worrying that her suitemates saw something not up to scratch in her that was real and incorrigible. For most of her adulthood, Slooz had washed between buoyant self-assurance and this doomed, hobbled sensation, a suspicion that she didn't have the goods and never would. Doubt of her endowments persisted into the heyday of her career (longer ago than she cared to admit), and had served as a useful spur to productivity: she was forever proving that she and the likes of Grier Finlayson were cut of the same fine cloth.

Arguably, if she were meant to know how Grier turned out, then they would still be in touch, and Grier would *tell* her what happened over coffee. Instead, Slooz had stooped to an anonymous fishing expedition – first clearing up the spelling issue, then establishing that Grier's married name was Danilowicz.

The results were in.

Her husband was a banker. They had twin boys, but not until 2000 – when Grier had to have been at least forty-three. A multiple birth at that age hinted at IVF, and so perhaps also at years of frustration and heartache before an implantation took. According to the public property registry, the couple owned an apartment on East 98th Street.

Grier wasn't on Facebook, but she was on LinkedIn, where the Prima Donna advertised the following:

'I plan parties, sometimes with themes. I write original lyrics for parties, and perform both commissioned work and standards in your living room. Let me write a birthday song for your child, specially tailored to their interests!

'I can also dress you for any special occasion, including making over your whole wardrobe. Let someone who has the eye transform you into all that you were meant to be!'

Grier Finlayson also showed up on an historical list of music internships at an arts institute in Colorado, under the interns for 1982. In the absence of any Wikipedia page, Slooz found evidence of two performances: in a small Chicago club in 1996 and a dinner theatre in Kansas City in 1998. Even allowing for the fact that the Web didn't really take off until around 1995, these were slim pickings. As of the twenty-first century, the sparse trail of digital breadcrumbs dried up completely. Under neither her maiden nor her married name had Grier left any professional footprint in almost twenty years.

So her husband supported her. The children could soon be off to college, hence the party-planning and makeover promotion: she'd need something to do.

There was a photo. One photo, as far as Slooz could discern, on the entire internet. It was a very bad photo. It was such a bad photo to choose to accompany your LinkedIn profile that it could only have been posted because the subject's horror of the camera made the selection at hand negligible. The phobia would have to have been so drastic that the ordeal of having another photo taken for social networking presented itself as even more forbidding than ensuring that nobody would ever hire you to design their themed party, sing at their house, write a birthday song for their child, or refurbish their wardrobe.

The shot had no date, and could have been old. She is shying from the lens, cutting her eyes askance. Though the eyes are recognisable, their gleam has retracted to pinpricks, and they look slittier. Her coat collar is raised. The grin is nervous, a little shit-eating. Her hair is full, dark with henna highlights, closing around her chin and trailing in an uneven zig into her eyebrows – so either the hair did grow back or she's wearing a wig. She's sitting in the passenger seat of a car, leaving the impression that the photographer, snatching a rare opportunity, has caught – his wife? – unawares. She is only a measure thinner than she was in college, so literal contraction doesn't explain the impression that this woman has shrunk.

She looks neurotic. She looks in retreat. She looks like someone you would have to cosset, of whom sons would be protective, lying to strangers that Mother is ill. She looks like a woman who can be difficult, who is fragile, for whom exceptions are frequently made.

To make herself feel better – though why Slooz felt bad could have stood examination – she impulsively input 'Myra Haas' into the search field. As her forefinger hovered above the return key, this time she took a moment to place her bets. What would have happened to Myra Haas? Myra was practical. She wasn't creative, but she was wily. So whatever arty or intellectual notions she nursed in college would have quickly fallen by the wayside. Applying that dry intelligence of hers, she'd have earned an advanced degree in business or law. It was the 1980s, after all. She'd have married a go-getter in financial services, for it was *Myra* who belonged with a banker. So she'd be well-to-do, and a live-in Eastern European nanny would have raised her kids. She'd solicit corporate donations to cancer charities, if only to attend the swank fund-raisers. She'd still be competitive, so she'd be rail thin.

Enter.

Myra Haas married Alan Metcalf, a representative of the same nutritional-supplement company whose wares she sold right out of college. They had no children. She was fond of animals, especially cats. She never left New York. She was a disciple of a 'spiritual healer' whose name Slooz didn't recognise, and worked part-time for years as a counsellor in the shyster's clinic.

This information was tidily all in one place on legacy.com, because Myra Haas was dead. In lieu of flowers, the bereaved were asked to donate to a variety of nonprofits with phrases like 'furry friends' in their names. The listing only asserted that Myra had died 'suddenly' in 2012 from causes unexplained. She would have been fifty-six. So much for the efficacy of nutritional supplements.

There was a lone picture too, and once again Slooz was flummoxed. If you were going to pick a single photograph of someone you presumably cared about for a memorial page on legacy.com, why would you choose this one? It was a bit out of focus, though even in black and white the eyes displayed a telltale sidling slyness: this was Myra Haas, all right. Age-wise, the photo was wildly out of date; she couldn't have been more than thirty-five in this shot. Still, the face had expanded.

Myra led a weird, fringy life, and she got fat. Beyond legacy.com, further searches on myra haas, myra haas barnard college, myra metcalf, myra haas metcalf, and even myra metcalf with the spiritualist thrown in turned up no relevant hits whatsoever. In internet terms, she was invisible. Yet on a sole point Slooz had been right: once you were rounding on sixty, the vote on what you'd amounted to was definitely in, since for Myra that tally was finalised by fifty-six. Closing the laptop, Slooz was embarrassed to find herself considering whether there was a song in all this.

Those two turned out rather badly. Most people turn out badly, at least by the grubby measure of a Google search. In parts per billion, the concentration of folks who distinguished themselves amidst the slosh of humanity resembled the proportion of active ingredients in quack-homeopathy cures. Which is why Slooz wasn't upset by being called a has-been. At least a has-been had been.

Of course, you could only convincingly piss on celebrity if you were already famous, and Slooz had been just success-ful enough to grow a bit Groucho about the club of worldly glory. That is, while she'd hardly clawed her way to the top of the heap – when her CD sales were at their highest, she might have been compared to Tori Amos, but nobody was comparing Tori Amos to her – she had clambered high enough to get a look at the view. No one would be listening to any of this middlebrow pop music a hundred years from now, and even if they were, a point-blank asteroid would hurtle along to melt their ear buds and everything else, too. All that will have mattered about Sloozie Twitch is that she two-timed a tender second husband who might otherwise have gone the distance, and she would die alone. In kind, whatever truly mattered about her old suitemates was prob-ably not available online – though, alas, by all appearances, neither had forged a career sufficiently illustrious for either woman to discount it.

Full circle, then: never mind the answers she actually found. What had she wanted to find?

She'd wanted to find what she found. She wanted to con-firm that Susan Twitchel had made good, while these snide, condescending classmates from her senior year of college had come to nothing. A stray journal entry from those dis-tant days had brought back an acrid memory and stirred old resentments. In running those mouldy names through a search engine, she'd wanted to gloat.

But the bad feeling that had nagged her ever since finding Grier's pitiable listing on LinkedIn was clearly guilt. Grier Finlayson commanded a more impressive instrument than Susan Twitchel from the get go, and had been much more disciplined about practising scales and doing vocal exercises. As Sloozie Twitch, our Susan may have cleverly palmed off the weaknesses of her voice as style, but by any standard measure Grier was the superior vocalist, which ought rightly to have reaped greater rewards than children's birthday parties. Even Myra: call her intelligence 'dry' or 'uncreative', she was still smart, medically smarter by a yard than her suitemate Susan, a B-plus-to-A-minus student with marginal SAT scores who could only have been admitted to Barnard by the skin of her teeth. Myra was a hard worker who followed directions and submitted papers on time, exhibiting just the reliability for which the working world was starved. She possessed excellent writing skills, and she was good at public speaking – why, Slooz could have written a boffo LinkedIn profile for Myra Haas. So how in God's name did this attractive, capable, well-educated young woman end up hawking sham nutritional supplements and purveying the nostrums of a spiritual huckster?

Plenty sucked, but there were thousands of photos of Sloozie Twitch online – some amateur snaps snatched from an audience, others from professional shoots. Yet for Slooz to hope that Grier and Myra would have tripped across any of these, in *Interview*, in *Rolling Stone* – for Slooz to hope that those two would have recognised their old classmate's voice on the radio, that they would have stared – or glared – at the posters in the windows of Tower Records in the days there was such a store ... Well, the notion was repellent. It wouldn't have taken a genius to sort out that Sloozie Twitch was none other than Susan Twitchel, but honestly she prayed that neither of the suitemates who had seemed to 'count' in 1977 had ever made the connection.

For gloating was out of the question. All she felt was a killing sorrow. Myra Haas and Grier Finlayson were strangers, and they had been strangers for a long, long time. As such, they were stand-ins for all the young people who'd ever felt anointed, and for whom the sensation of having a date with destiny would prove brief. Slooz knew better than anyone how readily her own laughable aspirations could have come to ash, had an influential producer not heard her warm-up set at CB's in 1981 and gone to the Vanguard instead.

In Googling rudely into private and professional lives that were none of her business, she'd also brushed against a universe in reverse: in which on a similarly chill, random, under-occupied evening, they were the ones who idly input *Susan Titchel* into a search engine, and they were the ones who misspelled the surname at first, only getting digital satisfaction after remembering to insert the *W*. They were the ones to note smugly that their old suitemate didn't even merit a Wikipedia page, which would have linked 'born as ...' to a stage name, in the improbable instance that Also-Ran ever required one. They were the ones who, just to make sure, ran the same search on Spotify, Amazon, and the iTunes Store, in order to confirm precisely what they'd have predicted: Susan Twitchel never recorded an ever-loving thing. They were the ones who tracked down photographs of their former classmate in the secret hopes that she would have got fat, and they were the ones who found only a cringing, poorly composed snapshot in which she looked neurotic – or for that matter, they were the ones who pulled up short against the fact that Susan had escaped their doggy snapping at her heels by being underhandedly dead. They were the ones who only remembered the aloof, acerbic girl in the first place because of her brazen counterfeiting of the dorm's sole budding virtuoso. They were the ones to suppose archly that this run-of-the-mill singer with her incongruous oboe was just the sort of no-hoper who'd have ended up working in lower-level municipal government her whole life – overseeing recycling, or pothole repair – and they were the ones perplexed to not find themselves quite as gratified by Susan Twitchel's obvious disappointment as they might have anticipated. She brushed up against the universe in which they were the ones left mystified by what they were looking for in the first place.

It all made for a particularly rich interview on *Injudicious Journals* and Slooz pinned the transcript, when they published it, to the top of her new Twitter feed.

AUTHOR BIOGRAPHIES

Elizabeth Day is an award-winning author, journalist and co-founder of Pin Drop.

Day is the author of four novels and numerous short stories. Her critically acclaimed debut novel, *Scissors Paper Stone*, won a Betty Trask Award for a first novel written by an author under the age of thirty-five. Her second novel, *Home Fires*, was published in 2013, followed by *Paradise City* in 2015 and *The Party* in 2017, all to critical acclaim.

Day is also a feature writer for UK and US publications including *New York Magazine* and *Vogue*, and is a contributing editor for *Harper's Bazaar*. She won a British Press Award in 2004 for Young Journalist of the Year and in 2013 was Highly Commended in the category of Feature Writer of the Year.

Day has appeared for Pin Drop on a number of occasions, including at the Simon Oldfield Gallery, Soho House, London, and at Pin Drop in Paris.

Bethan Roberts won the inaugural Pin Drop Short Story Award in 2015 with 'Ms Featherstone and the Beast'.

Roberts is the author of four novels and numerous short

stories. Her first novel, *The Pools,* was published in 2007 and won a Jerwood/Arvon Young Writers' Award. Her second novel, *The Good Plain Cook,* published in 2008, was serialised on BBC Radio 4's Book at Bedtime and featured in *Time Out*'s Books of the Year. *My Policeman* followed in 2012, and was chosen as that year's City Read for Brighton. Her latest novel, *Mother Island,* is the recipient of a Jerwood Fiction Uncovered Prize. Roberts' short fiction has been widely published and her dramas have been featured on BBC Radio 4.

Nikesh Shukla is the author of three widely acclaimed novels and was the editor of the hugely successful collection of essays, *The Good Immigrant.*

Shukla's debut novel, *Coconut Unlimited,* was shortlisted for the Costa First Novel Award 2010 and longlisted for the Desmond Elliott Prize 2011. This was followed in 2014 by *Meatspace,* which was hailed by the *Guardian* as capturing 'a cultural moment' and in 2018 by *The One Who Wrote Destiny.* His short stories have been featured in *Best British Short Stories 2013,* the *Sunday Times* and BBC Radio 4. A key voice in the conversation around diversity in publishing, Shukla is a champion of emerging BAME writers.

Shukla appeared for Pin Drop at the Simon Oldfield Gallery in 2013.

Claire Fuller won the Pin Drop Short Story Award in 2016 for 'A Quiet Tidy Man'.

Fuller's short stories and flash fiction have received numerous awards, including the BBC Opening Lines competition in 2014.

Her novels *Our Endless Numbered Days* and *Swimming Lessons* have been released internationally to widespread critical acclaim, including the 2016 American Bookseller Association Awards (finalist) and 2015 Desmond Elliott Prize (winner).

Ben Okri is the Man Booker Prize-winning author of eight novels, including *The Famished Road* and *Starbook*, as well as collections of poetry, short stories and essays.

He is a Fellow of the Royal Society of Literature and has been awarded an OBE as well as numerous international prizes, including the Man Booker Prize for *The Famished Road*, the Commonwealth Writers' Prize for Africa, the Aga Khan Prize for Fiction and the Chianti Ruffino-Antico Fattore. He is a vice president of the English Centre of International PEN and was presented with a Crystal Award by the World Economic Forum.

Okri has read for Pin Drop at the Bath Literature Festival and at the Royal Academy.

Anne O'Brien was shortlisted for the Pin Drop Short Story Award in 2017 for 'These Silver Fish'.

O'Brien's work has appeared in several anthologies and magazines and received recognition from numerous awards, including the Bath Short Story Award (winner), *The London Magazine*'s Short Story Competition (second prize) and short-listed for the Bridport Prize and BBC's Opening Lines.

A. L. Kennedy is the author of seventeen books: six literary novels, one science-fiction novel, seven short-story collections and three works of non-fiction. She is also a dramatist for stage, radio, TV and film and regularly reads her work on the BBC.

She is a Fellow of the Royal Society of Arts and a Fellow of the Royal Society of Literature and was twice included in the *Granta* Best of Young British Novelists list. She has won awards including the 2007 Costa Book Award and the Austrian State Prize for International Literature and was longlisted for the Man Booker Prize in 2016 for *Serious Sweet*.

A longstanding supporter of Pin Drop, Kennedy has read her short stories for Pin Drop to audiences in London on several occasions and featured on RTE Radio.

Anna Stewart was shortlisted for the Pin Drop Short Story Award 2017 for 'The Way I Breathed'.

Stewart's stories have been widely published in journals and magazines, and shortlisted for a number of awards. With a background in theatre, Stewart has performed her work internationally and collaborated on development projects with the National Theatre of Scotland.

Craig Burnett was shortlisted for the Pin Drop Short Story Award in 2017 for his story 'Feathers Thick with Oil'.

Born in Dundee, Burnett grew up in Oxfordshire and lives in south London. His short stories have been included in various publications and he was a prize-winner at the Cambridge Short Story Award 2018. He is an editor at a global politics think tank.

Douglas W. Milliken was shortlisted for the Pin Drop Short Story Award in 2017 for 'Heart's Last Pass'.

Milliken is the American author of the novel *To Sleep as Animals* and several chapbooks, most recently *One Thousand Owls Behind Your Chest*. His stories have been widely published and have received numerous awards, including the Maine Literary Awards and the Pushcart Prize.

Will Self is a highly acclaimed, award-winning British author, journalist and political commentator. He is the author of ten novels, five collections of shorter fiction, three novellas and five collections of non-fiction writing. His work has been translated into twenty-two languages, and his novel *Umbrella* was shortlisted for the Man Booker Prize.

Regularly appearing on television, Self is also a frequent contributor to BBC Radio 4 and writes for publications including the *Guardian, Harpers,* the *New York Times* and the *London Review of Books*. He also writes columns for the *New Statesman,* the *Observer* and *The Times*.

Since 2012, Self has been Professor of Contemporary Thought at Brunel University. In 2015 he read for Pin Drop at the Royal Academy of Arts during Ai Weiwei's landmark exhibition.

Jarred McGinnis was shortlisted for the Pin Drop Short Story Award 2017 for 'Rough Beasts'.

His short fiction has been commissioned for BBC Radio 4 and appeared in respected journals in the UK, Canada, USA and Ireland. McGinnis has worked on projects selected for the British Council's International Literature Showcase, teaches at Goldsmiths university and was the creative director for *Moby-Dick Unabridged* at the Southbank Centre.

Barney Walsh was shortlisted for the Pin Drop Short Story Award 2016 for 'Under the Waves'.

Walsh moved from a background in theoretical physics to literature and he is now the assistant editor of *Litro Magazine*. His stories have appeared in a number of respected journals in the UK.

Rebecca F. John was shortlisted for the Pin Drop Short Story Award in 2017 for 'Paper Chains'.

John's short stories have received widespread recognition, winning the PEN International New Voices Award, shortlisted for the *Sunday Times* EFG Short Story Award and broadcast on BBC Radio 4. Her debut novel, *The Haunting of Henry Twist*, was shortlisted for the Costa First Novel Award. In 2017, she was featured on the Hay Festival's 'Hay 30' list.

Joanna Campbell was shortlisted for the Pin Drop Short Story Award in 2017 for 'Brad's Rooster Food'.

When Planets Slip Their Tracks, Campbell's first collection of short fiction, was published in 2016 and followed her debut novel, *Tying Down the Lion*, published in 2015. Campbell's short stories are widely published and have won numerous awards.

Emily Bullock was shortlisted for the Pin Drop Short Story Award in 2017 for 'Freshwater'.

Winner of the Bristol Short Story Prize, Bullock's short

stories are widely acclaimed and have been broadcast on BBC Radio 4. Her debut novel, *The Longest Fight*, published in 2015, was featured in the *Independent*'s Paperbacks of the Year.

Cherise Saywell was the winner of the Pin Drop Short Story Award 2017 for 'Morelia Spilota'.

Saywell is a British-Australian author of two critically acclaimed novels, *Desert Fish* (2011) and *Twitcher* (2013) (both Vintage). Her short stories have won the Mslexia Short Story Prize and the V. S. Pritchett Prize and been shortlisted for several awards, including the Bath Short Story Award and the Asham Award. Her story 'Pieces of Mars Have Fallen to Earth' was selected for BBC Radio 4's Opening Lines in 2015.

Lionel Shriver is an award-winning and bestselling American author.

Her novels include the National Book Award finalist *So Much for That*, the *New York Times* bestseller *The Post-Birthday World*, and the international bestseller *We Need to Talk About Kevin*, which won the Orange Prize in 2006 and was made into a film starring Tilda Swinton.

Shriver won the BBC National Short Story Award for 'Kilifi Creek'. She is also widely published as a journalist for the *Guardian, New York Times, Wall Street Journal, Financial Times* and many others.

A longstanding supporter of Pin Drop, Shriver has read her short stories to captivated audiences at BAFTA and the Royal Academy of Arts during the Anselm Kiefer exhibition in 2015.

ARTIST BIOGRAPHIES

Eddie Peake (b. 1981, London) studied at the Slade School of Art and the Royal Academy Schools, where he graduated in 2013. Selected international exhibitions include *Friendship of the Peoples*, Simon Oldfield Gallery, London (2011), The Curve, Barbican, London (2015), *Where You Belong*, White Cube, Hong Kong (2016) and *Concrete Pitch*, White Cube Bermondsey, London (2018).

Kay Harwood (b. 1978, Lancashire) studied in London at the Slade School of Art and the Royal Academy Schools, where she graduated in 2004. Since then, Harwood has exhibited widely in Britain and abroad, including *Artfutures*, at Bloomsberg Space, Simon Oldfield Gallery and the Royal Academy of Arts.

Gabriella Boyd (b. 1988, Glasgow) studied at Glasgow School of Art and the Royal Academy Schools, where she graduated in 2017. Selected exhibitions include *Dreamers Awake*, White Cube Bermondsey, London (2017), *Glasgow International* (2018) and *Help Yourself*, Blain|Southern, London (2018). Boyd provided illustrations for the Folio Society's publication of Freud's *Interpreting Dreams* (2017).

Jonathan Trayte (b. 1980, UK) graduated from the Royal Academy Schools in 2010. Selected exhibitions include *Bloomberg New Contemporaries*, ICA, London (2011), *Art Icon, Under a Pine Tree*, Simon Oldfield Gallery, London (2011) and Whitechapel Gallery, London (2017), and *Tropicana*, Christies, London (2017).

Luey Graves (b. 1987, London) studied at the Slade School of Art and the Royal Academy Schools, where she graduated in 2012. Selected exhibitions include *Friendship of the Peoples*, Simon Oldfield Gallery, London (2011), *Image/Object*, Furini Contemporary, Rome (2013), *Symbolic Logic*, Identity Art Gallery, Hong Kong (2014) and Studio Voltaire, London (2015).

Marco Palmieri (b. 1984, Tulsa) graduated from the Royal Academy Schools in 2011. Selected exhibitions include *Bloomberg New Contemporaries*, ICA, London (2011), *Wonderwheel*, Depart Foundation, Miami (2015), *Three Romans*, Galleria Lorcan O'Neill Roma, Rome (2015) and the British Schools, Rome.

John Robertson (b. 1983, UK) studied at the Glasgow School of Art and the Royal Academy Schools, where he graduated in 2012. Selected exhibitions include *Art Britannia*, Miami (2013), *Tilt*, Royal Academy of Arts (2014) and Abbey Scholar in Painting at the British School in Rome.

Coco Crampton (b. 1983, London) graduated from the Royal Academy Schools in 2014. Selected exhibitions include *Fourth Drawer Down*, Nottingham Contemporary, Nottingham (2014) and *All Over*, Studio Leigh, London (2016).

Fani Parali (b. 1983, Greece) graduated from the Royal Academy Schools in 2017. Selected exhibitions include *Gender, Identity and Material*, Royal Academy of Arts, London (2017), *Drawing Biennial*, Drawing Room, London (2017) and *Glasgow International* (2018).

Murray O'Grady (b. 1987, Essex) graduated from the Royal Academy Schools in 2014. Selected exhibitions include *Bloomberg New Contemporaries*, ICA, London (2010) and *Young British Art* (2011/13). Murray was awarded the inaugural Vanguard Prize (2010) and was Artist in Residence at Burlington Arcade as part of the *Royal Academy Arts Festival* (2017).

Pio Abad (b. 1983, Manila) studied at the University of the Philippines, Glasgow School of Art and the Royal Academy Schools, where he graduated in 2012. Selected international exhibitions include *e-flux*, New York (2015), Centre for Contemporary Arts, Glasgow (2016) and *Art Basel Encounters*, Art Basel, Hong Kong (2017).

Declan Jenkins (b. 1984, Isle of Wight) studied at New College Oxford and Wimbledon College of Art before graduating from the Royal Academy Schools in 2015. He presented his first solo exhibition, *I Sing of Armoires...*, Sims Reed Gallery, London (2017).

Mary Ramsden (b. 1984, North Yorkshire) graduated from the Royal Academy Schools in 2013. Ramsden has exhibited widely, including *New Order II: British Art Today*, Saatchi Gallery London (2014), *Art Now: Vanilla and Concrete*, TATE Britain, London (2015) and *Couples Therapy*, Pilar Corrias, London (2017).

Carla Busuttil (b. 1982, Johannesburg) graduated from the Royal Academy Schools in 2008. Selected international exhibitions include *Newspeak: British Art Now*, Saatchi Gallery, London (2010), *We See (in) the Dark*, Museum of African Design, Johannesburg, South Africa (2015), *Art Los Angeles Contemporary*, Los Angeles (2015) and a Fashion Art Commission at 180 Strand, London (2018).

Jessy Jetpacks (b. 1987, Dubai) graduated from the Royal Academy Schools in 2017. Selected exhibitions include *Royal Academy America* (2016), *The Second Space*, Xi'an Maike Centre, China (2017/18) and Glasgow International (2018).

Nick Goss (b. 1981, Bristol) graduated from the Royal Academy Schools in 2009 and has exhibited widely. Selected exhibitions include *Jerwood Contemporary Painters*, Jerwood Space, London and national tour (2010), *Bluing*, Simon Preston Gallery, New York (2016).

Tim Ellis (b. 1981, Chester) graduated from the Royal Academy Schools in 2009. Selected exhibitions include *Newspeak: British Art Now Part I*, Saatchi Gallery, London (2010), *Seduction*, Simon Oldfield Gallery, London (2012), *We*

Belong Together, Hong Kong (2013) and *The London Open*, Whitechapel Gallery, London (2015).

Adam Shield (b. 1988, Newcastle-upon-Tyne) studied at Newcastle University and the Royal Academy Schools, where he graduated in 2017. Selected exhibitions include *Bearing Liability*, Strange Cargo Gallery, Folkestone (2017) and Glasgow International (2018).

The artists in *A Short Affair* have been selected from the Royal Academy Schools.

ABOUT PIN DROP STUDIO

Pin Drop, the home of short fiction, is a multifaceted arts and culture studio.

Pin Drop brings extraordinary short fiction to life, rooted in its critically acclaimed programme of live events, which sees world-renowned authors and actors take centre stage to read short fiction against the backdrop of prestigious institutions, such as BAFTA and the Royal Academy of Arts in London, and other iconic venues in major cities across the globe.

Pin Drop's audiences embrace the simple pleasure of listening to a story read aloud; the experience is the perfect counterpoint to a hyper-connected world. The essence of the events is captured in the Pin Drop podcast series for listeners to tune into wherever they may be.

As champions of the short story, Pin Drop also commissions original short fiction from bestselling authors and discovers new stories through the prestigious Pin Drop Short Story Award, an annual open-submission prize in collaboration with the Royal Academy of Arts.

Founded in 2012 by curator Simon Oldfield and author Elizabeth Day, Pin Drop is at the heart of a short-story renaissance.

pindropstudio.com

ACKNOWLEDGEMENTS

I am immeasurably grateful to countless people who have provided their support, guidance and encouragement. To you all, I offer my effusive thanks and immense gratitude.

Scribner invested their faith in me, Pin Drop and *A Short Affair*. For that I will always be indebted. To Ian Chapman and Suzanne Baboneau, I give my especial thanks.

To the authors who have contributed their stories to *A Short Affair*, you have my deepest appreciation, and to the artists who have created artworks in response to those stories.

Thank you to the extraordinarily talented authors, actors, artists and thinkers who have appeared live at Pin Drop and delivered spellbinding performances in locations across the globe, each one a step on the path to *A Short Affair*. I am indebted to you all: William Boyd, Sebastian Faulks, Stephen Fry, Dame Eileen Atkins, Dame Siân Phillips, Sir Peter Blake, Graham Swift, Juliet Stevenson, Julian Barnes, Professor Richard Dawkins, Russell Tovey, A. C. Grayling, Jason Atherton, Tom Rob Smith, Selma Blair, Juliet Oldfield, Tracy Chevalier, Sean Delaney, Lisa Dwan, Jacob Fortune-Lloyd, Ruta Gedmintas, Viv Groskop, Elizabeth Healey, Evie Wyld, Maura Tierney, Rachel Johnson, Andy Burnham, Lea Carpenter, Sadie Jones, Duke & Joe Brooks, Aysha Kala,

A. L. Kennedy, Olivia Laing, Sara Maitland, Lyndsey Marshal, Perdita Weeks, David Baddiel, Colum McCann, Prunella Scales, Alistair McGowan, Bel Mooney, Jeremy Neumark Jones, Lisa Hogg, David Nicholls, Ben Okri, Clara Paget, Gala Gordon, Tuppence Middleton, Molly Parkin, Alice Patten, Princess Julia, Polly Samson, Francesca Segal, Will Self, Owen Sheers, Lionel Shriver, Nikesh Shukla, Daniel Lismore, Nathan Stewart-Jarrett, Ed Stoppard, Sue Tilley, Mark Titchner, Tim Winton and Dame Penelope Wilton.

To the wonderful and dedicated Pin Drop team, you have my enduring thanks and gratitude, especially Anita Lawlor for working so closely with me on every line of this anthology. Thanks also to Julia Ravenscroft, Francesca Oldfield, Owen Richards, Flynn Warren and Thom Hill.

A special thank you to my dear friend and Pin Drop co-founder, Elizabeth Day, who worked tirelessly with me at the beginning to craft Pin Drop into the multi-faceted arts and culture studio it is today.

Thank you to all our incredible partners including BAFTA, Burberry, Soho House, Audible, the British Academy, Houses of Parliament, The New Craftsmen, Grosvenor Estate, Hauser & Wirth, Regent's Park Open Air Theatre, Dr Johnson's House and The Charles Dickens Museum.

My sincerest thanks to everyone at the Royal Academy of Arts, particularly Humphrey Ocean RA who championed Pin Drop from the outset, and the Artistic Director, Tim Marlow, for his unflinching support and the foreword to this book. Thanks also to Amy Bluett, Kira Milmo and Eliza Bonham-Carter, who have keenly embraced our collaboration.

I am indebted to all the magnificent people who give invaluable support and loyalty to Pin Drop and give my special thanks to our board of trustees, advisers, members and patrons. I am particularly grateful to our Chairman Etienne de Villiers, Niall Curran, Bill Damaschke, Felicity Jones, Jacqueline Hurt, John McIlwee and Leslie Stern for representing Pin Drop and guiding me through.

Thanks also to the extraordinary people who have been part of the journey: Christopher Bailey, Vanessa Xuereb, Tom Russell, Will Bax, Jessica Bax, Tracey Markham, Sven Becker, Alison Bracker, Charlotte Appleyard, Clare Taylor, Tom Godfrey, Toby Spigel, Susan Holding, Ben Ravenscroft, Jeffrey Hinton, Sara Sassanelli, Matt Farrell, Amy Edwards, Emma-Jane Taylor, Ben Webster, Lucy Ellison, Caroline Michel, Nathaniel Lee-Jones, Pippa Brooks, Matthew and Thomas Ryan, Karen Fraser, Chris McCrudden, Oonagh Carnwath, Helen Upton, Jo Whitford, Suzanne King, Dawn Burnett, Gill Richardson, Peter Zenneck, Troels Levring, Amy Williams, James Montague, Joe Stroud, Leslie Macleod-Miller, Maisie Lawrence, Will Atkins, Julian Shaw, Irha Atherton, Dea Vanagan, Simon Martin, Mark Henderson, Catherine Lock, Natalie Melton, Tino DeMartino, Barrie Livingstone, Marta Gut, Vicki King, Lisa Hall, Tig Teague, Candice Swift, Juliette Meinrath, Debbie Sim, Mandy Sim, Roya Nikkhah, Sue Reid, Nick Hornby, Tim Morris, Doug Miller, Kate Ellis, Julia Royse, Julie Lomax, Jean Wainwright, Oksana Kolomenskaya, Nick and Julie Harding, Keli Lee, Catherine Day, Ann Gilmore, Susan Boyd, Vivienne Sharpe and Tim McCormick, Stephanie and Julian Grose, Katherine Solomon, the Pilati family, Fawzia Kane, Helen Brocklebank, Helen Ervin, Rebecca Thornton, Andrea Wong, Matthew Appleton, Cormac Kinsella, Sinéad Gleeson, and Tom and Christine Day.

Finally, to my family, especially Tim Julian, Doris Julian, my sisters and my parents, Diane and Paul Oldfield.

Copyrights and Credits